SAFE HARBOR

ROSEMARY McCRACKEN

Safe Harbor

A Pat Tierney Mystery – Book 1

Rosemary McCracken

Copyright © 2012, 2018 Rosemary McCracken.

All Rights Reserved.

SECOND EDITION

Print Edition ISBN: 978-1-77242-090-6

Cover design by Sara Carrick

Carrick Publishing

http://www.rosemarymccracken.com

Praise for Safe Harbor

"With *Safe Harbor*, Rosemary McCracken proves why she's already won international acclaim. This is an absorbing page-turner you won't want to miss." —Rick Mofina, bestselling author of *The Burning Edge*

"Rosemary McCracken has a deft touch for writing believable relationships, especially among families. These particular characters will soon feel like people you know and won't want out of your life. Add to this an exciting plot and you'll be ready for a great read." —Maureen Jennings, author of the *Detective William Murdoch mysteries*

"The title of Rosemary McCracken's debut novel, *Safe Harbor*, resonates on many levels. *Safe Harbor*, a house that offers refugees with questionable legal status a home, is a central player in the novel's fast-paced and involving plot. But the words "safe harbor" also reflect the life financial advisor Pat Tierney has chosen to live after her husband Michael's sudden death. In the opening pages of the novel, Pat is ripped from her safe harbor by a dark secret from her husband's past. She is forced to meet challenges she could never imagine, but her courageous refusal to turn from danger makes her a very compelling protagonist. This novel will stay with you long after you've turned the final page."—Gail Bowen, author of the *Joanne Kilbourn mysteries*

"*Safe Harbor*, by Rosemary McCracken, is a clever, original combination of domestic cozy and international intrigue. Its heroine, a respectable widow with a good home, a loving family and a lucrative job, suddenly finds herself responsible for a young boy with a mysterious past somehow connected to her own. Torn between saving him and saving her comfortable life, she risks all she has in a story that is full of twists, turns, surprises and startling revelations. Touching, intriguing and sometimes downright scary, this story hooked me from page one until the final action-packed pages." —Rosemary Aubert, author of the *Ellis Portal mystery series*

"This family drama quickly spirals into an intriguing mystery. A highly entertaining read!" —D.J. McIntosh, author of *The Witch of Babylon*

McCracken's novel offers a coherent structure, an exact feel for Toronto locales and, in Pat, a hugely attractive sleuth figure. —Jack Batten, *Toronto Star*

To Ed, who is always there for me.

Prologue

"We are missing one of our, how you say…assets. You help us get back?"

Jude clutched the phone and went to the living room window. Across the street, she saw a black SUV parked at the curb. Its chrome fenders glinted in the sunlight.

She turned back to the room. Her son Tommy lay on the sofa, his knees propped up. He was playing a video game on the hand-held gaming device Santa had given him for Christmas.

She fixed her eyes on the boy. "Look, I don't know where?"

"Then you find out," the voice on the other end of the line demanded. "If you know what is good for you—and your boy."

Jude turned her back on Tommy. "You leave him alone. He's just a child."

"Then do what I say. Get us the Somali."

"Wait!"

The only response was the droning dial tone.

Heart pounding, she glanced at Tommy and felt the color drain from her face. "Oh God. What have I done?" she whispered.

Jude placed the receiver in its cradle and looked out the window again.

The SUV hadn't moved.

She had to stay calm and somehow get Tommy out of the house.

She rubbed both hands on her jeans, trying to restore the circulation, but they remained ice cold. She walked over to the sofa and crouched down beside her son.

"Come here, sweetie." She struggled to keep her voice steady as she pulled him into a hug.

He squirmed. "Not now, Mommy. I'm not finished."

"Tommy, you have to put that away." She moved to ease the device from his grasp.

"No! The game's not over."

Jude stood up, her face tight with fear. "Yes, it is. Give that to me." She held out a shaking hand.

Tommy scowled.

"I said *now*."

He pushed a few buttons, then handed the device to his mother. "What did I do?"

She crouched down, held his shoulders and looked into his brown eyes. "It's not you, Tommy. Mommy needs help."

Tommy frowned. Then his face lit up. "I know who can help us."

She looked at him quizzically. He pointed to his T-shirt.

Her heart sank, but she feigned a smile. "*Spiderman* can't swing to our rescue. But, I have an idea. Tommy, how would you like to go to a hotel?"

Tommy's eyes widened. "Cool." He paused. "Are we going to live at the hotel?"

Jude tousled his dark-brown hair. "No, it's just for a day or two." She wondered where they could go then.

Tommy stared at her, looking puzzled.

"Let's pretend we're spies, Tommy. We'll sneak out the back door and run down the alley. Then we'll look for a taxi on the Danforth. Okay?"

"Yes, Mommy."

She took his hand and led him toward the stairs. "We may be away longer than just tonight. We'll pack a few things to take with us."

"But, Mommy, can't we??"

"We don't have time for questions, Tommy. You have to do as I say. Got it?"

"Got it," he muttered. "Ten-four."

She stopped on the landing. "Now scoot to your room and get out your backpack. I'll be there in a sec."

"I wish Daddy was here. Not in heaven."

She drew in a deep breath. "Me too, honey."

In her bedroom, Jude sank onto the bed. Her heart hammered in her chest as her gaze fell on the pewter-framed photo on the dresser. She picked it up and stared at the photograph of a man in a dark suit and tie. He was handing a silver trophy to a teenage boy dressed in hockey gear. The photo had run in the *Toronto World*, and the newspaper had sold her a print.

She focused on the man in the photograph. "What should I do?"

Then it came to her.

"Tommy, your father may be able to help us after all."

Chapter One

Pat

It was just after four o'clock on the thirtieth day of December when an attractive dark-haired woman rushed into my office. Her china-blue eyes were pleading. "Mrs. Tierney, I need to speak to you."

"You can't just barge in here," said Rose Sisto, our administrative assistant. "I'm sorry, Pat, she ran past me."

Even though it was a Sunday, Rose and I were in the office finishing up work before the branch closed for a week's holiday. I'd been about to tell Rose to head on home and I decided that now would be a good time to do so. "I'll take care of it, Rose. Call it a day."

Rose scowled at the woman, then nodded to me. "Thanks, Pat." She offered me a cautious smile. "Happy New Year." She closed the office door.

I motioned to the woman to take the chair that faced my desk. "You've caught me at a bad time, Ms...."

She extended her hand. "Seaton. Jude Seaton."

I hesitated, then shook it. "I'm very busy."

"I'll pay for your time, of course." She dug into her shoulder bag.

I held up a hand. "Five minutes. Then, I'll write a note for Rose to book you an appointment in January. And my fees only apply to my clients. Until you and I decide to work together, there's no charge. Who referred you to us?"

"It...it's not what you think. I don't need an investment advisor."

4

I slid my chair back. "Then why come to me?" I was sure she was going to try to sell me something, until I saw tears glisten on her cheeks. I pushed a box of tissues across the desk. She patted her face and fixed her eyes on me again.

What was she up to?

"It's my little boy, Tommy. I'm afraid someone will…" She worried her hands together. "Hurt him."

"Your little boy?"

She took a deep breath. "I've heard a lot about you. Gemma Johannsen is a friend of mine."

Gemma had come to my late husband, Michael, for investment advice when she had inherited her uncle's large estate. I'd managed her money for the past four years since Michael's death.

"I realize this is a strange request, but…I need someone to take Tommy over the New Year while I sort things out. Would you…"

I stared at her and wondered if she was crazy. She was in her mid-thirties, nicely dressed in slim-fitting black trousers and a black cashmere turtleneck. Well groomed. Didn't look like a head case, but…

"How did you get into the building?" I asked her. "It's Sunday and the door downstairs is locked."

"A man opened the front door with a key, and I followed him inside. I saw that the light was on in your office so I knew you'd be here."

She knew exactly where my office was in the building. What else did she know about me?

"Ms. Seaton, if your son really is in danger, you need the police."

"No. No police."

I was taken aback. "They'll know how to handle whatever this is."

"Absolutely no police."

I frowned. She was up to something that she didn't want the police to know about. I wanted her out of my office.

I stood up. "Surely this is a matter for your family."

"I can't leave Tommy with my mother or my sister. Or any of my friends."

I didn't need this. I walked over to the door and opened it. "Look, Ms. Seaton, I've had enough. You must have noticed in the listings downstairs that our name is Tierney Pratt Financial. We're a financial services firm, not a child-care center."

The woman's eyes seemed to grow larger in her pale face. "I don't know where else to go, and I didn't think you'd turn Tommy away."

"Whatever made you think that?"

"Tommy," she started, in a voice not much louder than a whisper, "is Michael's son."

I stared at her and let her words sink in. She held my gaze.

"Michael? My husband?" I gave a nervous laugh. "Is this some kind of sick joke?"

The woman looked down at her hands clasped in her lap and shook her head.

I glared at her. "I don't believe you." And I didn't.

She stood and motioned for me to follow her to the door. "See for yourself."

In the reception area, a small boy was seated on a chair, swinging his legs as he focused on a gaming device in his hands.

"Tommy," the woman said.

The child looked up and grinned. Then he returned to his game.

My heart did a flip-flop. The boy was a miniature Michael?the same liquid brown eyes framed with long lashes, the same wavy brown hair. He even had Michael's dimple on the right side of his face. And he looked a lot like my older daughter, Tracy. There was no point in denying it. This was Michael's son.

I eased the door closed and bowed my head. Why hadn't I known about this child? Then I wheeled around to face the woman. "How dare you come here!"

She just stood there, looking at me.

I returned to my desk and dropped into my chair. I felt a sob gathering in my chest. She slid back into the chair across from me.

"Michael had a son," I said. "A son."

"He didn't know. I never told him about Tommy." She paused. "And I haven't told Tommy who his father was."

"Why?"

"I...I thought it would be better this way. For all of us."

"When...?" My throat constricted.

"Tommy is seven."

"Go on." My mind raced back to what had been going on in my life at the time Tommy was conceived.

"I met Michael at a summer party Gemma threw. You were out of town."

I'd taken the girls to England for a month that summer. Michael planned to join us for the last week, but he called to say he couldn't make it. Said he was bogged down with work looking after my clients as well as his own. I apologized. Bastard!

"The party was a barbecue," the woman continued, "but it started to rain so people drifted inside. Michael

7

went over to the piano and started to play. Standards, old show tunes. Soon everyone was singing."

She paused. "I sat down on the piano bench to play with him. Cole Porter, 'Just One of Those Things.' When he smiled at me, there was...something..." She bowed her head.

I struggled to speak. "How...how long...?"

"Less than three weeks."

I got up, went over to the window and looked out on the Toronto night. Christmas lights twinkled on Eglinton Avenue. The street looked exactly as it had for the past few weeks, but my world had changed beyond recognition.

Twisting the rings on my left hand, I studied my reflection in the glass. I saw a green-eyed blonde, hair artfully disarranged. Businesswoman, mother, a wife for nearly twenty years. A woman so stupid that she didn't know her husband was sleeping around. I swallowed back the bile that was rising in my throat.

"Mrs. Tierney," the woman was saying, "Michael broke it off the day before you returned. I never saw him again."

I turned to face her, crossing my arms over my chest. There she sat, her eyes fixed on me, the mother of Michael's son. I thought of the baby boy I'd lost when I'd miscarried at four months. "You never saw him again?"

She touched her fingers to her lips. "Once. One day Tommy and I were in the parking garage at the York Center. Tommy was two years old. Michael walked by with one of your daughters. A fair-haired girl in a pink rain slicker."

Laura. I fidgeted with my rings again.

"We were in the car, and Michael didn't see us. I've often wondered what would have happened if he had. But he probably wouldn't have realized that Tommy was his son?even though he looks so much like him. Men are like that."

"No, he would have known. It was pretty hard to put anything over on Michael."

She locked eyes with me and nodded. "When I heard he'd died, I felt so…sad that Tommy would never know his father."

My anger exploded. "You felt sad that your son would never know his father? You should have thought of that when you were sleeping with another woman's husband."

She drew back a bit. "Michael told me it was the first time he'd…strayed. I thought that made me special, but it didn't. The idea of choosing between us never occurred to him." She paused, looking downcast.

I stood at the window, my hands clenched.

"The last time we were together, he said he couldn't bear the thought of ever losing his girls." She looked up at me. "He wasn't just talking about his daughters."

"Why are you telling me this?" I wanted to slap her.

"I need someplace Tommy can go for a few days. I thought if you knew who he was, you'd help."

"You fucked my husband, but you are not fucking with me." I was out of control. The man I'd loved since I was nineteen had lied and cheated and played me for a fool, just as Jude was trying to. I gripped my hands together so she wouldn't see them shaking. "Get out. Now."

She rose from the chair and came over to me. I got of whiff of sandalwood and some other spice I couldn't place. "Please. I have nowhere else to turn." She touched my hand. I jerked it away from her.

"I'm not a bad person. I teach English at Queen of Angels Academy. I pay my bills and my taxes. And I'm raising my son to be an honest and caring person." She closed her eyes and paused for a few moments. "I'm in some trouble right now. I'm afraid that if I don't…do what he wants, something will happen to Tommy."

Looking at her ashen face, I wondered for a moment if she was telling the truth. "What kind of trouble?"

The door opened and Tommy stood facing us. I turned my head. I didn't want to see that little face that looked so much like Michael's.

"Mommy, how long we gotta stay here?"

He went over to his mother and she put an arm around him. "This nice lady is Mrs. Tierney."

I forced myself to look at the child and my heart ached.

"You're going to stay with Mrs. Tierney for a few days, while Mommy takes care of some work."

I gasped in surprise.

"But Mommy…" The boy looked at me with his father's eyes.

"It'll just be a few days." She gave him a hug. Over his head, she sent me a beseeching look.

I shook my head.

"Tommy, go wait on the chair in the next room," she said. "I'll come see you in a minute."

"How dare you," I cried when the boy left us.

"You have to take him." Her voice rose in pitch. "Something terrible will happen to him if you don't."

She was trying to play on my sympathy. "No."

Tears filled her eyes. "I'm sorry, but I can't risk anything happening to Tommy. Just give me a few days to sort things out."

She stepped outside the office and returned moments later with a blue nylon backpack and a booster seat.

"I've packed some of his clothes. And I brought along his booster seat for your car. I'll call you in a few days." She thrust the seat into my arms. Startled, I took it.

With that, she dropped the backpack on the floor and bolted out of the office.

Chapter Two

Pat

I stood there holding the seat for a few moments, stunned. Then I flung it on a chair, ran to the door of the suite and out into the empty hall. At the elevator, I heard the ancient contraption grinding its way down through the old building. I thought of taking the five flights of stairs, but I knew that Jude would be gone before I reached the ground floor.

Tommy looked up from his game when I returned. "Where's Mommy?"

"She left in a big hurry."

"We're staying in a hotel tonight."

Then we had better get your mother back here. But I kept my thoughts to myself and headed into my office.

I surveyed the papers on my desk, but my head was spinning with images of Michael and Jude. Clinking wine glasses. In bed.

And now their son was sitting outside my office.

I decided that I'd finish my work later and printed out the document on my screen. I looked out at the boy in the waiting room. I had to get rid of him before I left for cottage country with my daughters the next morning.

I grabbed a notepad and pen, went out and sat down beside Tommy. "What's your phone number?" I wrote down the number he gave me. "Your address?"

"Thirty-four Ramsey Road."

Jude had mentioned her mother and a sister. "Your grandmother, Tommy. What's her name?"

"Nana."

"That's what you call her, but what's your grandmother's other name?"

"Mommy calls her Mom."

"Do you know her phone number?"

He shook his head. "Mommy calls Nana, then I talk to her. But I know what street she lives on. Rosedale Park Drive."

I wrote that down. "Aunts and uncles?"

"Auntie Arlene and Uncle Lloyd. And Uncle Patrick."

"You know their phone numbers?"

He shook his head.

"Their last names? are they Seaton like yours?"

His eyes looked puzzled. "I think so."

"You'll have to wait here a little longer. Need to use the washroom?" I took him to the washroom and found a bottle of orange juice for him in the kitchenette. When he came out, I gave him the juice and he went back to his game.

I called Gemma Johannsen and got her voice mail. Then I remembered that she had planned to spend the week between Christmas and the New Year in St. Lucia.

Jude had said it would just be a few days. Did that mean two days? Three days? Did she intend to call the office when she was ready to take Tommy home? Or had Gemma given her my home number and my cell number?

I picked up the brass nameplate on my desk and turned it toward me. Pat Tierney, CFP, it read. Certified Financial Planner. Certified chump was more like it. I turned the nameplate back to face the client's chair.

I scrunched up a piece of paper. I aimed it at the wastepaper basket by my open door and lobbed the paper ball across the room. Bull's-eye!

"Bravo, *ma chère*. You should try out for the Raptors." Stéphane Pratt, my thirty-two-year-old business partner, stepped into the office suite. "I thought you'd be packing for the cottage."

Stéphane looked festive with his jaunty Christmas bow tie. There were more blond highlights in his brown hair, and a spiffy charcoal suit hung well on his slim five-foot-five frame.

I tried to slap a cheerful look on my face. "I have work to wrap up here. Had a good Christmas?"

He shrugged. "So-so. Big family get-togethers bring out the worst in everyone. Sister Hélène was determined to play the perfect Christmas hostess. Problem was hubby Serge, who's an obnoxious drunk."

I smiled, trying to look sympathetic. Stéphane had broken up with his lover in the fall, and I'd hoped that Christmas with his family in northern Ontario would restore his spirits. "Cross-country skiing over the New Year may make up for Christmas."

"I'm looking forward to it."

"I'll have to take my laptop."

"You need a holiday, Pat."

"An hour of work now and then won't kill me."

Stéphane studied my face. "I don't know. You look..." He shifted his gaze to the coat rack near the door, where I'd hung my white cashmere coat and forest-green scarf. "Nice coat. And long scarves look good on tall women."

"Christmas gifts from the girls."

He gave me a wink. "Was there a present under your tree from Mr. Devon Shaughnessy?"

My heart sank at the mention of Devon's name. I'd met him the previous summer when I'd rented a house on a lake north of Toronto. Devon owned the vacation home beside it.

In September, he'd returned to the software firm he ran in Connecticut. I hadn't heard from him until early December when he'd called to invite my daughters and me to ring in the New Year in cottage country. Stéphane was still shaky after his breakup with Claude, so I'd asked Devon to invite him as well.

I'd been looking forward to the holiday and to spending time with Devon. Until Jude Seaton walked into my office and turned my world upside down.

"Devon's giving all of us the perfect gift," I said. "New Year's at his cottage."

Stéphane's brow furrowed. "What is it, *ma chère?*"

"Nothing. Everything is fine." Seeing his puzzled look, I softened my tone. "Sorry. It's just..." I couldn't explain. "You're right. I do need a break."

"Well..." He looked at me anxiously. "I'll hit the liquor store in the morning. The wine and the bubbly will be my treat." He cocked his thumb over his shoulder. "Who's the kid?"

"The son of a friend...of Michael's." I struggled to keep my voice steady. "I'm looking after him for a few days."

Stéphane's eyes bored into me. "What's his name?"

"Tommy. Tommy Seaton."

He chuckled. "Are we wooing Tommy as a future client? A potentially very rich one?"

I looked at him, puzzled.

"Is he one of the Seatons, as in Seaton Ferguson?"

Seaton Ferguson, the giant auto-parts manufacturer. Why hadn't I made the connection? The Seatons and the Johannsens moved in the same moneyed world. But Jude had said she was a teacher. "I'm not sure if…if it's that family."

"If he's one of those Seatons, he could come into quite an inheritance one day."

When Stéphane had left for his own office, I looked up Seaton Ferguson on the Internet. Patrick Seaton was listed as the company's president and chief executive, and Lloyd Dobson was down as its vice president. Uncle Patrick and Uncle Lloyd? But I didn't find either of them in the telephone directory. Or a Seaton on Rosedale Park Drive. But I hadn't really expected to. The Seatons and the Dobsons would have had unlisted phone numbers.

I punched the number Tommy had given me into my cell phone and got Jude's voice mail. I decided not to leave a message. Instead, I called for a taxi. I locked up the office, and bundled Tommy, his backpack and his booster seat into the cab that was waiting in front of the building. I gave the driver Jude's address.

"I'm taking you home," I told the small boy in the booster seat beside me.

"Mommy and me are staying in a hotel tonight. She said we'd get room service and watch movies on television."

"We'll see if she's at home."

The taxi took us through Leaside and turned south on Laird Drive. On Danforth Avenue, we drove east for a few miles. Just past Woodbine, we turned onto a dark, tree-lined street and pulled up in front of a small semi-detached brick house. I saw Christmas lights twinkling through the living room window.

"I don't think Mommy's at home."

"Does she leave the Christmas tree lights on when she goes out?"

He just stared at me.

Jude had said Tommy was in danger. You have to take him, she'd said. Something terrible will happen if you don't.

I looked at the house again. She'd been stringing me a line. She needed someone to look after her son so she could party over the New Year. But I couldn't shake the uneasy feeling I had as I sat outside that house.

I turned to Tommy. "Do you have a key?"

He shook his head. "Mommy sometimes puts a key under the mat."

"I'll just be a minute," I told the driver.

Tommy started to follow me out.

"Stay here. I'll see if your mom's in."

I climbed the steps to the sagging front porch and looked in the living room window. No one was in the room, and the rest of the house seemed to be in darkness.

I rapped the brass knocker on the front door. Nobody answered, so I tried again. After a couple of rounds of rapping and waiting, I hit redial on my cell and put my ear to the door. I could hear a telephone ringing inside the house. I flipped up the mat in front of the door. Nothing there. Then I surveyed the neighboring homes. Some of them had lights on.

I opened the taxi's back door. "Are you friendly with any of your neighbors?"

"Sophie. She lives there." Tommy pointed to the semi next to his. Its windows were all dark. "She's gone to see her daughter."

I got in beside him. "Do you have a babysitter?"

"Cindy stays with me sometimes."

"Does she live around here?"

He shook his head. "Cindy's in high school."

"You know where she lives?"

17

"No. She comes to our house."

I gave the cabbie my address. On the way home, I called several of the big downtown hotels. Jude Seaton wasn't registered at any of them. She wasn't at any of the airport hotels I was familiar with either.

"Mommy said we'd get room service," Tommy said between calls.

"All these hotels I'm calling have room service. Once we find your mother, you can order whatever you like."

Chapter Three

Pat

Maxie, our golden lab, greeted us with a rapturous dance in the front hall. Then she got up on her hind legs and leaned her forepaws on my chest.

"Down, girl," I said. "Sit." She gave my face a lick before she obeyed.

"Tommy, meet Maxie."

He seemed to hesitate a moment or two before he reached out to pet the dog. Maxie sniffed his hand, licked it, circled us twice, then came to rest in front of me. Her eyes shone.

I grimaced. Maxie wanted to play. The last thing I was in the mood for.

A few days before Christmas, I had found her at the Toronto Humane Society and was seduced by her mournful eyes. I kept her in a kennel until Christmas Eve when I presented her, with a big, red bow around her neck, to my daughter, Laura. Laura immediately named her Maxie, a tribute to her beloved Max, hit by a car the year before.

Maxie was housebroken, but given to displays of impulsive affection. And she was fond of stretching out on the sofas. I'd been after Laura to discipline her pet.

I was helping Tommy take off his jacket when Farah Alwan, our housekeeper, came into the hall, her long, dark hair pulled back from her face with an elastic band.

"You're still here," I said. It was after six and Farah was usually long gone by then.

She fastened a black scarf over her head. "I wait for Raad. He come any minute."

I introduced her to Tommy, then the door bell sounded. I opened the front door and waved Farah's brother inside. I liked Raad, a serious man who held down a daytime job in a factory and worked as an office cleaner in the evenings.

He came in and pulled off his tuque. I noticed that his dark hair was graying at the temples.

"Hello, Mrs. Tierney." He turned to Farah. "I have something you must read, my sister. Mrs. Tierney, I want you read also."

He followed Farah into the kitchen where she'd put her coat and he thrust a section of the *Toronto World* into her hands. Farah sat down at the table. Raad sat across from her and stroked his short beard while she read.

I pulled out another chair for Tommy, and got him a bottle of apple juice. I sat down beside him.

Three years before, Farah and her mother had left Iraq by crossing into Jordan. They'd spent six months in a refugee camp and were sponsored into Canada by Raad, who had arrived five years earlier and was a Canadian citizen.

Now in her early twenties, Farah was adjusting well to life in North America. From the magazines she read and the comments she'd made in the year she had worked for me, I'd gathered she was looking forward to everything our consumer society could offer her: lovely clothes, travel and a beautiful home. Outdoors, she still wore the hijab. I knew she would cover her head in public as long as she lived in Raad's home.

"People are missing," Raad said to me. "Refugees. They disappear, no one see them again."

Farah slid the newspaper across the table and shrugged.

Raad handed the paper to me. An article had been circled with blue ink.

> *The head and limbs of a young African-American male have been found in a shallow grave northwest of Toronto.*
>
> *The discovery just outside of Brampton is the third of its kind in recent months. In November, Toronto city workers found the head of an Asian woman while dredging a pond in a Scarborough park. A few weeks before that, limbs were retrieved by a pet dog in a city ravine. Police found a head of an African-American male in the woods nearby.*
>
> *None of the body parts have been identified, and none match missing-person reports…*

"You think these are the refugees who have gone missing?" I asked.

Raad bowed his head. "I have terrible feeling."

"What this have to do with us?" Farah asked him.

He looked at her in dismay. "Not everyone blessed like you and me, Farah. Refugees, they sometimes turned down by Canadian government. But if they return home, they go to prison. Maybe they are tortured or killed. So they hide here in the shadows. Work for people paying them cash, asking no questions."

"I am sorry for these people," Farah said, "but is not my problem."

Raad blasted her with a torrent of Arabic. She lowered her eyes.

"There is Suleyman," he continued in English. "His claim get turn down in November. He disappear. No one know where he is."

"He go underground," Farah said.

"Why he not tell his friends?" Raad asked. "They have ears open for work for him."

Farah tried to affect concern, but she wasn't convincing.

"And there is Ali. And now this." He pointed to the newspaper article. "I worry about you, my sister. Streets not safe."

"This is Toronto. Allah protect us here."

Tommy pounded the empty tetra-pack on the table and got out of his chair.

Raad stood up. "Come, Farah. We make delivery." He turned to me. "Is now our holiday, Eid ul-Adha. We pray at mosque, and share food with family and friends. Is also our time to give to people less fortunate than us. Our mother, she cook special meal for Safe Harbor. Farah and me, we give people there feast tonight."

"Safe Harbor," I said. "The home for refugees in the west end?"

"Yes, I help there weekends. Come, Farah."

With a sigh, she put on her coat and followed him to the door.

As soon as Farah and Raad had gone, I hit redial on my cell and got Jude's voice mail. I glanced at Tommy who was throwing a ball down the hall for Maxie. It looked like he would be with us for the New Year.

I left a message telling Jude where we were going the next day and asking her to drive up north to get her son. I gave her directions. I left my cell and my home numbers, and told her to call me that evening. I needed to know if Tommy had any allergies and who I should contact in an emergency.

I wondered what I would tell the girls. They would take one look at Tommy and know their father... I decided I would deal with that in the morning. I sat Tommy down at the kitchen table and told him my plans for the next few days.

"Is Maxie coming?"

"Yes."

"Cool!"

"Tommy, are there any foods you can't eat?"

"Like Ben at school? He can't eat nuts so we don't bring peanut butter in our lunches."

"Yes, nuts or anything else. Do you have any food allergies?"

"I eat everything."

"Allergies to anything else?" I looked at Maxie. "Animals?"

"Mommy's allergic to cats and dogs, that's why I can't have one. But I'm not."

I could only hope he was right. "My girls, Tracy and Laura, won't be home till later tonight. I'll fix us some soup and sandwiches?"

"Mommy said we'd have room service."

"Tommy?"

"Can we order pizza?"

I closed my eyes and prayed for patience. "Not tonight. After we eat, you can have a bath and I'll make up your bed in the guest room."

"Can I watch television?"

"No. We have a big day ahead of us."

"But my mom lets me?"

"You're at my house tonight, Tommy."

He stared at me for a few seconds, then nodded. Just like Michael did.

The thought flashed through my mind that the boy might really be in some kind of danger. But I pushed it away. Jude had accomplished exactly what she had set out to do when she visited my office that afternoon. She'd found a babysitter for her son.

In the kitchen, I found a note from Laura under a fridge magnet. She said she had taken Maxie for a walk earlier and would walk her again when she got home around ten.

I needed time to myself that evening. I needed time to think.

After I had tucked Tommy in for the night, I changed into a flannel nightgown and a long, red bathrobe. My comfort clothes. I peered into the bedroom mirror. My dark blond hair had been layered and highlighted the week before and I'd tousled it with mousse that morning. But the perky hairdo was at odds with my drawn face. I looked every one of my forty-seven years. Maybe more.

In the kitchen, I opened a bottle of chardonnay and poured myself a glass. I started to return the bottle to the fridge, then hesitated. "What the hell." I took a swallow from the glass. With the bottle in my other hand, I headed for the sunroom.

I sifted through a shelf of CDs and programmed the stereo. The silky voice of Ella Fitzgerald singing "I Remember You"?one of Michael's favorites?filled the room.

"No," I said to Maxie who was eyeing the sofa. "On the floor."

The dog stretched out on the carpet. I settled myself on the sofa and surveyed the room Michael had designed.

We'd added it to the back of the house the year before Laura was born. During the day, it was filled with light from the French doors and the skylight. At night, with the shutters drawn and a fire in the fireplace, it was a cozy retreat.

When the girls were younger and went to bed earlier, Michael and I would curl up in front of the fire, and listen to jazz or watch old movies. I considered lighting a fire, but I didn't have the heart for it. Instead, I pulled a wool throw over myself and remembered the warmth I'd once found in Michael's arms. Arms that he had wrapped around Jude.

I poured myself a second glass of wine.

I'd met Michael when I was a second-year English major at Queen's University. Our paths might never have crossed if it hadn't been for the fall production of *Private Lives*.

When the curtain fell on the final performance, it went up on our romance. Until Jude walked into my office, I'd believed it had played out as a happy story that ended prematurely with Michael's fatal heart attack four years before. Now, his affair with Jude had given that story a nasty twist.

I clenched my fists. How could he have fallen for her? And how could I have not known?

The curtain parted. The four actors joined hands and took deep bows. Lynda Burke, who had played Amanda Prynne, moved forward for a solo bow. Dan Hooper, the play's director and the head of the English department, presented her with a bouquet of red roses and a kiss on each cheek.

Then Michael Tierney, the male lead, stepped up and took Lynda's hand. They bowed in unison. The audience got to its feet and roared its applause. In the wings, I clapped until my hands hurt. I had loved every moment of the eight performances, especially the leads' quicksilver sparring as the dueling divorcées.

"Neat, eh?"

I turned to see Jackie McKinnon, the petite brunette on the makeup team, beside me. I shrugged, annoyed. I'd thought I was alone and out of sight.

"Michael's a heartthrob." Jackie echoed my thoughts. "Looks like a movie star in that gold smoking jacket."

She heaved a great sigh. "But, hey, what does it matter? He and Lynda are an item."

My heart sank. Of course. Lynda Burke, with her long auburn hair and exotic clothes, could have any guy she wanted on campus.

"They both graduate in the spring, so they'll probably try for the same grad school. But then Michael's in commerce so he may wind up with a job instead."

I frowned. Michael was cool. Commerce was for squares with horned-rimmed glasses who beavered away in the library to get an edge on jobs in soulless corporations.

An hour later, I was sipping Purple Jesus at the cast party. Couples on the dance floor gyrated to KC and the Sunshine Band's "Shake Your Booty." I scanned the floor, hoping to catch a glimpse of Michael.

"Disco's dead," a male voice said behind me.

I took a sip of my drink. "Those people out there are into it. Not my thing, though."

"What is your thing?"

I turned my head and nearly sputtered. Michael Tierney, a bottle of beer in his hand, stood inches away from me. He'd changed into blue jeans and a pale blue shirt with a button-down collar.

"I…I…" I wanted to tell him how great he'd been in the play, but I found myself at a loss for words.

He grinned and extended his hand. "Michael Tierney. You're…?"

"P-Pat," I managed to say as I took his hand. "Pat Kelleher."
Grand Funk Railroad chugged through "The Locomotion."
"Stage crew, right?"
"Yeah."
"Well, Pat Kelleher, what do you say we dance?"

Ella was crooning "All the Things You Are" as the memories washed over me. Michael's fondness for jazz, old musicals and the Beatles. The first time we made love in the sagging bed in the student co-op where he lived. The small apartment we shared in Toronto while I was at teachers' college. The emerald ring he gave me that Christmas.

I held my left hand up to the lamp behind my head. The diamonds beside my wedding band sparkled in the light. On our tenth anniversary, Michael had presented me with a diamond eternity ring. We'd given the emerald to Tracy on her sixteenth birthday.

The circle of diamonds filled me with sadness. I hadn't realized eternity would be so brief.

Chapter Four

Yuri

"There! There she is." Oskar slouched further down behind the steering wheel.

Yuri's eyes narrowed and focused on the house with the sagging front porch. The front door was ajar and someone leaned out to pick up a newspaper. The SUV was parked across the street and two houses down, so he couldn't make out whether the figure was a man or a woman. Then the door closed and the street returned to its early morning slumber.

He yawned and checked his watch. Five past six. He needed another coffee. Mornings were not his favorite time of day.

"We go in now. While street still quiet."

Yuri held up a hand. "One more day, we watch. See who is in there. Maybe she not alone."

"She have young boy. But that no problem."

"No man?"

"No."

"No boyfriend she spend night with?"

"No. Come, we go."

Oskar reached for the door handle, but Yuri grabbed his arm. "Wait."

Oskar jerked his head around and glared at him.

Yuri had long before known that recklessness trumped caution when Oskar wanted to take action. If anything, his foolhardiness had grown over the years and it worried Yuri. He remembered Oskar's mistakes in combat that had cost comrades-in-arms their lives. He had no desire to be counted among the glorious dead.

"Oskar, remember I tell you in Bosnia to watch and wait before you make move? Wait for right moment? Is holiday time now. Maybe she have visitors. Family."

"Watch and wait good back then, but now something need to be done." Oskar opened his door. "Before she tell everyone."

Oskar had a point. With a sigh, Yuri followed him out of the van. The woman needed to be taken care of before she talked.

But, as they crossed the street, instinct told him they were making the wrong move.

Chapter Five

Pat

"Mom, why do I have to go?" Laura asked for the tenth time the next morning. "It's New Year's Eve and there's a party at Kyle's tonight. Everybody will be there."

"Not everybody. You'll be up north. Now grab your bag and get into the car. Tracy and Tommy are waiting for us." I hit redial on my cell and got Jude's voice mail again. Where was the woman? She hadn't called the night before and she wasn't at home now. I didn't bother leaving another message.

"Mom, don't you get it?" Laura said. "Devon wants to spend time with you. We'll just be in the way."

I had wondered what Devon expected from this holiday. The summer before, there had definitely been a spark between us, but we'd made an unspoken agreement to move slowly. At least I'd thought we had, and if Devon wanted to spend time alone with me, he wouldn't have included our kids. But after Jude's visit the day before, I was glad he had.

"Devon asked all of us and we'll all be there," I said. "No exceptions."

Laura rolled her eyes. "And why is that kid coming along? If you think I'm babysitting some brat—"

"Laura."

"Who is he, anyway?"

"His mother's a client. Something came up—"

"Yeah, a hot date."

"Something urgent came up," I continued, "and I agreed to take him."

"Mom, you're the world's biggest pushover."

I glared at her. "That's enough." If she knew Tommy was her brother, she'd have called me something a lot more colorful than a pushover.

"This woman's taking advantage of you. Like, what could be so urgent on New Year's Eve?"

"What's urgent right now is that you get in the car so we can head out before we get stuck in traffic. Move it."

Laura groaned and picked up her backpack.

I locked up the house and took my carryall to the car, wondering when the fun would start.

Vivaldi's "Mandolin Concerto" flowed from the stereo as I drove the silver Volvo up the Don Valley Parkway. The sun shone down on us from a true blue sky. The temperature outside hovered around zero.

Beside me in the passenger seat, Tracy studied a legal text. I looked in the rear-view mirror. Tommy sat on his booster seat with Maxie beside him. On Tommy's other side, Laura had tuned out everyone as she listened to her iPod.

In the mirror, I saw her take the buds out of her ears and fasten her blond ponytail into a knot at the back of her head. Then she turned her head and looked at Tommy. "Have I met you before?" she asked him.

I saw him shake his head.

"Yeah, but you look familiar."

"Mommy says I look like my dad."

"Speaking of fathers and sons," I said, "I wonder if Ryan looks like Devon."

That got Laura's attention away from Tommy. "Devon's son will be there? Since when?"

31

"Since Devon phoned a few days ago about a change in his flight plans. They should be up there by now."

She slumped back in her seat. "Great, just great. I've got to miss my boyfriend's party to spend New Year's with a couple of kids."

Tracy looked up from her book. "Ryan's no kid."

"How old is he?" Laura demanded.

"Nineteen Devon told us last summer. Probably twenty by now. A few years older than you, Laura. A third-year history major at UC Berkeley."

"You may have a lot in common," I said.

"Yeah." Laura put the iPod buds back in her ears. "I bet he doesn't want to be there either."

"Welcome to Chez Shaughnessy." Devon held the driver's door open and tipped an imaginary hat on his silver head. "We hope you find everything to your satisfaction."

He put his arms around me as I stepped out of the car. When he kissed me, I pulled back.

His eyes widened in surprise. "What is it?"

"Nothing. I'm just a little..." Hurt. Betrayed. And unsure how I felt about him.

"Tired?"

"Just a bit." And I was, even though the drive had been smooth and our only stops had been to buy groceries in Kincaid and to rent cross-country skis at Highland Outfitters.

He brightened. "We'll fix that. Let's get you settled?"

"Mister, is this place yours?"

Devon and I looked down at Tommy.

"Yes, indeed." Devon crouched down so he was at eye level with the boy. "And you're...?"

"Tommy." The boy held out a mittened hand. "Tommy Seaton."

"Pleased to meet you, Tommy Seaton. I'm Devon Shaughnessy." Devon shook the boy's hand and glanced over his shoulder at me.

"Tommy's mother...there was an emergency. She asked me to take him."

"No problem." Devon straightened up. "Plenty of room." He turned his attention back to Tommy. "Why don't you take the dog for a run around the house while I help the Tierneys unload the car?"

Tommy scampered after Maxie, who was sniffing the other two vehicles parked in front of the house?a gold van, which I assumed was Devon's rental, and Stéphane's green Jag with a pair of skis on a custom-made roof rack.

Devon turned to me. "How long has the little guy been on skis?"

"This'll be his first time. I found that out when we rented our skis."

"How much do you know about him, Mom?" Tracy asked as she and Laura hauled baggage and grocery bags out of the trunk. "Is it some kind of custody thing, abusive father?"

"Nothing like that."

"Then what's his story?" Laura wanted to know.

"Let's unload the car."

"What's the big deal that you can't tell us?" Tracy asked.

"Yeah, what?" Laura added.

"Girls, you heard your mother." Devon pulled a bag of groceries from the Volvo's trunk. "Let's get your stuff inside."

"But?" Laura began to protest.

"Your mother will fill us in in good time. Right, Pat?"

I smiled weakly and took my bag from the trunk. I didn't know how much of Tommy's "story" I should tell them.

Chez Shaughnessy was a two-story log structure on five acres. It had a wrap-around deck, generous windows that let in plenty of light, four upstairs bedrooms, a study and another bedroom in the basement. And it faced one of the largest lakes in Haversham County.

The Talking Heads' "Life During Wartime" blasted through the house as we got settled in our rooms.

"Someone's into the oldies," Tracy as we headed back downstairs.

"Oldies?" I asked.

"Yeah, Mom," Laura said. "The Eighties. Like where have you been?"

"Ryan, put something else on," Devon shouted over the music when we reached the foot of the stairs. "And turn down the volume while you're at it."

The main floor of the house was open-concept. A long pine refectory table separated the country kitchen from the living area where a black leather couch and armchairs were arranged in front of a large stone fireplace.

Devon knelt in front of the fireplace. Stéphane was seated in an armchair, a glass of red wine in his hand. Devon's son, Ryan, slouched on the couch, eyes closed, head nodding in time to the music, Doc Martens propped on the coffee table in front of him.

If a studio ever remade *Blade Runner*, I thought as I sat down beside him, Ryan should try out as an extra. He was dressed in black, his head was shaven, a metal ring pierced his right nostril and more rings adorned his left earlobe.

He had his father's black eyes under dark brows, aquiline nose and square jaw. But his good looks were marred by the scowl on his face and the brooding expression in his eyes.

"Ryan," Devon said.

"All right, all right." Ryan picked up a remote from the table and stopped the music. "Something for the old folks. How about...ah, just the thing." He punched some buttons. "You should all know this one."

Punk rock sprang from the stereo, as a harsh, nasal voice spat out the lyrics to Frank Sinatra's "My Way."

Laura seated herself on the other side of Ryan. "Sid Vicious. Awesome!"

Devon got up from the fireplace and hit the buttons on the stereo. "That's enough of Ryan's selections." He glared at his son before slipping a CD into the system. Edith Piaf's "Milord" wafted through the house.

"Everyone up for skiing?" he asked.

He was trying so hard to be the perfect host and his son wasn't co-operating. I should have rallied, showed some enthusiasm, but I just wasn't up to it.

"Conditions should be perfect," Tracy said. "It's been snowing here for the past two days."

"I'm good to go," Stéphane said.

Laura jumped up. "Me too. Let's hit the trails."

"Me and Maxie wanna come," Tommy said.

"Tracy and Laura will help you with your skis and keep an eye on you, Tommy. Right, girls?" I gave my daughters my no-arguments look.

Laura rolled her eyes. "Whatever. C'mon." She took Tommy's hand. Ryan and Devon remained seated as the others went off to collect their ski gear.

I racked my brain for something to snap Ryan out of his sullenness. "Do a lot of cross-country skiing?"

"In California? Duh!" A silver stud in his tongue flashed as he spoke. "I'm at Berkeley now, or did Dad forget to tell you?"

Devon turned to me. "Ryan wanted to head back after Christmas, but I convinced him to try out his skis up here. And meet the Tierneys."

"Meet the Tierneys." Ryan got up from the sofa. "Sounds like a bad sitcom."

"Ryan!" Devon said.

Ryan scowled. "Okay, sorry," he said to me. He turned to his father. "Satisfied?" He headed for the stairs.

"Where do you think you're going?" Devon called after him.

"Got to get back to that history paper on my laptop." A bedroom door slammed.

"I'm sorry." Devon shook his head. "He's changed in the past few years. Used to be a fun-loving kid, captain of the high-school football team. Now…" He shrugged.

I laid a hand on his arm. "Hey, Tracy and Laura are no angels."

"So, ready to hit the trails?" He tried to sound chipper but didn't succeed.

"I'll take a pass today. I'm a little tired. I wouldn't be able to keep up."

"Nonsense. You'll—"

"Devon, please."

He put an arm around my shoulders and studied me. "What is it, Patty? Something's eating away at you."

"It's Pat, not Patty."

"All right. Just let me know if there's anything I can do."

I shook my head.

He clasped my shoulder and leaned forward to kiss me, but I turned my head away.

"I'm sorry," I said. "It's not you. It's…"

"Too much domestic drama?" He inclined his head toward the stairs.

I tried to smile. "It didn't play like *Father Knows Best*, but no. You join the others. I'll keep Maxie here with me."

He kissed me on the cheek. "I'll light a fire for you."

In the kitchen, I poured myself a glass of chardonnay and returned to my seat in front of the fireplace. I reached down to stroke Maxie who was stretched out on the floor by my feet.

I picked up my handbag from where I'd dropped it on the floor, took out my cell phone and hit redial. "Service is unavailable," appeared on the screen.

Devon had said the phone service had been disconnected for the winter, but I picked up the telephone on the end table just to be sure. Dead. Jude wouldn't be able to reach me. I rested my head on the back of the sofa and groaned. Damn woman!

In the background, Edith Piaf had given way to Glenn Gould playing Bach's "Goldberg Variations." The music, its emotion firmly contained in its tight structure, soothed me. If only I had my feelings under such control.

The image of Michael and Jude, arms wrapped around each other, floated into my mind. And there I was on a holiday with Devon who expected more than I had anticipated.

I took a gulp of wine. I had claimed a room upstairs with twin beds for Tommy and myself, glad for the first time that the boy was with us. Michael was the only man I'd ever slept with and…

Damn you, Michael. I drained the glass and went to the kitchen for a refill.

Michael had shaped my life in so many ways, I thought as I returned to the sofa. I was nineteen when we met. He was my first lover, my husband and the father of my children.

And he was Tommy's father.

"So, Pat Kelleher, you never answered me. What is your thing when it comes to music?"

"Right now, my favorites are women, even if they don't all write their own stuff. Joni Mitchell, Laura Nyro, Janis Joplin, Joan Baez, Judy Collins—"

"I get the picture." He smiled. "You're an English major."

So what? "Second year."

"And you want to write the great Canadian novel—or play."

"Of course." I smiled at him. "And you?"

"Commerce. I'd like to get into an MBA program next year."

"That sounds…" I hesitated.

"Not cool?"

I shrugged.

"What about Mick Jagger? Isn't he cool?"

What did the Rolling Stones' lead singer have to do with—

"Jagger went to the London School of Economics."

"Well," I countered, "it seems like he found a better gig."

I didn't share his ambitions then, but I couldn't help falling for Michael. He was a sexy-looking guy, of course. He was also smart, confident and dismissive of what he called phonies. At the top of his list of phonies were the guys who got girls by reading poetry and talking about the meaning of life. A good many of them were in my English classes.

After his MBA, Michael took a job at Norris Cassidy, the big brokerage house in Toronto. We married after I'd finished teachers' college and found a job at a private girls' school. Not the school where Jude taught—now wouldn't that be a coincidence? But, like Queen of Angels, it attracted the daughters of Toronto's wealthy families. Tracy was born the following year and I left teaching.

During the 1980s, investment firms were starting to get into the new field of financial planning, which involved managing clients' money to provide for their children's education, unforeseen events and their own retirement years. A few years after he'd joined Norris Cassidy, Michael opened one of its first financial planning branches. His enthusiasm for his work sparked my interest. I took night courses and joined him at the branch when Tracy started kindergarten.

Right from the start, I loved my work as a financial advisor. I still do. It's important work, getting clients' financial houses in order.

I took another sip of wine and stared at the snow-covered lake outside the sliding deck doors. I decided to put this business about Michael and Jude behind me. In a day or two, Jude would drive up and get Tommy. Then the two of them would be out of my life.

When the skiers returned I would drive over to the inn we had passed on the highway and call Jude from there. Hopefully, she would answer her phone. If she didn't, I'd leave another message telling her about the phone situation at the house. I'd say I would call her back in the morning.

But when Jude and Tommy returned to the city would that really be the end of it? What about Tracy and Laura? They had a right to know they had a brother.

I gulped down the rest of the wine. "You ruined everything, Michael!" I set the glass down on the coffee table with a bang. "And Jude…I wish you were dead!"

Chapter Six

Pat

The door to the deck slid open and Tommy ran into the room. "I skied the whole way," he cried. Maxie danced around him.

"Take off your boots," I told him, and he returned to the mat by the door. "You had fun out there?"

He looked up from his boots and nodded solemnly.

Boots off, he joined me on the sofa. "What should I call you?"

"Well...how about Mrs. T?" That was what Laura's friends called me.

"Okay." He smiled at me. "What about the others? Mommy says I can't call grown-ups by their first names."

"You can call Tracy and Laura and Ryan by their first names. Devon and Stéphane are older, so why don't you ask them what they'd like?"

He snuggled up to me. "It's nice here." He reached down to pat Maxie.

I was surprised that he wasn't shy around strangers. At his age, Tracy and Laura had been tongue-tied with people they didn't know. I put an arm around him. "What grade are you in, Tommy?"

"Grade One."

Then I remembered that he was Michael's son. I withdrew my arm and stood up. He looked at me, puzzled. "I'll get you some juice." I hurried into the kitchen.

At seven, I sat Tommy down at the table, and gave him a snack of crackers and cheese. The goose had turned a golden brown in the oven, Tracy's mushroom soup simmered on the stove and Devon had mixed a pitcher of cranberry vodka cocktails. Glass in hand, I went upstairs.

I had changed into my new black silk trousers and turquoise shirt when I realized I'd forgotten about my plan to call Jude from the inn. Would there be enough time before dinner? I shook my head. It was New Year's Eve and I figured she was probably out with her friends. I made a mental note to call her in the morning.

I knocked on the door to Ryan's room and pushed it open. "Dinner in twenty minutes. We're having appetizers now."

"Be right down," the figure on the bed mumbled.

I sniffed. The room reeked of cannabis.

Ryan sat up on the bed, coughed and extended a joint. "Try some?"

I shook my head and closed the door. How had Ryan brought the drug into Canada?

But it wasn't my problem. Then I stopped in my tracks. Maybe it was. Two years before, Laura had coolly informed me that she'd tried pot and found it overrated. Would she try it again? Should I speak to Devon? No, Ryan was beyond his control.

Downstairs, Willie Nelson was crooning "Stardust." I joined Stéphane and Devon in front of the fire.

"It's a temporary market correction. The bull run will go on for years," Stéphane said. "The younger baby boomers will be power investing for the next ten years to finance the kind of retirement they want."

Devon raised an eyebrow. "What's your take on technology?"

"Technology is here to stay. Investors got burned a few years ago by Tekstar, but everyone's on the Internet now. There's no going back."

"Speaking of technology," I said, "my cell phone doesn't work here."

Devon smiled. "We're in a dead zone. The rock cuts on the highway block the signal."

I remembered the towering walls of rock we'd driven through about a mile down the highway. They had cut us off from the rest of the world.

Tracy came down the stairs, her hair still damp from the shower, and headed for the kitchen. "Laura, give me a hand in here."

Laura heaved herself up from the couch. "Okay." She paused near the stairs. "Hey, somebody should check on Ryan."

"Laura!" I called as she ran up the stairs.

"Never mind." Tracy made a noisy show of hauling out dishes. "I'll manage."

I glanced at Devon. When did we lose control of our kids?

"Don't worry, *ma chère*," Stéphane said. "They'll be down as soon as they get a whiff of dinner."

Devon shrugged. "Let them be."

"Right." I could only hope that Laura would turn down Ryan's offer of a toke.

Tracy collapsed on the sofa beside me. "The timer will go off any minute. We'll eat soon."

Devon handed her a glass of wine. "Stéphane's been telling me about the human body parts that have been turning up around Toronto."

"Now there's a cheerful holiday topic." She took a sip. "Scary stuff, though. I can't believe we used to be called Toronto the Good."

"Toronto is a big city," Stéphane said. "And despite what Agatha Christie would have us believe, crimes are more likely to take place in big cities than in St. Mary Mead."

I shivered. "Who would do something like that? And why?"

"Sounds like the work of one of the ethnic gangs," Stéphane said. "Drug turf wars, probably."

"What makes you think that?" Devon asked.

"The victims are non-Caucasians."

"Assumptions based on stereotypes won't get you a conviction in court," Tracy said.

Stéphane chuckled.

A buzzer sounded in the kitchen and Tracy jumped up. "The goose is ready to carve. Volunteers?"

I looked from Stéphane to Devon. "Either of you guys up for the challenge?"

Devon unfurled his long legs and got up from the sofa. "I'm your man. Won a blue ribbon at carvery school."

"Should I...?" I pointed at the ceiling.

He shook his head. "They'll be down."

"Why can't I have some of that?" Tommy looked at the wine Devon had poured into glasses around the table.

I emptied a box of grape juice into the glass in front of him. "That's grape juice just like this. Only stronger. For older people."

Tommy looked at me, clearly unconvinced. Stéphane tucked a napkin into the neck of the boy's sweater.

Laura and Ryan came down the stairs. Ryan's head bobbed to an inaudible beat as he lurched to the table. Laura held a hand over her mouth.

I closed my eyes.

"Hey, Mom. Hey, Trace." Laura gave a little wave as she sat down. "Something in here smells good enough…to eat." She burst out laughing.

"No thanks to you," Tracy said.

"Ooooh, sis, c'mon. Like where's your holiday whatchamacallit?"

I held up a hand. "Girls that is enough."

Tracy folded her arms across her chest and glared at her sister. Laura cupped her hand over Ryan's ear and whispered something, setting off another fit of giggling from the two of them.

I passed the soup tureen to Tracy. "You can serve the soup."

She frowned at Laura, then ladled soup into bowls.

Devon cleared his throat. "Shall we say grace? Pat? You're at the head of the table."

I tried to remember the prayer before meals the nuns had taught us at school. "Bless us, Lord, on this New Year's Eve for this food, which…"

"And thanks for the grub, amen," Laura cried.

I lifted a spoonful of soup and glanced at Ryan. His eyelids drooped. His head started to lean forward.

No!

There was a crash as Ryan's head fell into his soup bowl. He sputtered as he raised his head and shouted, "Fuck!" He pushed back his chair. "This shit is hot."

"Ryan said the F word. Ryan said the F word," Tommy chanted.

Maxie stood up and barked.

"You're in trouble now, you're in trouble now," Tommy said as Ryan wiped his face with a napkin.

Maxie barked in agreement.

"Maxie, down," I said. "Tommy, stop it."

Devon was on his feet. "Ryan, leave the table. Come back when you can act civilized."

"Yeah, yeah, whatever." Ryan flung his napkin on the table and stomped upstairs.

Devon glared after him as he took his seat.

Laura had a hand over her mouth. Her shoulders shook with laughter.

"What's so funny?" I asked.

"Mom, really. Falling into his soup? That's not funny?" She burst out laughing and banged her hand on the table. Soup sloshed over the side of her bowl.

"Better take some time out, too," I said.

"Sure thing." Laura rose, giggling again. "Who wants to eat some greasy old goose anyway?" She headed up the stairs, a hand over her mouth.

Devon and I looked at each other.

"Pat, I'm so—"

"Sorry," I said. "Me, too. Who taught them their manners?"

We both smiled weakly.

"Kids today." Stéphane shook his head. "Pass the rolls, please."

After Tracy's cherries jubilee, I announced it was time for Tommy to go to bed. He got off his chair and said goodnight to everyone at the table.

"Devon and Stéphane said I can call them by their first names," he said on the way upstairs.

"That's fine."

He smiled as I tucked him into the twin bed next to mine. "I had the bestest day. I drove here. I skied. I met lots of new people." His eyes popped open. "I forgot my bedtime prayer." He squeezed his eyes shut. "Now I lay me down to sleep, I pray the Lord my soul to keep. God bless Mommy and Nana, and keep them safe. And bless Laura and Tracy and Mrs. T. And Maxie. Amen."

I was touched. "That was a lovely prayer, Tommy. Thank you for including us."

He snuggled down under the quilt. "You're my family too."

My hand trembled as I switched off the bedside lamp. What had Jude really told him about his father?

A half-hour later, Ryan and Laura bounded down the stairs dressed in their parkas.

"Where are you two off to?" Devon asked.

"Laura, what—" I began.

"Easy." Ryan ran a hand over his head. "We're sorry. We shouldn't have smoked up with the kid around."

Devon looked at him sternly. "You shouldn't have smoked up, period."

"Yeah, yeah," Ryan muttered. "So we're sorry, okay?"

"We need some fresh air," Laura said, "to clear our heads. Then we can do the Auld Lang Syne thing."

"Your sister and Stéphane need help in the kitchen, but I suppose you could do with some fresh air."

"We need more firewood," Devon said. "It's at the back of the house. Think you can handle that?"

"Sure thing," Laura said as she and Ryan went out the door.

Minutes later, I heard an engine start up outside. Devon fumbled in his pants pocket, then sprinted for the door. He flung it open. "Damn!"

Standing beside him, I watched the van's tail lights disappear down the drive.

"My stupidity. I left the keys on my dresser." He took a jacket from the hall closet and pulled it on. "Have to get that firewood myself."

I put on my parka and followed him outside.

Stéphane was pouring glasses of champagne at the table when we'd finished bringing in several armfuls of wood. "Where can they have gone?" Devon asked me.

Drugs and driving is a deadly combination. "They shouldn't be on the road," I said. "Do we call the police?"

Devon looked thoughtful.

"Impaired driving is a criminal offence," Tracy said. "Whoever is at the wheel could lose his or her license. Maybe spend time in jail."

A criminal record. I hesitated. "No, we can't get the police involved. We'll just have to…"

Devon put an arm around me. I pictured Laura behind the wheel of the van. Could she concentrate, judge distances, see what was on the road ahead? Or Ryan…?

I rested my head on Devon's shoulder. "There's nothing we can do."

Stéphane touched my arm. "Stop beating yourself up. We'll have a glass of bubbly now… is that okay? Or wait until midnight?"

I looked at Devon. "What do you think?"

"Well…we're not going anywhere and the bubbly is poured." He picked up a glass.

Stéphane handed out the rest of the glasses and raised his own. "To a superb meal, and to our cooks, Pat and Tracy. Tracy, your talents will be wasted on the legal profession."

Tracy scowled, but I knew she was pleased.

"And to our gracious host, Devon."

Pounding sounded on the front door.

"They're back." Devon headed for the door.

He opened it, and I could see two figures outside. Devon huddled with them, then motioned them into the house. He beckoned me to join them. At the door, he put an arm around my shoulders. "Police."

Fear clutched my heart. "An accident? Laura? Ryan?"

"No, nothing like that. They're here to see you about a Jude Seaton. Any relation to...?"

I nodded and scanned the officers' faces. Their expressions were solemn and watchful. I knew that something was terribly wrong. My mind flew back to what I'd been thinking just hours before. I'd wished— no!

"Ontario Provincial Police." One of the officers displayed his ID. "You're Pat Tierney?"

I swallowed. "Yes."

"Sergeant Marcel LeMay, OPP Kincaid Division." He pushed back his fur-trimmed hood and ran a hand through his salt-and-pepper hair. He turned to his partner. "And this is Sergeant Andy Kovaks," he added with a hint of a French accent.

The partner, a stocky, fair-haired man in his late twenties, inclined his head.

"Officers, let's continue this downstairs," Devon said.

Tracy came up behind me as Devon led the policemen into the basement. "Mom, what is it?"

I turned and clasped her hands. "It's about Tommy's mother."

"You should have a lawyer present. I'll go down there with you."

48

"Honey, you've been watching too many legal shows on TV. You and Stéphane have to stay up here in case Tommy wakes up."

"But—"

I held up my hand. "I need you up here."

She stared at me for a few moments. "Okay."

As I started down the stairs, Dean Martin was crooning "Baby, It's Cold Outside" over the sound system.

I shivered.

Chapter Seven

Pat

"How well do you know Jude Seaton?" LeMay's long nose pointed at me like a retriever's.

I pulled out a chair from the desk in the basement study and sat down before I answered. The officers took off their parkas and sat on a couch across from me. Kovaks held a notebook and a pen.

"I met her yesterday. What's happened to her?"

"We haven't been told much," LeMay said. "Toronto Homicide likes to keep things on a need-to-know basis."

Homicide. The fine hairs stood up on the back of my neck. That meant…

"All I can say is that Ms. Seaton was found dead in her home today."

Blood pounded through my ears. I closed my eyes.

"Just a moment," Devon said from his post at the door. "If this woman was found in Toronto, that's outside your jurisdiction."

"Toronto police asked us to contact Ms. Tierney. At the request of…" LeMay turned to Kovaks.

Kovaks flipped back a few pages in his notebook. "Hardy. Detective Sergeant Neil Hardy. Homicide Division."

"What does he want with Pat?" Devon asked.

"There was voice-mail message from you on the victim's phone," LeMay said to me. "And your business card was found at the scene. Next to the phone."

I hadn't given my card to Jude. Then I remembered the case that displayed my cards on Rose's desk. Jude must have taken one.

"Hardy reached your housekeeper at your home," LeMay continued. "She gave him your numbers, but the phone here has been disconnected and you weren't answering your cell phone. Fortunately, she had this property's roadside number."

"My cell doesn't work here."

LeMay nodded. "Big rock cut down the road."

"Can you back up a bit, officers?" Devon interjected. "What happened to Ms. Seaton? It would help if we were all on the same page."

"Her sister paid her a visit around one-thirty this afternoon and found her," LeMay said. "She may have been dead a couple of hours. The coroner's report isn't in yet, but the case is being treated as a homicide." He leaned forward and clasped his hands in front of him. "Hardy thinks he may be looking at a double homicide." He paused. "There's a little boy, Ms. Seaton's son. He's missing."

I glanced at Devon, then looked at the police officers. "He's not missing. He's here with us."

"The Seaton boy is here?" LeMay looked surprised. "Ms. Tierney, you hardly knew this woman—you just met her, you said—and you have her child?"

My mind started clicking. How much did I need to tell them? "Jude was referred to me by a long-standing client. We met yesterday. She told me about her son—Tommy—and I offered to take him here with us."

LeMay looked skeptical. "Just like that?"

"In my business," I replied, "we do a lot on goodwill."

"Hmm. Who referred her to you?"

"Gemma Johannsen. She's on vacation in the Caribbean right now."

"Buy why you? Why are you babysitting instead of one of Ms. Seaton's relatives?"

"Jude asked me to take Tommy for a few days." I chose my words carefully. "Said she was afraid that someone would harm him. And that it wouldn't be safe to leave him with her mother or sister."

Kovaks scribbled furiously in his notepad.

"She tell you who this person was?" LeMay asked.

"No, she didn't." I pictured Jude's lovely face and blurted out the first thing that came into my mind. "It might be a man she was seeing. She told me if she didn't do what he wanted, she was afraid that something would happen to Tommy."

Kovaks' head jerked up and he stopped writing.

"The boy's father?" LeMay asked.

I swallowed. "No, Tommy's father is dead."

"She tell you who this guy was?"

"She never said who this person was. It's just a feeling... that it might be a man she was involved with."

LeMay shook his head. "It didn't occur to her to call the police?"

"That's what I told her. I said if her son was in danger, she needed the police. But she said no. No police."

LeMay looked at Kovaks and shrugged. "It's Toronto's case. We'll leave the other questions to Hardy."

He turned back to me. "What the kid knows may be crucial to the investigation. We have to get him to Toronto. Now if you'll get him ready, we'll—"

"Tommy is asleep upstairs. He's seven years old and he's had a long day. Can't it wait until morning?"

LeMay glanced at his watch. "By the time we get him there tomorrow, the case will be almost twenty-four hours old. Time is of the essence in a homicide case." He was interrupted by a burst of static from a walkie-talkie clipped to his belt.

Scowling, he lifted the instrument to his ear. "Pardon?" He walked to the other side of the room to be out of earshot, but I could hear his end of the conversation.

"How bad? Where? Uh-huh. Got it. The boy Toronto wants? He's here. Who's going to—okay, fine. We're on our way." He signed off and sighed. "Looks like it will have to be tomorrow morning after all. There's been a bad accident. Van hit a patch of ice and slammed into a rock cut."

My heart skipped a beat. Please, not Laura.

"What color was the van?" Devon asked.

LeMay stared at him. "Why do you want to know?"

Devon glanced at me. "Our kids borrowed my rental. A gold van."

"This vehicle is maroon."

Devon let out his breath. I closed my eyes and offered a silent prayer of thanks to God Herself.

LeMay's walkie-talkie summoned him again. He answered it and stood listening for a few moments. "Got it." He turned back to me. "Ms. Tierney, have the boy ready at seven. One of Toronto's finest will take him to the city. Officer named Mancini. He works with Hardy."

"I'll go with them," I said.

He shook his head. "You're not family."

"Tommy's spent some time with us. With a stranger, he'll be frightened and upset."

LeMay shrugged. "It'll be Mancini's call."

At the foot of the stairs, he turned. "A child can't be questioned without a parent or a guardian present, so someone from Ms. Seaton's family will need to be there."

"Sergeant LeMay, you mentioned Jude's sister," I said. "I could call her from the hotel down the road. Ask her what she wants me to tell Tommy…about his mother."

LeMay looked at Kovaks. Kovaks flipped through his notebook. "Arlene Dobson. She and her family are with her mother, Norah Seaton, tonight. That's Seaton as in Seaton Ferguson. The family owns the company." Kovaks scribbled briefly, tore a sheet from his notepad and handed it to me.

Stéphane had been right about Tommy's connection to the auto-parts giant, I thought as the officers headed up the stairs.

I took a seat in front of the fireplace and Devon settled in beside me. Tracy and Stéphane looked at us expectantly.

"Well?" Tracy asked. "What happened to Tommy's mother?"

I glanced at the stairs to the second floor. "She was found dead in her home today. The police are treating it as a murder."

"Oh, Mom."

"Poor kid," Stéphane murmured.

"Isn't it time you told us about her?" Devon asked.

I took a deep breath. "Jude Seaton taught at Queen of Angels Academy, the private girls' school. Her family owns Seaton Ferguson."

Stéphane gave a low whistle. "*Tabernac!* So the kid is one of those Seatons."

"She told me the boy was in danger, and that she needed a few days to sort things out."

"Who—?" Tracy started to ask.

"She didn't say who this person was, but I have the feeling it was a man she'd been involved with."

"So the police will have an obvious suspect," Devon said.

"I may have jumped to conclusions because she was so attractive."

"Tommy would have been killed too if he'd been at home," Tracy said. "Mom, you saved his life."

I shook my head, feeling miserable. I'd got what I wished for. Some kind of dark magic had to be at work if my thoughts could be answered that quickly.

Then the meaning of Tracy's words hit me.

Tommy would have been killed if he'd been at home. Jude had said the boy was in danger and she was right. Someone had threatened to hurt her child. That person was probably her killer and he would have killed Tommy too if the boy had been with her.

What was it Jude had said? That if she didn't do he wanted something would happen to Tommy. Who was this "he" and what was he up to? I looked at Tracy and Devon and Stéphane. "Tomorrow morning, I'll go to Toronto with Tommy. The police think he may know something that will help the investigation."

"I'll come with you, Mom."

"No, Tracy. We'll drive in with a police officer so you'll need to take the Volvo and Maxie back to the city. And the skis back to the rental place."

"Stéphane, if the prodigals don't return tonight, we could scout the area for them in the morning," Devon said. "If we don't find them, can you give me a lift back to the city?"

"Done," Stéphane said.

"What about Tommy's father?" Tracy asked. "Shouldn't he be told?"

I hesitated a few seconds before I answered. "He's no longer on the scene."

Stéphane uncorked a bottle of champagne. "Two minutes to midnight."

When our glasses were filled, we raised them slowly. Our faces were serious, our eyes sad. It was a wake, not a New Year's Eve party.

Devon broke the ice. "To more gatherings here in the New Year."

"To a hot new boyfriend for me," Stéphane put in.

"To health and happiness for—" Tracy's voice caught and she started to cry. I gave her a hug.

Devon began to hum "Auld Lang Syne" and raised his glass. "Never could remember the words. To family and friends!"

We clinked our glasses and kissed one another. I started to melt at Devon's kiss, but I drew back, confused by my feelings. Not yet. Not until I had thought through all I'd learned about Michael and Jude. And Tommy.

Stéphane topped up our glasses, but no one was feeling festive. When we'd finished the champagne, Tracy and Stéphane washed the glasses, said their good-nights and headed off to their rooms.

I slouched down on the sofa and propped my feet up on the coffee table. "I'd be all over Laura and Tracy for putting their feet on the table," I told Devon. "But with all that's happened…"

"Understood." He went over to the mini-stereo, and held up a CD case. John Williams, Spanish guitar. "How about this?"

"Sure."

He held up a bottle of cognac. "Nightcap?"

I smiled, and he poured cognac into two snifters. He handed one to me. "Everything okay? You've been quiet today. Long before the police arrived."

"Just tired. I was working full-tilt the past few weeks, with only two days off at Christmas. That's what happens." I tried to smile. "You finally take a break and you collapse."

"There's something else." He put a hand over mine. "It's not the kids, is it? Thank God they weren't in that accident, but that stunt of theirs was inexcusable."

"It's not that," I murmured. "It's...it's..."

I felt tears gathering in my eyes. Devon moved beside me and put his arms around me. I liked the feeling of his warmth and the solid mass of his body.

He rubbed my back. "Want to talk about it?"

I found that I did. The story of Jude's visit to my office and her revelation that Tommy was Michael's son spilled out. "I haven't told the girls. And I'm not sure what Tommy knows about his dad."

"Whew! No wonder you seemed distracted." He paused. "You haven't told me much about Michael, but I gather you had a pretty good marriage."

"That's what I thought."

He took my hand. "I see it at conferences, where there are men, women and opportunity. But the fact that Michael ended the affair before you came home means he chose you."

I felt tears on my face and pictured mascara sliding down my cheeks. "I wonder what else I didn't know about him."

He held me until I pulled away. He handed me a tissue and I dried my eyes. "I'll cope," I said. "But now there's Tommy."

"That does complicate things. You're sure this woman told you the truth about the boy's father?"

I took a sip of cognac. "My first reaction was to deny it. But as soon as I saw Tommy, that was no longer an option. The boy is the picture of Michael. Laura noticed the resemblance today, but she didn't make the connection."

"Will you tell the girls?"

"I'll have to. They have the right to know they have a brother. But later. First thing tomorrow, Tommy will have to be told about his mother."

He gave me another hug. "You shouldn't have to do that."

"He'll want to know why he has to go back to the city. And he'll find out as soon as he gets there."

"Leave it for his family."

I closed my eyes and thought of Michael. I shook my head, trying to clear it. "I was going to call Arlene in the morning, but maybe I should do it now."

"Good idea."

"It's twelve forty-five."

Devon stood up. "I don't think Jude's family will get much sleep tonight. Let's go over to the lodge."

"C'mon, someone pick up." I tightened my grip on the pay phone in the lobby of the Limberlost Lodge, a cheesy imitation of an Alpine inn with window-boxes filled with plastic flowers. "Don't give me voice mail."

Beside me, Devon nodded encouragement.

I glanced at the tinsel and the red and green streamers that made the lobby look forlorn rather than festive. The bald man behind the desk yawned and checked his watch. On the tenth ring, the phone was picked up.

"The Seaton residence." The woman on the line spoke with a European accent.

"I'm sorry to call so late, but I need to speak to Arlene Dobson."

"All media calls are to go to—"

"Wait! I'm not from the media. It concerns Tommy, her nephew."

I heard a sharp intake of breath. "One moment, please."

A few seconds later, another woman came on the line. "Where's Tommy?" She sounded on the verge of hysteria.

"Tommy's fine, Mrs. Dobson. My name is Pat Tierney, and Tommy is spending a few days with my family north of Toronto. The police came by tonight and told us about your sister. I'm very sorry for your loss."

The woman began to cry. "H-how c-come Tommy's with you?"

"Jude asked me to take him."

"Y-you're a friend of Jude's?"

I hesitated. "Yes." I decided to let my relationship with Jude stand at that.

"I was the one who found her," she said. "It was horrible. She was on her living room floor covered in blood."

The image of Jude's face flashed through my mind and I flinched. "I hope the police told you that Tommy is okay."

"It was late when they called, but yes. We were told that he's safe. That was a relief. My poor mother. She feared the worst."

I took a deep breath. "Tommy doesn't know about his mother yet."

"God, I'm no good at things like that."

"The Toronto police need to talk to him tomorrow. He'll ask why he has to go back to the city."

"Could you possibly…"

It had to be done. "I can tell him. But when we get to Toronto, you or someone else in your family will need to be present when the police talk to Tommy. They can't question a child unless he's with a parent or a guardian. Can you meet us at the police station around ten?"

The woman gasped. "No, I can't. And Mom's not up to it. The doctor came by this evening and gave her a shot. My brother Patrick would be the one, but he's in Mexico. He won't be back until tomorrow evening. Can't the police wait one more day to see Tommy?"

"They need to talk to him as soon as possible. It may be crucial to the investigation. We leave here at seven in the morning."

"Ms…what did you say your name was?"

"Tierney. Pat Tierney."

"I know I'm imposing on you, Pat, but would you accompany Tommy to the police station?"

"I just met your nephew yesterday, Mrs. Dobson—"

"I can't. It's all just…just…"

"Someone from his family should be with him."

"You're Jude's friend."

"Well, yes, but—"

"We've got so much to handle here. The funeral and…" The woman sobbed. "And I don't know if Mom's heart is up to it. Please, Pat?"

"All right. But you'll have to call the police to authorize me in your place."

"I have that detective's card here somewhere. I'll call him right now."

"I'll bring Tommy to you after he's seen the police."

"Actually, I...I have one more favor to ask." Before I could reply, she blurted out, "Could Tommy stay with you tomorrow night?"

What planet did the Seatons come from? Just because they...

"It's crazy here right now," she added. "Tommy wouldn't get the attention he needs."

What made her think a stranger would give Tommy the attention he needed? "The boy's just lost his mother. He should be with his family."

"Please, Pat, just one more night."

"All right." I gave her my Toronto home number.

Then I called my home in Toronto. I hoped Laura would pick up. But all I got was my voice-mail message.

Chapter Eight

Pat

I was wide awake at six o'clock the next morning. Tommy was sound asleep in the twin bed next to mine.

I pulled on my housecoat and peeked into the room across the hall that Tracy and Laura had taken. Tracy was asleep in one bed. The other bed was empty. Where was Laura? Was she okay? I hoped she was at home in Toronto, but I'd have to wait until I got to the city to find out.

Back in my room, I looked down at the sleeping boy. The police car would arrive in an hour, and we needed to get dressed and eat breakfast. I gently shook Tommy's shoulder. "Tommy, wake up."

"Humph." He rolled over, rubbing his eyes.

"Tommy, we have to get dressed and have some breakfast."

He yawned, then brightened. "Is it time to go skiing? You should have seen me yesterday. I—"

"We won't be skiing today." I sat down on the edge of his bed.

"Why not?"

I swallowed. "Something's happened, Tommy, and we have to go back to the city. When you're finished breakfast, we'll pack up our things."

"You said we were going skiing."

"Tommy." I took his hands in mine.

"What?" He dropped his chin to his chest.

I wondered what I should say. "Look at me, Tommy."

The boy looked up at me and my heart turned over. Michael's son! I ran a hand over his hair. "Tommy, something has happened to your mother."

His eyes were enormous in his face. "Mommy?"

"Yes." I paused, then plunged in. "Your...your mother is dead."

He looked at me silently. I wasn't sure that he'd understood what I'd told him. I wrapped my arms around him, but he wriggled in my embrace. I released him.

His eyes were filled with tears. "That means I won't see her again? Like Grandpa?"

"That's right."

"What did I do?"

I kissed his forehead. "It's nothing you did, Tommy. A bad person...killed her."

"Everybody liked Mommy."

"Sometimes terrible things happen to good people."

He burrowed his head in my chest. I hugged him and felt his small body tremble in my arms. He had no parents now. I tightened my arms around him. "Tommy, we have to go to your aunt and your grandmother in Toronto. And the police want to talk to you."

I patted his back as he sobbed into my chest. "A policeman will be here in an hour. He'll take us back to Toronto and..." He sniffed and looked up at me. "Then we can help them find whoever did this to your mother."

"Will the policeman have a gun?"

"Gun? I don't know, Tommy."

The strains of Verdi's "Va, Pensiero" from the car stereo washed over me as I leaned back in the car seat, head on the headrest, eyes closed.

"Magnificent, isn't it?" said Detective Constable Mario Mancini.

"Beautiful." I glanced at the heavyset detective with the dark moustache. He'd kept small talk to a minimum for the first hour of the trip. "Verdi. 'Chorus of the Hebrew Slaves' from *Nabucco*."

"Very good. Most people, they know—or guess—that it's Verdi, but that's about it."

"So?" I wondered where this was heading.

"So, it's a sort of test. If you hear that and it doesn't move you…" He shook his head.

"There's something wrong with you?"

He smiled. "It's not foolproof, but…"

"I passed?"

He flashed me a grin. "Uh-huh."

"I didn't think I'd hear this in a cop's car. I'd have expected something like, I don't know, country music."

"I grew up with this music. It's what my parents played at home."

"Your boss share your taste in music?"

"Hardy?" Mancini smiled and shook his head. "He didn't know the name, "Va, Pensiero," but he liked it. So he passed the test."

I turned around and saw that Tommy had fallen asleep. Was he still in danger? Now that Jude was dead, would her killer still want to harm her son? And what had she been involved in? I took a deep breath. Tommy would be with me another night. After that, it would be up to his family to see that he was safe.

On the stereo, Verdi had given way to Bach. "Jesu, Joy of Man's Desiring." A musical balm. I turned back to Mancini. "I'm surprised Detective Sergeant Hardy agreed to me being here with Tommy. I'm not family."

"He didn't. But the higher-ups, they said don't upset the family. The family wants you here, so…" He shrugged. "Besides, it saves us from having to track you down for questioning."

We arrived at Toronto Police Services headquarters on College Street just before ten. Detective Sergeant Neil Hardy, man with a wiry build and cropped ginger hair, was waiting for us in the lobby. In contrast to the custom-fitting brown suede sports coat that Mancini sported, Hardy wore a rumpled, navy suit, and he looked like he'd been up all night. Taking in his red-rimmed blue eyes, I realized that he had.

"You must be Ms. Tierney," he said to me.

The he bent down and held out his hand to Tommy. "Hi, Tommy. I'm Detective Hardy."

Tommy seemed to hesitate. Then he shook Hardy's hand.

"Do you know why you're here, son?"

"Mommy."

"We need to ask you some questions. You could be a big help." Hardy paused. "Think you can do that?"

"Yes," Tommy said. "I want to help Mommy."

"Then let's get to it."

Hardy took us to an interview room on the tenth floor where a woman with wavy white hair was waiting for us.

"This is Detective Liliana Markowicz," Hardy said to Tommy and me. "Markowicz, meet Pat Tierney and Tommy Seaton."

"Hello." Markowicz's smile cracked the skin on her face into dozens of tiny fissures, like a dried apple. "I'll have to ask Ms. Tierney to sit at the back of the room."

She turned to Tommy, concern in her caramel-colored eyes. "Tommy, I'm very sorry about your mother."

I gently squeezed Tommy's shoulder, then moved to a chair at the back of the room where Hardy and Mancini were seated.

"We have to ask you some questions," Markowicz continued. "We need to know as much as we can about your mother so we can find the person who did this to her. Will you help us?"

Tommy stared at his boots. Suddenly, he looked up at the policewoman. "Do you have a gun?"

She smiled. "It's locked away. I don't need it for the work I do."

He looked down at his boots again.

"Tommy, do you think you can help us?"

He nodded.

"We'll videotape this talk so you'll have to speak up. Have you ever seen yourself on a video, Tommy?"

The boy shook his head.

Markowicz turned on the equipment. She gave the date and time into a microphone. "Detective Constable Liliana Markowicz interviewing Tommy Seaton. Also present are DS Neil Hardy and DC Mario Mancini, and Pat Tierney. Interview commences." She paused. "Tommy, did your mother tell you why she took you to stay with Mrs. Tierney?"

Tommy shook his head.

"Will you say it out loud for the recording, Tommy?"

"No. Mommy and me, we were playing spies. We went out the back door and ran down the alley. She said we were gonna stay in a hotel."

Jude thought this guy might be watching the house. She wanted to get Tommy out of there without alarming him so she turned it into a game.

"Did your mother tell you what she planned to do while you were with the Tierneys?"

"Work."

"What kind of work did you mother do?"

"Teacher."

She paused for a moment. "Tommy, did your mother have many friends?"

"Yes."

"Who were her friends?"

"Sister Celia."

"Who is Sister Celia?"

He shrugged. "A friend. Mommy and I didn't go to her Christmas party, but she brought me a book and a DVD."

"Do you know her last name?"

"No."

Markowicz looked at me. I shook my head.

"Who else was your mother friendly with?"

He shrugged again. "Sophie. She lives next door. Gemma. People who came to the house."

"Gemma? Who is she?"

"Mommy's friend. She's got two dogs, Beans and Bacon."

"Did your mother have a boyfriend?"

Tommy looked up at her, puzzled.

"A special gentleman friend."

"Clive came for dinner on Saturdays. Sometimes Mommy would get Cindy to stay with me when they went to a movie."

"Cindy is…?"

"She's in high school. She talks to her friends on the phone when she's at our house."

"Do you know Cindy's last name?"

"No."

"Was Clive at your house around Christmas?"

"Clive stopped coming. He and Mommy had a big fight."

"What did they fight about?"

"I was in bed upstairs. I heard them shouting and I put my head under the pillow."

"When was this fight they had?"

"A long time ago. After the summer holidays."

"Do you know Clive's last name?"

He shook his head.

"Say it out loud, Tommy."

"No."

"What kind of job does Clive have?"

"Don't know."

"Did he talk about his work?"

"No."

"What does Clive look like?"

"Taller than Mommy."

"What color is his hair?"

"Brown."

"Color of his eyes?"

He shrugged. "Don't know."

"Does he have a beard?"

"No."

"A moustache?" She ran a hand across her upper lip. "Here."

He didn't answer for a few seconds. "I think so."

"Tommy, do you remember anything special about Clive? Something about how he looked? How he talked? Something that made him different from other people?"

He paused for a few seconds. "He had a neat watch. With dials and stuff."

Markowicz smiled. "All the gadgets. Date, second hand, compass, stopwatch. My son-in-law has one. Tommy, when did you last see Clive?"

"Don't know."

"Did he bring you a Christmas present?"

"No."

She paused a few seconds. "That will be all for now. Tommy, you've been a really big help. We'll have a few more questions in a day or two." She patted the boy's hand. "Interview concluded. Ten hours and thirty-two minutes."

When she had turned off the recorder, Hardy motioned Markowicz over. "Detective, could you take Tommy down to the cafeteria, get him some cookies or pop or something? We need a few minutes with Ms. Tierney." He fished some change out of his pocket. "The vending machines should be running today."

He held the door open for me. "My office."

Hardy tapped a file folder on his desk with a pen. Mancini sat stoically at my side, notepad in hand.

"Do you really expect us to believe that story?" Hardy asked. "A woman from one of this city's wealthiest families—whom you say you never met before—just happens to drop by your office, just happens to ask you to look after her son, and you just happen to agree. Don't you think that sounds far-fetched?"

"We do a lot on goodwill—"

"Did you sign up Ms. Seaton as a client?"

"No."

"Don't you think what you did went way beyond goodwill, especially for someone who wasn't a client?"

I didn't answer.

"What aren't you telling us, Ms. Tierney?"

"What I've told you is the truth."

He stopped tapping his pen and dropped it on the folder. He folded his hands on top of his desk and leaned forward. "What are you hiding?"

I remained silent.

He pushed back into his chair. "You told the OPP about the boyfriend. What did Ms. Seaton say about him?"

I locked eyes with him. "She never mentioned a boyfriend. It was just a feeling I had. She mentioned that someone, a man, might hurt Tommy if she didn't do what he wanted."

"She was an attractive woman so she must have had a man in her life."

I hesitated for a moment. "Something like that. Pretty fuzzy thinking, I admit, for someone who's trying to raise her daughters to be independent women."

"Think this Clive was giving her a hard time?"

I gave a small shrug. "I don't know. She taught at Queen of Angels. Maybe the other teachers know something."

"We're checking. But it's hard to get hold of teachers over the holidays."

"Tommy said in the interview that a woman called Gemma was his mother's friend. That would be my client, Gemma Johanssen, who referred Jude to me. She's in the Caribbean right now, but she'll be back sometime this week. Tommy also mentioned a Sister Celia. Maybe she teaches at Jude's school."

"We'll find her."

I stood up to leave. "If there's nothing more, I'll get Tommy—"

"Not yet. We need to see the boy again." He flipped through the folder on his desk. "Ah, here it is."

He took out a pewter picture frame and propped it up to face me. "Found this in Ms. Seaton's home. Could be our killer."

He turned the frame around so that the photo faced me.

I sucked in a breath. The grin, the dark, wavy hair with a touch of gray at the temples, the brown eyes framed with long lashes—Michael! I choked back the sob that rose in my throat. The picture had run in the *Toronto World* the year before Michael died. Norris Cassidy had sponsored the city's high-school hockey championship, and the photo captured Michael presenting the trophy to the captain of the winning team.

Hardy started to rise from his chair. "We'll show this to the boy."

"Wait. That man didn't kill Jude."

Hardy glanced at Mancini and settled back in his seat. "Go on."

"That's…" I struggled to find words as my memories of Michael and my hurt at his betrayal washed over me.

"Someone you know?" Hardy leaned forward, hands folded in front of him on the desk.

"Yes."

"How do you know he's not our man?"

"Because he's been dead for four years. That's my husband, Michael."

"They say confession is good for the soul." Hardy held out a box of tissues. "Feel better?"

I wiped away the tears that had started to flow as I told the detectives of Jude's visit to my office.

"What you've told us explains why Ms. Seaton wanted you to take Tommy," Hardy said.

"Still kind of weird," Mancini put in.

"Yeah, but I can buy it." Hardy studied Michael's photo. "The boy and your husband. I see the resemblance." He put the photograph down on his desk and tilted back in his chair. "You realize, of course, that your story makes you a prime suspect."

"What?" I was outraged. "That's preposterous."

"Jealousy is a great motive."

"But I had no idea that Michael had an affair with Jude. Not until she told me."

"But once she's told you, your anger simmers. It eats away at you. You decide to confront her—"

"But Michael is dead. It's over."

"Hell hath no fury like a woman scorned. You meet her, your anger rises, you can't help yourself—"

"Enough!" I sprang to my feet and leaned on Hardy's desk. "Nothing like that happened."

"I believe you, Ms. Tierney," Hardy said. "Now sit down."

I glared at him, and slowly eased myself back into the chair.

"The reason I believe you is that you have the perfect alibi."

"Which is?" I was still seething.

"Tommy. He was with you when Jude Seaton was killed. Tommy gets you off the hook." He stood. "That's it for now. Mario, take Tommy and Ms. Tierney over to the Seatons' place."

"Tommy is staying with me tonight."

Hardy looked surprised, then thoughtful. "Good idea."

"Arlene Dobson asked if he could stay with me one more night." I paused. "Jude was afraid something would happen to him. Is he still in danger?"

"Yeah, if he knows his mother's killer. The killer might think the kid could identify him—or her." Hardy looked up at the ceiling. "It's better that he doesn't stay with the Seatons. And he can't go back to school next week."

I realized then that Tommy could be with me for some time. "Do you need to talk to him tomorrow?"

"He could probably tell us more, but we'll wait until the funeral's over. It's the day after tomorrow, Thursday. No visitation, just a funeral Mass and burial."

"I should pick up a few things for Tommy at his house. Would it be all right if I went over there?"

Hardy rubbed the back of his neck. "I suppose. But it's still a crime scene so you'll have to go with me." He looked at his watch. "Today's out of the question. Tomorrow okay?"

"Fine."

"Tomorrow it is. Mario, take them home."

From the top of the stairs, I watched Tracy lead Tommy down the second-floor hall to the guest bedroom. The boy paused in front of a gallery of family photos on the wall.

"Laura?" He stood in front of a shot of Laura that Michael had taken when she was about Tommy's age.

"That's right," Tracy said.

He pointed to another photo. "That's not Maxie."

"That's Max. Our first dog."

"Where's Max?"

I held my breath. Tommy didn't need to hear about another death.

"Max was hit by a car," Tracy said.

Tommy moved on, and I released the breath I'd been holding. He stopped in front of a wedding picture of Michael and me. "That looks like my daddy."

My heart skipped a few beats.

"Where is your dad, Tommy?" Tracy asked.

He shook his head. "He died. Mommy has a picture of him." He squinted at the photograph. "Sorta looks like him."

"Do you know who the woman in the picture is?"

He moved closer to the photo. "That's Mrs. T. She looks young there."

Tracy nodded. "And that's my dad. He died, too."

At the end of the hall, she steered Tommy into the room on the right. "You'll sleep here again tonight."

I closed my eyes and sank down on the top step.

"Phone call for you, Mom," Tracy called out an hour later.

I picked up the extension in my bedroom, hoping Laura was on the other end. Luella Cruickshank's high-pitched voice assaulted my ear. "Patricia, Arnie would be a wonderful addition to your firm."

I pinched the bridge of my nose and suppressed a groan. Sometime over the years that she'd been Michael's client and then mine, Luella had got hold of our home phone number. She didn't hesitate to call whenever she felt like it.

"Patricia Tierney, did you hear me?"

Apart from my third grade teacher, Luella is the only person who has ever called me by my given name. I was Patty then and I shortened that to Pat when I turned thirteen. I'm Pat to everyone today.

"Mrs. Cruickshank—"

"Luella, please, Patricia. After all, we're like family."

Please! Then I felt a stab of remorse. Luella was a lonely old woman. She was also one of our top clients with plenty of money to manage, although she demanded constant attention. "Luella, what's Arnie—"

"He's back in Toronto, staying with me till he gets his bearings. He's weighing his options, but his prospects are excellent. He's taken that stockbrokers' course and he intends to make his mark on the investment world. He just needs to get a foot in the door."

Luella's son had lived in Vancouver since he graduated from the University of British Columbia ten years before. From what I'd gathered, his subsequent careers had not been successes.

"Luella—"

"And let's not forget his management skills. Look at what he did for that rock band, the Cosmic...Cosmic..."

"The Cosmic Messengers. My daughter's a fan."

"See? My Arnie takes them under his wing, and the next thing you know they're on top of the charts."

There was no point in reminding her that the Cosmic Messengers had skyrocketed to success after they'd ditched Arnie and found new management.

"Arnie wasn't cut out for that, though. All those arguments about artistic integrity drained him. But he'll take to the world of finance like a duck to water."

"If he wants to work at our firm, he'll have to contact head office. As you know, Tierney Pratt is a branch of Norris Cassidy Investments."

"They'll see that they have a diamond in the rough." She paused. "Anyway, Patricia, I wanted to let you know that Arnie will be at our meeting next Monday. I showed him my last quarterly statement. He has an investment idea he wants to discuss with you."

I knew trouble was brewing.

"Until then, *adieu*. And Happy New Year."

I winced as I placed the receiver in its cradle.

I picked up the next phone call on the first ring.

"Laura's on her way home," Devon said.

"Thank God."

"I just dropped Ryan off at the airport. Stéphane is driving Laura in. They should be at your place soon."

"Where were they?"

"Stéphane and I spotted the van at a place called—get this—Honeymoon Haven." He paused. "They've got a sign out front that advertises their love tubs."

I groaned.

"So Stéphane waited in his Jag while I pounded on the door. Ryan opened it, with a towel wrapped around his waist. Next thing I know, I hear Laura shout 'Bastard!' and a glass whizzes toward the door and shatters just above Ryan's head."

I gasped.

"Lovers' spat."

"Devon!" He was talking about my little girl.

"Okay, I'm with you. I'm afraid I lost it. I yelled at them and told them to get dressed."

"Where are you?"

"I'm heading back up north. I'll close up the house and come down to Toronto tomorrow afternoon." He paused. "Think I could hang around for a few days?"

Devon would be one more thing for me to worry about. But I wouldn't have to deal with him until following day. "Of course." I heard the front door open. "I think Laura's home now. I'll see you tomorrow."

The front door banged shut. "Laura?" I called.

"Yeah, what?"

"You and Ryan had everyone worried sick." I came into the front hall where my daughter was taking off her snow boots. "We need to talk."

I motioned her into the kitchen. "Devon told me he found you and Ryan in a motel."

"So?" She sat down at the table and pulled off the black band that held her hair back from her face. "Mom, I'm eighteen, not twelve."

My anger flared. "You just met this…this boy…and you jumped into bed with him."

"You make it sound so sordid." Laura's eyes flashed and her nostrils flared. "Devon roared in like King Shit. He was, like, totally Neanderthal. He's not my father."

My mind flashed to Michael, but I put that thought aside. "Did you have sex with Ryan?"

"Motherrrr!"

"Well, did you?"

She glared at me.

"Laura, we've talked about how sex is best with someone you love and trust. It's ultimately your decision, but…I hope you had the sense to use condoms."

She just looked at me.

I wanted to scream. Instead, I fell back on my own mother's stock response. "I'm disappointed in you, Laura. I thought you were more responsible."

"Oh, please!"

"After you two took off, the police arrived."

"You called the police?"

"No, they came to us." I paused. "It was about Tommy's mother. She's been murdered."

Laura put her hand to her mouth. "Oh my God!"

"Tommy is staying with us tonight. He's upstairs."

She glanced at the ceiling.

"I'll save the lecture on being irresponsible and inconsiderate for another time. What I want to know is why you two took off?"

"Oh, Mom, that New Year's Eve thing was totally lame. I thought we'd be able to make Kyle's party. But once we were on the road, I didn't think I should turn up at Kyle's with another guy. We saw the motel sign, figured we were already in deep do-do so…"

I groaned. "You didn't think you should show up at your boyfriend's party with another guy, so you spent the night in a motel room with this fellow."

She studied her hands. "Seemed like a good idea at the time."

"Devon told me that when he found you two, you threw a glass at Ryan."

"Yeah, well, Ryan's a first-class jerk. I'd had all I could take of him."

I wanted to shake her. "Then why did you go to bed with him?"

"Can I have a drink?" Tommy stood at the kitchen door, clutching the teddy bear he'd found in the guest room.

"Sure can." I took a glass from the cupboard.

"Who were you in bed with, Laura?" Tommy asked.

Laura snorted and stalked out of the room.

Chapter Nine

Pat

"Your mother's funeral is tomorrow," I said when Tommy had finished breakfast the next morning.

He looked at me, his eyes wide, and nodded.

"Have you been to a funeral before?"

"Grandpa's. I was only four then."

I smiled. "That was a long time ago."

"They put him in a stone house. Is that what they'll do with Mommy?"

"I don't know."

"I want her here with me."

I put an arm around him. "I wish she was here with you too, honey." Then I pulled back and looked at him. "I have to go out this morning, but you'll stay here with Laura. I don't want you to leave the house on your own. Do you understand?"

"Not even with Maxie?"

"Not even with Maxie. Laura will let Maxie out into the backyard. Promise me you'll stay inside, Tommy?"

"Okay."

The phone rang and I picked up the kitchen extension.

"Arlene Dobson here. The police say Tommy is in danger."

And a good day to you, too, I wanted to say. "Just a moment, please." I put a hand over the receiver. "Tommy, go upstairs and brush your teeth."

When the boy was out of earshot, I spoke into the receiver. "Tommy seems to be bearing up well, all things considered." Not that Arlene had asked about her nephew.

"And they say it would be better if he isn't with us right now. So I wonder if you'd—"

"Mrs. Dobson, I have a family of my own to look after and a business to run."

"You're a friend of Jude's."

"The police don't want Tommy at his school next week and I can't take a seven-year-old to work. You'll have to find somewhere else he can stay."

"Don't worry about next week. Hopefully, everything will be back to normal by then."

Normal? Her sister had been murdered.

"Just for a few days," she went on. "My friends are all away at this time of year. We'll pay for a sitter while you're at work."

"I don't know a sitter. My youngest child is eighteen."

"I'll find you one. You'll be at the funeral tomorrow?"

"Yes."

"Then you can take Tommy to the church. That would be a big help."

I was speechless at Arlene's assumption that the rest of the world would fit in with her plans.

"Tommy will need proper clothes for the funeral," she went on. "I...I can't go to Jude's. Not after...I don't suppose you'd...?"

"Go over to your sister's house?"

"It would be a big help."

"As it happens, I'm going there this morning with a police officer."

"Good." She paused. "You'd better pack up all his clothes. He won't be returning there."

Hardy turned the key in the ignition and Bob Dylan let loose with "Like a Rolling Stone."

"Sorry." He punched a button that shut off the sound. "Mario told me you're into opera."

"I passed the 'Va, Pensiero' test. He mention that?"

"Yeah, he told me. That's why I went easy in questioning you."

I rolled my eyes. "Easy?"

He laughed.

"I take it you're not a fan of the classics," I said.

"I love the classics. The Stones, the Beatles, Creedence—"

I smiled. "Classic rock. I like Dylan, too. Just turn the volume down a notch."

He pushed a button, adjusted a knob and "Like a Rolling Stone" returned. The lyrics brought my thoughts back to Tommy. Was he all on his own? His family didn't seem to want him.

Snow was falling and Hardy turned on his windshield wipers. "They're calling for six inches today."

I looked out the side window. "I don't like to leave Tommy."

"Your daughter's with him."

"Yes." Laura had grudgingly agreed to keep an eye on Tommy for a few hours. I was counting on Tracy for backup. She'd spent the night with a friend, but she had called to say she'd be home soon.

Hardy pulled up in front of Jude's small semi-detached house and stared at it for a few moments. Yellow crime-scene tape was strung across the front stairs. "She came from one of the wealthiest families in this city." He shook his head. "And she didn't even have a will."

I wasn't surprised. I'm always after my clients to draw up wills and powers of attorney, and many of them try to put it off. They don't like to think about dying or becoming incapacitated.

Hardy lifted up the crime-scene tape. I scrambled under it and climbed the stairs. The wooden front door had been stained a walnut brown. It looked sturdy and there were no gouges on it. "Did Jude's killer break into the house?" I asked.

"No signs of a break-in."

"Then Jude let him in."

He shrugged.

"She knew the person who killed her."

He didn't answer.

From the front hall, I surveyed Jude's home. I wanted to know more about this woman who had attracted Michael. The main floor held a small living room, an adjoining dining room and a kitchen behind it. Futon sofas, a pine coffee table, an old upright piano and a large pine table and chairs filled the rooms. Framed posters of art exhibitions covered the walls. But three small, signed oil paintings hung among the posters. I thought one of them might be an A.Y. Jackson. Four pine bookcases were crammed with books. A film of white powder covered every surface.

"Crime scene squad was here yesterday." Hardy pointed to the hardwood living room floor. "They took the carpet."

"That was where—"

"Yup. Right there on the carpet."

Jude's face slashed. Her body limp and covered with blood. I shuddered.

"I'll get Tommy's clothes." I headed for the staircase. "Do I need to be careful about touching things?"

"No, we've taken prints. I'll wait for you down here."

Three bedrooms were on the second floor. The largest, with frilly white curtains and a queen-sized bed covered with a patchwork quilt, had clearly been Jude's room. I stood, transfixed, in the doorway. Was this where...?

Photos of Tommy as a baby and a toddler covered the dresser. This must have been where the police had found Michael's photo. A framed headshot of Jude stood on the highboy. I took it for Tommy.

The smallest room was a study with a desk and a chair, a cot made up with sheets and blankets, and more bookcases. I headed for the third room with the Harry Potter poster, and took Tommy's navy blazer, dress pants, a white shirt and a bow tie from the closet. I removed all the socks and underwear from the dresser, and returned to the closet for everyday trousers, shirts and sweaters.

In Jude's room, I found two large suitcases. I stuffed them with Tommy's clothes and tossed Jude's photo into the second case. I spotted something in a mesh pocket on the inside of the lid.

I pulled out a business card. "Clive Pettigrew LLB. Tax disputes and litigation." A downtown address, a telephone number and an e-mail were on the bottom of the card.

Clive Pettigrew. This was Jude's guy.

"Everything okay up there?" Hardy called from downstairs.

"I've got two heavy suitcases. Can you give me a hand?"

I looked at Clive's card and fought the urge to slip it into the pocket of my jeans. But I was too busy to play Nancy Drew. When Hardy reached the second floor, I handed him the card. "Found this in one of the suitcases. Clive Pettigrew. Must be the man Jude was seeing."

He gave me a curt nod and pocketed the card.

"Slaughtered!" the headline screamed in large type.

The Toronto Tattler's front page, with a blown-up photo of Jude, was in full view through the newspaper box's glass door.

"Heiress killed in her home," the deck below the headline added.

I shook my head as I walked to the street corner. What wouldn't *The Tattler* stoop to?

The office tower across the street was the address on Clive's business card. His law office was somewhere in that building.

While I waited for the light to change at the busy Bloor Street intersection, I saw Hardy leave the building. He had lost no time in checking out Clive. I watched him walk west on Bloor toward Avenue Road and merge into the crowd on the sidewalk. I crossed the street when the light turned green.

After Hardy had driven me home with the suitcases, I'd made a quick lunch for Laura and Tommy. Then I called for a taxi to take me downtown.

I wanted to get a look at this guy Jude had been seeing. Did he resemble Michael? I wondered if there was a certain type of man she was attracted to. "No," I whispered. "Michael was in a class all of his own."

Not true, I told myself as I approached the building. Michael had plenty of company in the cheating class.

Still, I wondered if Clive looked just a bit like him. Wavy brown hair, nice...

A woman has been murdered, I told myself sternly. Clive may be Jude's killer.

I walked through the revolving doors. I figured it wouldn't hurt to talk to the man for a minute or two.

In the lobby, I looked at my watch. Two thirty-five. I figured Clive should be back from lunch by now, but would a tax lawyer be in his office on the second day of the New Year?

There was only one way to find out.

The forty-something redhead looked up from her computer screen. "Can I help you?" She peered at me over her glasses.

"I'd like to see Mr. Pettigrew." I looked around the twentieth-floor reception area and took in the abstract paintings, potted plants and leather couches. They added up to nondescript.

"Your name?"

"Pat Tierney."

She turned back to her computer. "I don't seem to have you here."

"I don't have an appointment."

"I can put you down for—"

A door opened across the room and a man in a gray suit stepped into the reception area.

"Clive Pettigrew?" I asked.

"Yes?"

"I'm here about Jude Seaton."

His eyes flicked over me, sizing me up.

The redhead glanced from Clive to me, then back to Clive again.

"No calls," he said to her. He motioned me into his office and took the chair behind the desk. "Have a seat, Ms...."

"Tierney. Pat Tierney." I sat across from him.

"You're with the police?"

"No."

I appraised him. Clive Pettigrew had a small brown moustache, thinning brown hair and an unattractive way of pursing his mouth. He sat on the edge of his chair. Hardy had clearly rattled him.

I caught a glimpse of a heavy stainless steel watch bracelet under his white shirt cuff. The watch that had fascinated Tommy was no doubt waterproof, probably gave weather reports and altitude readings. The ultimate toy for many men, but I couldn't picture this prissy guy climbing mountains or scuba diving.

"You probably know that Jude was killed on New Year's Eve."

He blinked. "Yes, shocking."

"I found your card at her house."

His head jerked back. His small eyes grew wary. "Who are you?"

"I already told you. Pat Tierney."

"No, I mean who are you with? You say you're not police. What do you want?"

"I'm a financial advisor."

He gave a short laugh. "Jude had a financial advisor? She didn't give a hoot about money. Not that she needed to, with her family."

"She must have decided she needed one."

He examined his platinum cuff links. "And I suppose I have you to thank for the visit I just had from that homicide detective."

"I found your card in a suitcase when I packed up Tommy's clothes. I gave it to Detective Hardy."

He pursed his lips. "So why are you here?"

"I thought Jude's will might provide a motive for her murder."

"You're her financial advisor." He gave me a sour smile. "You should have a copy of her will."

"She'd just come to me before she was killed. We hadn't got as far as wills yet."

"Then, why are you—"

"She left a son."

"Tommy." I couldn't tell from his expression or his tone of voice whether he liked the boy.

"Yes. Tommy is a relative of mine on his father's side. For his sake, I want to get to the bottom of this." I paused and wondered if I had said too much. I didn't want him to know that Tommy was staying at my house.

He leaned forward on his desk. "I don't have a copy of Jude's will and I have no idea if she even had one. I wasn't her lawyer. I was a friend."

"You were dating her."

"Is that any of your business?"

"I've been speaking to her friends, trying to get a handle on...what happened."

"As I told the detective, we met at a wine tasting last spring and saw each other for a few months after that."

"You broke up?"

"That's right."

"You had an argument."

He rose from his chair. "What are you implying?"

"Nothing. Just asking if you broke up."

"We didn't have a lot in common." He moved behind his chair.

He drew in a deep breath, then grasped the back of the chair. "As I told the police, I haven't seen Jude since September."

It flashed through my mind that the police hadn't known about Clive Pettigrew until Tommy mentioned him and I found his card. That meant they hadn't found his phone number in the records of Jude's calls.

"It's funny," I said, "that there were no records of calls you made to Jude—or calls she made to you."

"I called her from pay phones and I discouraged her from calling me."

"Sounds like something a married man would do."

He walked to the door. "It's very sad about Jude. But as I told Detective Hardy, I know nothing that can help the investigation. Good day, Ms. Tierney."

I reached into my handbag and put my business card on his desk. "My office number, should you want to speak to me again."

I was half-way across the reception area when he called my name. He cleared his throat. "You said you're a relative of Tommy's father. Who was Tommy's father?"

"Jude didn't want that known. We should respect her wishes." I left the office suite and closed the door behind me.

I shook my head as I headed down the hall to the elevator. Clive was certainly no Michael. Jude had eclectic tastes in men.

I stared at the vase of roses on the kitchen table. "What's this?"

Devon put an arm around me. "Blooms for my hostess."

I stroked the velvety petal of an apricot rose. "They're lovely."

Then I looked around the room. "Where's Tommy?"

"Upstairs with Maxie." He turned me around and kissed me.

"Mom."

Out of the corner of my eye, I saw Laura in the doorway. I pulled away from Devon.

"Sorry to interrupt," she said with a smirk, "but there was a phone call for you. Guy named Leckie. Called about an hour ago."

Devon looked at me quizzically.

"Ray Leckie. One of the VPs at head office. I'd better see what he wants."

Devon sighed.

"Pat!" Ray boomed at the other end of the phone line. "Charisse and I are having a few people over for drinks tomorrow. We hope you can join us."

"Love to, Ray, but I have a houseguest." I was glad I had an excuse.

"Bring her along."

"It's a him."

"Good for you, Pat. Drop by after six. Date?"

I stifled a groan. "Date."

In the sunroom, Tracy had opened a bottle of shiraz and was filling glasses. Laura sat off to the side, pointedly ignoring Devon who was looking over our CD collection.

He selected a disc and placed it in the CD player. The voice of Bryan Ferry singing "Lover Come Back to Me" filled the room. Another of Michael's favorites.

Devon handed me a glass. "I'm taking us all out to dinner."

I suddenly felt drained. The thought of driving even a few blocks and looking for parking overwhelmed me. "It's snowing. Let's order in, and stay warm and cozy in front of the fireplace."

"We'll take a taxi. Pick a place Tommy would like."

"Will that be safe for him?" Tracy asked.

"He'll be with the group of us," Devon said. "We'll take cabs to the restaurant and back here afterwards. The boy hasn't been out all day."

"I'm staying here," Laura muttered.

"Fine." I glared at her, then turned to Devon. "The rest of us would be delighted to accept your invitation. I'll call Milo's and see if they have a table."

Dinner at my favorite neighborhood bistro was subdued. We talked about the snow that was falling outside, and the next game for the Leafs. My thoughts were on Tommy, who was silently eating his dinner beside me. After we'd finished our gelato, we took a taxi back home. The snow was coming down heavier.

I heard music in Laura's room when I took Tommy up to bed, but I didn't look in on her.

Downstairs, Devon had lit a fire in the fireplace. He produced the bottle of cognac from his home up north, and turned on the CD player. Bryan Ferry warbled "Sweet and Lovely."

Tracy kissed my cheek. "I'm turning in."

I closed my eyes and leaned back on the sofa.

"At last," Devon said. "Just the two of us."

I took a sip of cognac. "Umm, good."

He lifted his glass. "To us."

I took another sip.

He eased himself next to me on the sofa and put an arm around my shoulders. "Now we can get back to where we were—"

"Before we were interrupted." I smiled at him. "But first let me tell you something."

"About what?" He leaned over to nuzzle my neck.

"I met Jude's guy today."

He pulled back and raised an eyebrow.

"I found Clive Pettigrew's card at her house. I figured this was the Clive that Tommy mentioned to the police, so I visited his office this afternoon. He's a lawyer. Probably married."

"And he could be dangerous."

"I gave the card to Hardy. He'd already spoken to Clive when I got there."

"This guy—"

I shrugged. I wasn't in the mood for a lecture. "He said he was seeing Jude last summer, but they broke up in September."

"I wish you hadn't gone to see him."

We sat there for some time, sipping our drinks.

I closed my eyes. "The funeral's at ten tomorrow. I'll see you back here afterwards. We can do something with Tommy in the afternoon."

"I'm going with you."

"Sure you want to?"

He took my hand and we sat in silence again.

"Tommy has the guest room," I finally said, "so I can only offer you this sofa tonight."

Devon pressed a button on the remote and Bryan returned to "Lover Come Back to Me." He put an arm around me. "It hasn't turned out to be quite the holiday I'd hoped for, but it's good being here with you."

I drew a sigh. "My holiday was ruined when Jude showed up at my office."

He touched the tip of my nose with his. "I'd hoped..." He ran a finger over my lips, sending warmth spreading over my neck and chest.

I closed my eyes and saw Michael's face.

"With Jude and Tommy and everything, maybe this isn't a good time," Devon said.

I brushed my lips across Devon's cheek. My turn had come.

"No time like the present," I whispered.

He took me in his arms.

Chapter Ten

Pat

I awoke the next morning with Devon's arms around me. I was purring. I opened one eye. The bedside clock told me it was just after six. Then I opened the other eye.

I told myself that this should not have happened. I'd been angry at Michael, lonely, and Devon had been sitting next to me. And now…were we involved? Devon would expect things. Weekend visits, vacations. He would want help with that awful son of his. Impossible. I had my own kids to worry about. My business to run.

Slow down, I chided myself. I had spent one night with Devon. He lived in another country. He had his own business, his own friends, his own life.

He opened his eyes. "Much nicer here than on the sofa." He tightened his arms around me.

I gently disengaged his arms and propped myself up on one elbow. "The funeral is at ten. I'd better get up. Get breakfast…"

He ran a finger over my lips. "Not yet."

I eased myself down beside him, luxuriating in his warmth. I had forgotten how good skin on skin felt. Just a few more seconds, a minute tops. "I'd better…"

"It's too early to get up, Patty." He moved on top of me. "Way too early."

Tracy and I were toasting bagels, and Tommy was eating cereal at the table, when Laura appeared in the kitchen doorway. "Mom, you haven't fooled anyone with that bedding on the sofa. It wasn't slept in. You jumped into the sack with Devon last night."

"Laura!" What was I going to do with her?

Tracy stared at me, her mouth open.

Laura slipped into a chair beside Tommy. "So did you? Do it?"

"None of your business, Laura," Tracy said.

"Why not?" Laura asked. "Mom wanted to know all about me and Ryan."

"Devon is Mom's guy. They've been seeing each other since—"

"Did he use a condom, Mom?" Laura asked.

Tommy looked up from his bowl of cereal. "What's a condom?"

"That's enough." I said. "The street hasn't been plowed and we have to be at the church by ten."

"No, I want to—" Laura stopped short, seeing Devon in the doorway dressed in a sweatshirt and jeans.

"What's all this about?" he asked.

Tracy waved a hand. "Just a mother-daughter thing. Happens all the time around here."

Laura smirked.

"Bagel or cereal?" Tracy asked Devon.

"A bagel and a coffee would be good." He looked out the kitchen window. "There's a pile of snow out there. Tell me where you keep the shovel and I'll get started on the driveway."

"Our street hasn't been plowed," I said. "I don't know if we can make it over to Mount Pleasant. That's a major thoroughfare and it should be cleared by now."

Devon pulled a chair out from the table and sat down. "I'll do what I can with the driveway. Then we can only hope the plow comes by."

"The girls will give you a hand." I gave both of them a meaningful look. "I'll get Tommy dressed."

"I have to get ready myself," Laura said. "Got things to do today."

I gave her my no-nonsense look. "Laura, Tommy has to be at the church for his mother's funeral. Help Devon clear the drive and pray that the city plow comes along soon." I turned to Tommy. "Upstairs, young man."

"What's a condom?" Tommy asked again as I clipped his bow tie to his shirt.

"Something some people use when they're older."

"Like wine and cigarettes?"

"That kind of thing."

It wasn't my place to teach Tommy the facts of life, but I wondered who would. Certainly not his aunt. I gave him a hug. Poor kid, what would become of him?

He turned his face up to mine. "Mrs. T, what happens to people when they die?"

Another loaded question. "What did your mother tell you?"

"She said dead people go to heaven. She said that's where my daddy is. And Grandpa."

His daddy. I felt a rush of sadness, the precursor of tears. I took a deep breath. "That's where they are."

"Yeah?" He looked up at me again.

I kissed his forehead. "Your mother's in heaven, Tommy."

"What's heaven?"

Whew! I tried to remember what the nuns had taught us at school. "Heaven is a place where everyone is perfectly happy. They're with friends and family. They have no worries, and they know they'll be happy like this for ever and ever."

"Do they play video games in heaven?"

I smiled. "I'm sure they do, sweetie."

"Pat," Devon called from downstairs, "the plow's coming down the street."

The organist was playing "Ave Maria" when we arrived at the church. We were half-way down the center aisle, when Tommy tugged at my arm and pointed to a front pew. "There's Nana."

I took him to the front of the church where a small, silver-haired woman, smartly suited in black, was seated. She kissed Tommy on both cheeks. "My sweet boy, we must pray for your poor dear mother." Her voice had an Irish lilt.

Then she fixed her blue eyes on me. "You must be Mrs. Tierney. I'm Norah Seaton. We are grateful for all you have done for Tommy. Please come back to the house for lunch."

She pointed at the pew behind her. Strange, I thought, when Devon and I were seated on either side of Tommy, that the Seatons hadn't made room for the boy with them.

The plump blonde with a double chin who was seated beside Norah turned and gave me a thin smile. "Arlene Dobson." But she said nothing to Tommy. Didn't even acknowledge his presence.

The organist moved on to "Amazing Grace," and a priest in a purple chasuble, his gray hair pulled back into a ponytail, appeared at the foot of the center aisle. He waited there as a procession led by four altar girls holding oversized candles, followed by six men pushing a casket of dark, polished wood on a metal bier, moved down the aisle toward him. The priest sprinkled water on the casket. The men headed for the pews, two of them joining Norah and Arlene. I figured one of them had to be Jude's brother and the other was Arlene's husband.

The priest introduced himself as Father Jack Krespic. He told us he taught theology at the University of Toronto and that he had met Jude when she volunteered at Safe Harbor.

"An admirable woman." Father Jack ran a hand over his eyes. "With a real concern for her fellow human beings."

Tommy began to cry, and I put an arm around him. Norah turned and reached out a hand to him. Tears ran down her face. "It's difficult, my boy, but we must be brave," she said in a loud whisper. "Your mother would want us to be strong and soldier on."

Arlene stared straight ahead. The man beside her put an arm around her.

The funeral Mass began and I looked around the church. The sanctuary was filled with flowers, but the group of mourners was relatively small. About thirty people, many of them women, filled the front pews of the large church. I assumed some of them were Jude's colleagues at Queen of Angels.

But anyone could attend a funeral, I realized with a jolt. Everyone who saw me arrive at the church with Tommy would assume that he was staying with me. Why didn't I have Devon drive him in his rental van?

Father Jack's eulogy provided scant solace. "As Christians, we take comfort from knowing our loved one has gone to the fellowship of the risen Lord."

He paused. "But when the departed was a young woman like Jude with her life full of promise, it can be difficult for us to understand why a loving God would allow this to happen. Sure, there are sayings to make us feel better. Remember Billy Joel's song 'Only the Good Die Young'?"

There were titters among the congregation, then an awkward silence. Devon smiled at me. I took Tommy's hand.

"The death of Jude Seaton," Father Jack continued, "a beautiful, talented woman with a young son to raise and everything in life to look forward to, can really test our faith..."

I glanced behind me and spotted Hardy seated behind the mourners.

A movement at the back of the church caught my eye. A tall figure dressed in black stood in a side aisle beside a marble pillar. I craned my neck for a better look. Male, dark skin, early twenties. He was dressed in black jeans and a worn black jacket. Not someone I would have expected to see among this predominantly white, well-dressed congregation.

The man turned and glided back up the aisle. A heartbeat later, he vanished into the shadows at the back of the church.

"What is it?" Devon whispered.

"There was someone back there..."

He glanced at the back of the church, then looked at me.

I shook my head. "Probably not important."

We turned our attention back to the pulpit. Father Jack was telling anecdotes about Jude at Safe Harbor. "Several years ago, some of the volunteers built the back porch and they were painting it. I'd told them that this was blessed work because Jesus Himself was a carpenter."

I turned and looked at the back of the church again. Nothing.

"The job was nearly done," Father Jack said, "when one of the volunteers on a ladder dumped a bucket of paint over Jude. She let fly some pretty colorful language. 'Jude!' I said to her. 'Excuse me, Father Jack,' she replied, 'but Jesus Himself would be swearing too right now.'"

The faces of the people around us broke into weak smiles. Where had Tommy been while Jude was helping refugees at Safe Harbor?

"Ms. Tierney, a word."

Hardy hurried over to us as we made our way to the church parking lot.

"Can't it wait, Detective?" Devon said.

Hardy ignored him. "Who was that at the back of the church?"

Devon took Tommy's hand and pointed to a squirrel that was running along a hydro wire.

"I don't know what—"

"Come on. I was watching you. You turned around to look at the back of the church. Saw someone who's not part of the white-bread crowd. Tall guy, looks like he could try out for small forward with the Raptors. Slipped out as soon as you spotted him. What gives?"

"Nothing gives, Detective. I didn't get a good look at him. But anyone can walk into a church. Anything else?"

He studied me for a moment, then shook his head. "Not right now." He lowered his voice. "Call us if you see that guy again or any strangers hanging around. There's a killer out there. The boy may be his next target."

Chapter Eleven

Yuri

Yuri lit a cigarette and sat at the battered kitchen table while he stirred sugar into his mug of instant coffee.

A dark-skinned woman with an infant in her arms appeared beside him. "Sister not allow smoking at Safe Harbor."

Yuri gave her a smile, displaying a mouth full of broken and stained teeth. "I think you not tell Sister. Not if you know what is good for you." He tweaked the child's cheek. "And your kid."

The woman gasped, tightened her hold on the baby and scurried out of the room, leaving Yuri alone with his thoughts. Sister Celia and Oskar were at the funeral of the Seaton woman. Yuri frowned. He had told Oskar not to go, told him the police would be there.

But Oskar had laughed him off. "Jude and me, we work together when she volunteer at Safe Harbor," he'd said. "Is right I go to funeral."

Damn that Oskar. The Seaton woman's picture had been in all the newspapers. Yuri flung his cigarette onto the floor and ground it into the linoleum with the heel of his boot. But that was Oskar, always rushing in without considering the consequences.

When the Soviet Union collapsed in 1991, Yuri had been eighteen and training with the Spetsnaz, the Kremlin's elite fighting force. The British SAS? America's Delta Force? Hah, weaklings! Spetsnaz wasn't afraid of dirty work—sabotage, assassinations—for Mother Russia.

But he had missed his shot at glory. With the dissolution of the Soviet Union, morale plummeted in Spetsnaz and the rest of the military. Corrupt bastards were in charge and no one in uniform was making a decent wage. Yuri resigned and sought his fortune elsewhere.

The war in Bosnia-Herzegovina was attracting fighters from all over Eastern Europe, including Russian mercenaries and volunteers fighting for a Slav Orthodox brotherhood. But he had no principles left to uphold. He attached himself to the Bosnia Serb Army as a *kontraktniki* or contract soldier. He would get paid for the risks he took and move on. He no longer needed to be a hero. He gave himself a *nom de guerre* and became Yuri.

For the first few months in Bosnia's killing fields, he'd been part of a unit that smuggled gasoline to the Serbian forces. He quickly picked up the Serbian language, which was similar to Russian. Then, in the summer of 1993, he was assigned to a cell in northeastern Bosnia to back up its young leader, Oskar Jacovic. Against his advice, Oskar ordered a surprise early-morning attack on a Muslim village called Tica. The villagers put up more resistance than Oskar had expected and several of Oskar's men were killed.

Yuri shook his head and lit another cigarette. With a little reconnaissance, that could have been avoided.

In the end, they'd smashed through the village's defences. They rounded up the able-bodied men and shot them. They dumped their bodies in a mass grave. They burned the houses. And they raped twenty-four women.

The Serbian soldiers had been under orders to rape Muslim women. Spread around as much Serbian seed as possible so the victims would produce little Chetniks.

That day in Tica, most of the soldiers followed their orders with gusto, but a few had to fortify their resolve with alcohol. "I have two sisters," said a young man Yuri had found retching into the bushes. "I am ashamed to be a Serb."

But Oskar had no such reluctance. "We need to wipe out the Turks as if they were never here," he told Yuri over a bottle of *slivovitz* that evening. "No more Muslims, no more war. Simple. But what would we do then?" He laughed. "Taking our turns with their women," he added with a leer, "we do our duty and have a bit of fun at the same time, yes?"

Yuri knew there was more to the war than expelling the Muslims from Bosnia, but he avoided discussing politics. The country's problems had nothing to do with him. He was there for work. And as a *kontraktniki*, he was not expected to take part in the rapes, which was fine with him. He had no desire to force himself on crying, struggling women. There were plenty of girls in the Serbian towns who welcomed the soldiers. These were spirited wenches who were eager to satisfy a man and enjoy themselves between the sheets.

And he knew that Oskar hadn't given a damn about any Slav brotherhood. Oskar had only been out for himself then, just as he was now. They had that in common.

After Bosnia, Yuri had honed his skills as a soldier of fortune in Kosovo, then in Africa and Colombia. But he was getting older now. It was time to switch to another line of work. He'd slipped into Canada the year before and planned to lie low for a while. The country was too stable to practice his arts of war, but he knew there would be other opportunities.

Three weeks after he arrived in Toronto, he had run into his old comrade-in-arms, Oskar, in an Eastern European deli. It really was a small world. Oskar said he had work for him. It wasn't difficult and the money was good.

Yuri got up from the table. He had better scram before that nun got back. She didn't like him hanging out here unless he was doing a job for her.

Chapter Twelve

Pat

Father Jack blessed Jude's casket in the Seaton family vault at Perpetual Life Cemetery and gave it a splash of holy water. Norah stood beside him with her head bowed, her hands on Tommy's shoulders. There were tears on her face, but the boy's eyes were dry. The funeral director handed him a pale pink rose and whispered something to him. Tommy placed the flower on his mother's casket.

On our way back to the Volvo, a small woman with short dark curly hair approached us. "Tommy," she cried. The boy ran into her arms.

After a few moments, she released him and turned to me. "I'm Sister Celia De Franco, a friend of Jude's. And I know you're Pat Tierney. Arlene told me that Tommy is staying with you."

"For a few days."

"I run Safe Harbor, the home for refugees that Father Jack spoke about in his eulogy. I have to get back there now, but I'd like to talk to you. Could we…"

Tommy had mentioned Sister Celia at the police station. I looked at Devon. He placed a hand on my arm. "Tommy and I can hang out this afternoon," he said.

"I could drop by later today," I told Sister Celia.

Tommy tugged at my sleeve. "Can I come? I want to see Benny."

"Our cat," Sister Celia said. "You can visit us another time, Tommy. I have something to discuss with Mrs. Tierney." She smiled at me. "I'll be there all day."

Norah lived in a handsome, red brick house in Rosedale, the enclave for Toronto's wealthy residents just north of the downtown core. A tall spruce tree on the front lawn was festooned with Christmas lights, unlit during the day. And probably the past few evenings since Jude died.

Inside the house, there was no Christmas tree, no holly or mistletoe. Living rooms on either side of the front hall were tastefully furnished in mahogany and cherry wood. Large oil paintings, stained-glass side windows and handsome Persian carpets provided color.

"Tommy, my love." Norah enveloped her grandson in a hug. She lifted her head to greet Devon and me, and told us to help ourselves to drinks and the buffet in the dining room. "I want to spend a few minutes with my boy."

A gray-haired man in a navy blazer mixed drinks behind a bar in the east living room. In the dining room behind it, a long table was laden with dainty sandwiches, platters of poached salmon and roast beef, salads and baskets of rolls and bagels. At the sideboard, a middle-aged woman in a maid's uniform poured coffee and tea into china cups.

The sight of all that food twisted my stomach into knots. I took a cup of tea, and Devon and I moved into the room across the hall.

Arlene stepped up beside us, a frosted glass in her a hand. A stocky man with a ruddy complexion, one of the pallbearers, was at her side. "My husband, Lloyd Dobson. Pat Tierney and—"

"Devon Shaughnessy," Devon said. The men shook hands.

"Our kids are over there." Arlene waved at the sofa across the room, where a boy and a girl, who looked about ten years old, were seated with Norah and Tommy. "Evan and Bettina. Twins are such a handful." She heaved a dramatic sigh. "It's been horrific. And the worst was finding her. The most horrible thing that ever happened to me."

Lloyd patted her arm.

I stared at her. The most horrible thing that's happened to you, I wanted to say. What about Jude?

"I'll see if I can get anything for Norah," Lloyd said and moved away.

"Pat, Arlene." A woman joined us, her platinum hair spiking out from her head like a dandelion gone to seed.

"Gemma," I said.

She hugged Arlene, then turned to me. "I'd just got back from St. Lucia yesterday when the police called about Jude." Her face crumpled. "Horrible."

"Do you know Gemma?" I asked Arlene.

"We all went to Queen of Angels. Of course, I was years behind Gemma and Jude."

Gemma gave her a weak smile. "Two years."

I introduced Devon to Gemma. Then I turned back to Arlene. "Jude taught at the same school she went to?"

She wrinkled her pug nose. "Hard to believe anyone would want to go back there. After university, Jude drifted around the world for a few years. Taught English with Friends Beyond Borders in China and Tanzania. She had Mom and Dad worried sick. When she finally came back to Toronto, she got a job at our old school."

"Teaching at a private girls' school seemed pretty sedate for Jude," Gemma said. "I thought she'd go back to one of those underdeveloped countries. She had a real social conscience. At university, she was involved with the Animal Rights Front."

Arlene snorted. "And she was allergic to dogs and cats."

"She settled down because of Tommy," Gemma said.

"She never should have had that child."

Devon looked uncomfortable. I tried to change the subject. "You saw your sister at Christmas?"

Arlene shook her head. "Mom likes to have us all here for Christmas dinner. But Jude had the flu and stayed at home. On Boxing Day, Lloyd and I took our kids skiing in Vermont for a few days. When we got back, I called Jude because we hadn't exchanged Christmas presents. She said she still wasn't feeling well."

Jude had looked well enough when she came to my office.

"Mom talked about looking in on her, but I didn't want her to catch Jude's bug," Arlene continued. "So I dropped by on New Year's Eve morning with our gifts. I could see the Christmas tree lights through the front window, but she didn't answer when I rapped on the door. I tried the door knob and it turned. Inside..." She started to cry.

A tall man with dark hair came over and put an arm around Arlene. "I'm Patrick Seaton," he said to Devon and me. He smiled at Gemma.

I introduced myself and Devon to the president and chief executive of Seaton Ferguson, and noted how much he looked like Jude. Same dark hair, blue eyes, good bone structure.

He threw me a smile. "You're Jude's friend, the one who's been looking after Tommy."

"That's right."

"Thank you. It's been a great help to us." He ran a hand through his hair. "I can't believe that Jude is dead. She was two years younger than me, and hell on wheels when we were kids. Always coming up with schemes to outfox the folks. And now poor Tommy?" He shook his head.

"Tommy. All anyone can think about these days is poor Tommy," Arlene cried and moved away.

Gemma and I exchanged startled looks and stared at Arlene as she crossed the room.

"She's upset," Patrick said.

"And Tommy?" I asked. "What will happen to him?"

His face tightened. "Arlene has her hands full with her two. And Charlotte, my wife, is Crown counsel in the Queenston insider trading case. She's working eighteen hours a day. Mom's keen to have Tommy live with her, but I don't think her health is up to it. A young boy would be a handful."

"He can't go back to his school on Monday," I said.

"We'll come up with something by then. If you'd be good enough to have him for the next few days, he'll be off your hands by Sunday evening. I've made some calls to boarding schools."

"But…"

"We really appreciate it." He flashed me another smile. "Now, if you'll excuse me…"

"Smooth operator, that Patrick," Gemma said as he crossed the room. "He knew you wouldn't say no. Who could say no to a kid as cute as Tommy?"

"He's got a lot of nerve."

"I'll help myself to some food," Devon said. "Can I get either of you anything?"

Gemma and I both declined. As Devon headed for the buffet, Gemma looked wistfully at Patrick who had joined a group across the room. "I had a major crush on him when I was fifteen."

"He looks a lot like Jude and Norah. Arlene must take after their father."

"Arlene was adopted."

"Oh?"

"She was told when she was about ten and ever since then she's tried to be the perfect Seaton daughter."

"I take it Arlene and Jude weren't close."

Gemma smiled. "Two very different women. And Arlene was always jealous of Jude. Her great looks, her confidence, the fact that she was a real Seaton."

"Had Jude been dating anyone recently?"

"She may have been seeing someone last summer. I say this only because she never had time to spend at my cottage in Muskoka." She shrugged. "I've known Jude for twenty-five years. She was my dearest friend, but there are huge parts of her life I know nothing about. She never told me who Tommy's father was. She was a very private person."

I felt my face grow warm at the mention of Tommy's father. "I gave the police your name. Jude said you'd mentioned me."

Gemma looked puzzled. "I guess I must have. So that's how you know her. She never told me that she needed a financial advisor. But, as I said, she was a private person." She suddenly stopped. "Is that what the police are saying? That a lover killed her?"

"I don't know what they're saying. But Tommy mentioned that a friend of his mother's was at their house a fair bit last summer, although he hadn't been around for a while. A Clive Pettigrew. Did you meet him?"

"No. But I hope the police are following that up."

"They know about it."

She looked over my shoulder. "Speaking of the police…"

I turned to see Hardy making a beeline toward us.

"My cue to mingle." She drifted across the room.

Hardy pulled up beside me, a bottle of water in his hand. "I hear the boy is staying with you."

"I was asked—told, you might say—to keep him."

"By him." He motioned with his head toward Patrick.

"I don't get it. Why doesn't this family want to take Tommy in?"

He shrugged. "It's better that he's not with them. I'll take him back to your place."

"We'll be leaving soon. Tommy can come with us."

"He shouldn't be seen leaving with you."

A shiver ran down my spine.

He turned to go, then wheeled around to face me again. "Why were you questioning Pettigrew?"

"I wanted to—"

"Get a look at Jude Seaton's new man?" He impaled me with his ice-blue eyes.

"I—"

"What you did was really stupid, Ms. Tierney. This guy can get to Tommy now through you."

"He doesn't know Tommy is at my place. He doesn't know where I live. And I have an unlisted home phone number."

"It's not difficult to find out where someone lives. He probably knows people in your line of work."

"And he may not have seen Jude since they broke up in September."

"So he claims." He paused. "Did he tell you what their argument was about?"

"No. Maybe he'll tell you."

"Oh, sooner or later, he will." He fumed. "Leave the detecting to us, Ms. Tierney. It's no work for amateurs. I'll see you at your place."

I found Devon talking to a heavy woman in an outdated brown suit. "Rita Lonnegan is Queen of Angels' principal," he said. "This is Pat Tierney."

"I'm new at the school," Rita said. "I just got there in September so I didn't know Jude well. But she was popular with the students. A counselor will speak to them on Monday."

She looked at Norah and Tommy across the room and bit her lower lip. "Her poor family."

"Any of her colleagues hold grudges against her?" I asked.

Rita looked startled. "That's what the police asked me. We don't settle our differences with murder at Queen of Angels."

"Somebody did." With a pang of remorse, I remembered my death wish. Had someone else felt that way and acted on it?

"Ready to move on?" I asked Devon.

He smiled his assent, and we went over to Norah to say our goodbyes. The elderly woman took my arm. "We've been imposing on you, my dear, but it will just be for a few more days. You've been a wonderful friend to Jude." Tears filled her eyes. "She was a good girl, my Jude, for all her crazy notions and impetuous ways. She loved people. But I don't have to tell you that."

She stepped back and scrutinized our faces. "Tierney and Shaughnessy, those are Irish names. County Clare and County Galway."

I smiled. "Tierney was my late husband's name. His family has been in Canada for three generations."

"My father's family left Ireland during the potato famine," Devon said. "They were O'Shaughnessys then."

"No matter. You have the best of hearts." She gripped my arm again. "Promise me you'll do whatever you can to help the police find my girl's killer."

I gave her a hug. "Of course, I will."

But it was Tommy I really wanted to help. I knew then and there that I would do anything to keep that little boy from harm.

Chapter Thirteen

Pat

I put the key in the ignition and turned to Devon. "What did you make of that?"

"Norah." He shook his head. "Sad. Losing a child has to be one of the worst things that can happen to a person. And Arlene...quite the drama queen."

I smiled. I would have used a few other words to describe Arlene.

"And we've learned more about Jude," he continued. "A maverick. Definitely left of center."

I wondered whether Jude went for married men because they were a challenge or because she really preferred to be on her own. I pushed that thought aside. What did I care why she'd been attracted to Michael? What concerned me was why he had turned to her.

"The family rebel had a social conscience," I said. "Not the worst thing that could happen in a wealthy family."

"Tommy and I could take in a movie this afternoon. Or would that be inappropriate after his mother's funeral?"

I glanced at him. How do we keep a little boy amused? It was so domestic.

"A movie's a great idea. Ask him if he's seen the new Lord of the Rings film, *The Return of the King*. Even if he has, he may like to see it again. It's playing all over town."

I stared at the street, remembering the night before. Why had I let it happen? I glanced at Devon's silver head and thought of the roses he'd given me. Suddenly, I craved a close relationship with a man again.

I gripped the wheel. Stop being maudlin, I told myself. I thought I had a great marriage, but Michael had a son I didn't know about.

"Let's go out for dinner after the party," Devon said. "Just you and me. Our last evening for a while."

I pulled up in front of our house. "Sounds good."

He gave me a peck on the cheek before he got out of the car.

In the rearview mirror, I saw him waving as I drove down the street. He would leave the following day. His home was hundreds of miles away. Which was a good thing.

I told myself to focus on Safe Harbor and find out more about Jude.

Safe Harbor, I thought with a sigh. I could have used a safe harbor myself right then. A refuge where I could sort through everything that had happened in the past few days.

I located Safe Harbor a few blocks east of High Park in the city's west end. The three-story brick house was probably about a hundred years old, but its exterior was in excellent shape. Its front door and eaves had recently been painted dark green.

Sister Celia came to the door dressed in jeans and a red pullover. "Tea?" she asked when I was inside.

"I won't refuse."

I followed her past a lounge with shabby furniture and an old television set, and down a hall with scuffed walls and worn linoleum. In the kitchen, a kettle was boiling on the stove and a dark-skinned woman was feeding a baby in a highchair.

Sister Celia fixed two mugs of tea and put them on a tray. I followed her to a cozy sitting room at the back of the house. From my seat on the sofa in front of the fireplace, I saw a bed through a doorway to my right. I realized that these were the nun's private quarters.

Sister Celia sat sipping her tea. Finally, she put the mug on the coffee table and turned to me, sadness in her large, black eyes.

"I met Jude eleven years ago when she began teaching at Queen of Angels. We hit it off from the start. We were both bucking establishments. In her case, Toronto's upper crust. In mine, the Roman Catholic patriarchy. When I left teaching to start up Safe Harbor a few years later, she offered to do volunteer work for us."

A large gray cat jumped into her lap and she scratched him behind the ears. "This is Benny."

"Did Jude work here last fall?"

"No. She helped out for a year or two, but she stopped when Tommy was born. She wanted to spend her time away from the school with him."

"But you kept in touch?"

"I saw Jude and Tommy several times a year. Usually dinner and a movie at their home. And they came to our Christmas and summer parties here. They didn't show up this Christmas, though."

"Did she tell you about the men she was dating?"

"No. There was someone recently?"

"She was seeing a Clive Pettigrew last summer. Did you meet him?"

"No, I didn't. Do the police know about this man?"

"They're looking into it."

"Jude told me about Tommy's father." She locked eyes with me. "But she never spoke about any other men in her life."

I froze. "You know," I managed to say.

"Yes. I thought you might too when I heard that Tommy was staying with you."

Tears stung my eyes. "Jude came to my office the day before she died. She told me Tommy was Michael's son and asked if I'd take the boy for a few days. She was worried that he was in some kind of danger." I gave a mirthless laugh. "I had no idea Michael had a son. I gather Michael didn't either."

Sister Celia put the cat on the floor and moved closer to me on the sofa. "Jude told me just before Tommy was born. She wanted to confide in someone, I guess." She smiled. "Maybe she saw me as a mother confessor."

She paused. "I think I may be the only person she told about Tommy's father. Jude said she was going to keep it a secret. The fact that she told you meant she was really worried about the boy. She was impulsive but she wasn't cruel."

Knocking sounded on the door. "Come in," Sister Celia called out.

The door opened and a man in his late thirties entered the room. He wore round, wire-rimmed glasses and his short brown hair stood up around his head, giving him a youthful appearance.

"I go for groceries now, Sister." He spoke with an Eastern European accent. "Everything you need on list?"

Sister Celia nodded. "The list covers it."

The door closed. "My assistant, Oskar Jacovic. Besides me, we have six people in the house right now so our grocery runs are pretty frequent."

"Why did you want to talk to me?"

"I wanted to talk about Tommy. The Seatons don't seem eager to take him in."

"But he's family."

"Norah's crazy about Tommy now, but she was pretty upset when Jude was pregnant. And Arlene was outraged. So Jude kept her distance. Turned up for the must-show occasions(Christmas, Easter, Norah's birthday. Her father set up a trust fund for her, but I don't think she ever touched it."

Jude hadn't seen her family at Christmas.

"Norah would like to take Tommy, but her health isn't good. And Arlene and Patrick don't want him."

"No other relatives?"

"That's it. Norah has family in Ireland, but she hasn't seen much of them in recent years. Harold Seaton, her husband, was an only child."

I gave her a stern look. "If this is leading where I think it is(no. I have my own children. My husband may have been Tommy's father, but that doesn't make me responsible for the boy."

She shook her head emphatically. "I didn't mean that. Although I assume you'll want to stay in contact with him. Your daughters are Tommy's half-sisters."

That made me angry. "Don't make me feel guilty because Michael cheated on me."

She put a hand on mine. "I just wondered if, between the two of us, we could come up with some ideas. The boy needs a stable home for the next ten years."

What ideas did she think I'd have? I wasn't a social worker. "I hardly think the Seatons will let him be adopted."

"I'd hate to see him grow up in a boarding school. There may be someone who could give him a good home and see that he spends time with his grandmother."

"You could talk to Jude's friends. The only one I know is Gemma Johannsen. She's single, wealthy and likes to travel. I can't see her taking on a seven-year-old, but she may know someone who would. And the teachers Jude worked with…" I held out my hands, palms up. That was all I could suggest.

She looked thoughtful. "Queen of Angels would be the place to start. I'll give the principal a call. Gemma, too, if you'll give me her number."

"The new principal is Rita Lonnegan. And I'll ask Gemma to call you." I checked my watch. "I should go."

Sister Celia stood up. "You've had all this thrown at you in the past few days. You'll want to get back on track with your life."

At the front door, I turned to her. "Why are you so concerned about Tommy when you have all this"(I swept my arm to encompass Safe Harbor("to deal with?"

She looked at me quizzically.

"Tommy lost his mother," I said, "but he has advantages the people here will never have."

"You mean the family money."

"And the opportunities money buys."

"You saw the woman feeding her child in the kitchen?"

"Umm."

"That's Aziza and her son Asad. They're from Somalia. They arrived here with nothing but the clothes on their backs."

"What's that got to do with Tommy?"

"I'm curious about names, so I looked them up. Aziza means beloved. Asad means lion."

"I don't see("

"Despite Tommy's advantages, as you put it, Asad has something precious that's been taken away from Tommy. A mother's love."

"You're saying Tommy is a cub who needs a new lioness?"

Sister Celia smiled. "Yes."

In the driveway, Oskar was loading boxes into a black van with a man with shoulder-length blond hair. "Need lift to subway?" he asked as I headed down the front stairs.

"Thanks, but my car's over there." I pointed to the Volvo across the street.

"You friend of Jude? I see you in church today."

"Yes. I guess you knew her when she worked here."

"She work here many years ago. Before son was born. Tommy. You were with him in church today."

He noticed that Tommy was with me. I smiled blandly. "Mrs. Seaton asked me to take him to the funeral."

"He stay with you?"

"He's with friends."

Oskar shook his head. "Poor little boy. You tell him hello from Oskar."

I shivered as I headed for the car.

It was just after three when I left Safe Harbor. I knew Devon and Tommy wouldn't be back from the movie yet, so I drove down to Lake Shore Boulevard, turned east and headed for Jude's neighborhood.

Ramsey Road hadn't been plowed, so I left the car in a parking lot on the Danforth and made my way on foot. A young man wearing a Davy Crockett hat was shoveling the walk across the street from Jude's house.

I introduced myself, saying I was a friend of Jude's. "Did you see anyone at her place on Tuesday morning?"

He shook his head. "My girlfriend and I were away skiing for a week. Only heard about it today. Man, you read about these things but you never think they'll happen on your street."

119

"Did you know her well?"

"No. We moved here in October, then winter set in. We waved whenever we saw her, but that's as far as it went."

He pointed to the semi beside Jude's. "It's Sophie you should talk to. She's lived on this street for years and knows everyone. She came over this morning to tell us."

I thanked him and turned up Sophie's walk.

A short, heavy woman in her late sixties, dressed entirely in black, opened the door. When I said I wanted to talk to her about Jude, she invited me in. Her eyes, I noticed, were a striking aqua color.

"You like Greek coffee?"

I wondered if my kidneys would hold up, but I followed her into the kitchen.

"Terrible, terrible thing. Jude nice woman. Good neighbor." She shook her head as she stirred sugar cubes into a pot of dark liquid on the stove. She poured the liquid into two small cups and sat down beside me at the table.

I took a sip from the demitasse in front of me. "Heavenly!"

Sophie beamed at me. She pointed to the red poinsettia on the table. "Jude give me that for Christmas. Who could do this terrible thing to nice lady?"

"That's what the police want to find out. Did you see anyone at her house that day?"

"The police, they asking me that, too." A tear ran down her cheek.

I reached into my handbag for a tissue.

She wiped her eyes and blew her nose. "That morning, I come back from visit to my daughter. I get here around ten then I go out to buy groceries. When I come back, I make cookies, and I take some to Jude and

Tommy. I knock, no one answer door. I look in front window. I see Christmas tree and(" She clapped a hand over her mouth. "I come back here. I look at phone, but my hand shake. I reach for it but...I can't."

I smiled sympathetically and urged her to continue.

"I wonder what happen to little Tommy." Sophie sniffed and wiped her eyes again. "Is he in there hurt? I have my coat on to go across street for help when I hear car outside. I look out window and see sister of Jude. She come up steps, knock, call out. I know she get no answer. She go in and I hear scream."

She paused. "Then sister of Jude...I forgetting her name."

"Arlene."

"Arlene, yes. Arlene come to my door. She crying and telling me Jude is dead. She say Tommy not there. She come in here and she call police."

"Tommy is fine," I told her. "He was visiting friends when his mother was killed."

"Thank God."

"You saw nobody other than Arlene that morning?"

She shook her head. "If people talk loud, I hear through walls, but I hear nothing till Arlene, she bang on my door."

"How long were you out shopping?"

"One hour maybe."

"You often heard Jude and Tommy through the walls?" I chose my words carefully. I didn't want to imply that Sophie spent her time listening to what went on next door.

"I hear her calling him for dinner. Things like that. But they very nice people. Not shouting, not having noisy parties. Only once I heard shouting. Jude and her boyfriend, they shout, have big fight."

"When was this?"

"Many months ago. Maybe early fall. That Clive guy, I haven't seen him since then."

"Did you hear what they argued about?"

"No, but they sound very angry. He say something about 'those people'."

"Those people. People he didn't like?"

She shrugged. "I guess."

"Maybe Jude's friends." I imagined Clive would be critical of anybody who wasn't a clone of himself.

"Maybe."

"Did you tell the police about this argument?"

"No. They ask me what I hear on Tuesday. Later, they come back and ask about boyfriend. I tell them I not see him for long time. You think he kill Jude?"

"I don't know."

I wrote my home phone number and my cell number on my business card and slid it across the table. "Sophie, if you think of anything that might be helpful to Jude's family, you can reach me at these numbers."

She drew the card toward her, stared at it and nodded.

I was surprised to see Farah at the house because I had given her the week off with pay. She was playing a card game at the kitchen table with Tommy and Devon.

"Concentration." Devon smiled up at me. "Tommy's won the last two games."

Farah put on her hijab. "I think you need help with your visitors, Pat. So I come."

"Tommy talked us into a game of cards," Devon said.

I suppressed a smile. Farah had been with us for a few days at the cottage I'd rented the summer before, and I remembered that she'd been quite taken with Devon.

"How was the movie, Tommy?"

The boy didn't look up from the cards. "Good. I liked Frodo."

"Laura called to say she'd be here in an hour," Devon said. "And she'll be in all evening so we're clear for dinner after your VP's party."

Farah kicked a table leg. Cards scattered to the floor.

"Farah! I was winning." Tommy scrambled to the floor to pick up the cards.

I took Farah's coat from the back of her chair and inclined my head toward the front door. "Thank you for thinking of us, Farah, but we will manage just fine until Monday."

She followed me into the hall, then turned back to the kitchen. "Devon," she called, but he was helping Tommy set up for another round.

"You were here when the police called on Monday."

She looked embarrassed. "I leave my sweater here. I come for it."

I smiled. I figured she wanted to get away from the small apartment she shared with Raad and her mother. I pictured her stretched out on our sofa, watching daytime television. She'd told me that the Alwans didn't own a television set.

I handed her the coat. "I'll see you on Monday."

"Tommy here on Monday?"

"I'm not sure."

She pouted. "With cleaning and walking dog, I got no time for young boys."

"Enjoy your days off. I'll see you on Monday."

Chapter Fourteen

Pat

For Ray and Charisse Leckie, a few people over for drinks on a Friday meant a few dozen guests in their sprawling Bridle Path home. From the front hall, I saw waiters circulating with trays of drinks and *hors d'oeuvres.*

"Ho, ho, ho! Happy New Year, Pat." Charisse, a thirty-something brunette with Cleopatra hair, air-kissed my cheek.

Ray, a beefy man in his early sixties, put an arm around my shoulder. "Good to see you, my dear."

We followed them into the main room and I introduced Devon. Charisse gave him a sidelong look. "I take it you're both having a good holiday," she said.

We were about to reply when distinguished-looking man with white hair stepped up beside us. "Keith," I said.

Ray and Charisse returned to the door to greet another guest, and Keith kissed me on both cheeks. "One of my favorite people at the firm," he said.

"Keith Kulas is our chief executive," I said to Devon. "Keith, this is Devon Shaughnessy."

Keith looked across the room to where Ray was waving. "Ray wants me to meet his doctor friend. That must be him."

A man in an overcoat and a brown fur hat stood beside Ray. Keith headed over to them.

"Is Charisse in the investment business?" Devon asked.

"Charisse is an investment. She's Ray's trophy wife." I took two glasses of champagne from a waiter. "She runs a clothing boutique in Yorkville, but she seems to own more clothes than her store carries."

"Meow! Saucer of milk, Pat?" Stéphane, with a glass in a one hand, a plate of food in the other, stood beside us. "This is some bash."

"Just a few people over for drinks," I said.

"And a command performance during our holidays." Stéphane looked across the room at Keith, Ray and the new arrival who was handing Charisse his coat and hat. "Something must be up if *le beau* Keith is here. He doesn't usually socialize with minions from the firm."

"What does Ray do at Norris Cassidy, other than being a VP?" Devon asked.

"Ray is executive vice-president and chief compliance officer," I said.

"Which means," Stéphane added, "that he supervises all trades to make sure advisors are complying with securities regulations."

"Here they come again," I said as Ray and Charisse and the new arrival approached us.

"The Tierney Pratt team," Ray boomed. "Norris Cassidy's presence in North Toronto."

Ray and Charisse flanked a man wearing an out-of-date tuxedo. "My friend from medical school, Dr. Jan Vrancic. Jan is Mount Hope's chief nephrologist. Or, rather, he was. He just retired."

Jan bowed to me, displaying the center part of his gray hair.

"I'd forgotten," I said to Ray, "that you studied medicine."

"Never practiced. No bedside manner."

"I wouldn't say that," Charisse put in.

Ray clapped a hand on Jan's shoulder. "Jan and I go back a long way."

Jan gave us a genial smile. "Ray was my first friend in Canada." His English was flawless, although he spoke with an accent. "I grew up in what was then Yugoslavia and I won a scholarship to McGill University in Montreal. I met Ray when I started my undergraduate degree. He showed me the ropes."

Ray snorted with laughter. "He means the bars."

"I learned the ropes so well that I went to medical school at McGill and stayed in Canada after my studies. Now Ray takes care of my investments."

Ray turned to me. "Speaking of managing investments, a guy was in to see me today about a job. Has a lot of good ideas."

"Ray." Charisse tugged at his sleeve. "You're talking about work again."

"Just a sec, hon." He put an arm around his wife's waist and drew her closer to him. "Pat knows him."

"I can't think of anyone("

"His mother's your client."

I looked at him with narrowed eyes. "Luella Cruickshank?"

Ray beamed. "That's it, Cruickshank. There's potential there. Arnie Cruickshank may be a good addition to your team." He looked from me to Stéphane. "Aren't you two short-handed at your branch?"

I sucked in a breath. "We're fine as we are."

Devon and I lingered over cappuccinos after dinner.

"How about a weekend in New York?" he asked, taking my hand. "We'll stay at the Plaza, see some shows."

"Sounds great."

"When?"

"When Jude's killer is found and Tommy's out of danger."

"Where will Tommy go then?"

"I don't know."

"Do you want him with you?"

I stirred my cappuccino. "He's a dear little boy, but he should be with his family. I hope his grandmother will take him. With the help she can afford, he shouldn't be much trouble."

"And Tracy and Laura?"

I frowned. "You're implying that because they're Tommy's half-sisters he should live with us"

"No, but they'll want to keep in touch with him when you tell them they're related." He squeezed my hand. "And so will you."

"He's a special little guy. We'll see what his family comes up. Patrick said something about boarding schools, but I hope they don't send him to strangers."

My cell phone pealed the opening bars of "The Ode to Joy." I checked caller display. Laura.

"Mom, it's Tommy," she cried at the other end of the line.

"Calm down, dear. We'll be home soon and("

"Mom, he's not here. Tommy's gone."

Laura was waiting for us on the front porch, clutching her parka around her. "He was watching a DVD and I went up to my room to listen to music," she said as we came up the front walk.

"Why was he up so late?" I asked.

"He wanted to watch the end of a Disney movie and I figured he'd fall asleep. When I came back downstairs to check on him, he was gone. I looked all over the house. He's not here, and his jacket and boots are gone too."

I locked the front door. There was no point in giving Laura the you-were-supposed-to-be-keeping-an-eye-on-him lecture. The girl was worried sick.

"We'll split up and do a quick check of the neighborhood," I said. "But if we don't find him in, say, half an hour…"

"We'll call Hardy," Devon said.

"Right. Devon, you start("

Laura gripped my arm. "Look, Mom."

I turned to see Tommy rounding the corner of the block with Maxie on her leash. "Thank God."

Laura ran down the street to Tommy. I started down the stairs, feeling drained.

A black SUV turned the corner, throwing Laura, Tommy and Maxie into silhouettes in its headlights. It slowed as it drew up alongside them.

"Anyone you know?" Devon asked behind me.

"Can't tell with those tinted windows."

Maxie barked at the vehicle. Tommy and Laura tugged on the leash to restrain her.

"We'd better check this out." I sprinted toward them.

The SUV suddenly roared forward, bearing down on me. I leapt off the sidewalk and fell into a snow bank on a neighbor's lawn. The vehicle swerved from the sidewalk to the street and sped away.

Devon helped me up. "Are you all right?"

"No harm done." I held onto his arm as I got to my feet.

"We'd better call Hardy."

I shook my head. "What can we tell him? We didn't see anyone, didn't get a license plate number. And how many black SUVs do you think there are in Toronto?" I brushed myself off. "Let's get inside."

Laura made cocoa and Devon went upstairs to pack for his flight the next morning.

"Where did you go?" I asked Tommy. "We were about to call the police."

He slouched down in his chair at the kitchen table. "I took Maxie for a walk. We saw kids skating in the park."

I cocked an eyebrow. "Kids? At this hour?"

"Well, big kids, like Laura. There's music and("

I put an arm around him. "You can't go out alone, Tommy. I told you that you need to be very careful right now. Why didn't you listen to me?"

"Maxie had to go. She went to the door and started barking. Laura was upstairs, so I put on my jacket and my boots, and I got Maxie's leash. I knew she couldn't go out if she wasn't on her leash."

"You also knew you can't go out on your own right now."

Laura put mugs of cocoa in front of us. Tommy stuck out his tongue and licked the froth from the top of his drink.

"I wasn't on my own. I was with Maxie." He took a sip, then he looked at me sideways and smiled Michael's smile. My heart turned over.

"Finish your drink and Laura will put you to bed." I tousled his hair and kissed his forehead.

I took my mug into the sunroom and collapsed on the sofa. I clicked on the remote and Ella launched into "The Man I Love." I clicked Ella off and brought up the Brandenburg Concertos. Cool, soothing, cerebral music.

Devon joined me on the sofa. "Call Hardy now." He handed me the phone on the end table.

"What can I tell him? We didn't get the license plate number."

"Just tell him."

Hardy grunted when he heard what I had to say. "I'll get forensics over there to check for tire prints. If the vehicle drove up on the sidewalk, they should be able to pick up something."

He paused. "And Ms. Tierney, keep the boy inside the house."

"Hey—"

"And you be careful, too. Don't go out alone at night."

Thanks for the concern, I thought as I hung up.

Norah called while we waited for the forensics squad. "Patrick has found a place for Tommy at a good school. Central Canada College, just north of the city in Norwood. Patrick went there, and so did Harold, his father. Patrick will drive Tommy up on Sunday afternoon."

"The boy's only seven." I couldn't believe the Seatons would send a child who had just lost his mother off to a boarding school.

"I know. It breaks my heart. Patrick didn't go to CCC until high school. But it's what he and Arlene think is best. I've told them I can hire a nanny and have a tutor work with Tommy here until all this…is cleared up. But they won't hear of it. They've even got the doctor saying it would be too much for me."

I kept my thoughts to myself.

After a pause, she went on. "I'd like to have Tommy with me until Sunday. If you don't mind, I'll send my driver for him in the morning. You'll want to get on with your life."

"I'll drive him over after breakfast."

"Come for lunch."

"I will."

I curled myself around Devon and smiled. Take that, Michael, I thought.

"Promise me you'll be careful, Pat. That SUV…"

"Whoever that was, they were after Tommy, not me." I was trying to convince myself as well as him. "Once he's at that school, he should be safe. Maybe not happy, but safe."

"And you think you'll be out of the line of fire."

"Yes."

"I hope you're right." He turned over and wrapped his arms around me. "But I'm not so sure."

That made two of us. Someone was after Tommy and I was an obstacle in this person's way.

Chapter Fifteen

Pat

"I don't want to go away to school," Tommy said on the drive to Norah's home on Saturday. "I want Mommy to come back."

I looked at the small boy behind me through the rearview mirror. I wanted to take him in my arms and hug him.

"Can't I stay at your place, Mrs. T?"

I took a deep breath and thought of the Harry Potter poster in his bedroom. Laura had been a Harry Potter fan a few years before and she had DVDs of all the movies. I'd brought along her copy of the first Harry Potter movie for Tommy to watch while I talked to Norah.

"You may like this school, Tommy. Harry Potter went to boarding school and he liked it. That's where he learned magic."

He seemed to ponder the idea for a moment or two. Then he shook his head. "I'll hate it."

Norah opened the door as we walked up the front steps. She had aged since the previous day. The furrows were etched deeper into her face. Her sad, blue eyes were rimmed with red. Her shoulders sagged. With the funeral over, the full force of her daughter's death had hit her.

Norah hugged Tommy and clasped my hands. Then she led us into the dining room where three places had been set at the table. The woman who had poured tea and coffee at the funeral reception served us roast chicken, baby potatoes and carrots. Norah introduced her as Mrs. Bonokowski.

"Don't play with your food," Norah chided Tommy who was pushing pieces of chicken around his plate.

"He'd be happier with kids' food," I ventured. "Zoodles or Kraft Dinner."

"Nonsense. Children can eat the same food as everyone else. Do you have children, Pat?"

"Two daughters. Tracy's a junior lawyer in her articling year. Laura will be in university next fall."

"I see." But she looked as if she didn't.

After raspberries and cream, Tommy moved to the room across the hall. He settled in front of the television with *Harry Potter and the Philosopher's Stone* and Norah's miniature poodle, Gigi. Norah and I remained at the table with our coffee.

"I've been going through my photos of Jude." She turned to the buffet behind her and took a photo album off it. "I've put my favorites in here."

There were pictures of Norah as a young woman with a baby in her arms. Pictures of Jude as a toddler blowing out candles on birthday cakes. Jude dressed for tennis, Jude on horseback. Jude in a long, white dress at her high school graduation ball. The usual mementoes that are in every family photo album.

"Jude is an unusual name," I said.

Norah smiled. "She was christened Judith Eileen. Eileen after my mother. I'd paid my dues to the Irish by naming my firstborn Patrick and I wanted something grand for my daughter. I came up with Judith, a queen from the Bible. And my girl hated it. Shortened it to Jude when she was ten."

"She was quite the individual."

"Well, you knew her." Nora paused. "How long did you know Jude, Pat?"

I looked at the older woman and wondered if I should tell her. I decided that I should. "I didn't know your daughter at all, Mrs. Seaton."

She stared at me. "But…"

"She came to my office the day before she died and asked me to take Tommy for a few days. She seemed to think he was in danger."

Norah's hand flew to her mouth. "So he is in danger. Whoever killed…"

"You'll need to be careful. Tommy shouldn't go outside on his own. The police think Jude's killer may have targeted him."

"But why you? Why did Jude ask you to take care of Tommy?"

"That's what I wanted to know." I sat up straight in the chair. "She told me that my late husband, Michael, was Tommy's father."

Norah's eyes were circles of blue in her white face. "Oh, my goodness."

We looked at each other in silence for a moment or two.

"Your husband. How could she have done that?"

"I take it that you didn't know who Tommy's father was."

"No. I asked her many times, of course. She always said it was none of my business. But why would she look you up now and ask you to take Tommy?"

"She believed he was in danger." I paused, hoping that would sink in. "She thought I'd take him because he was Michael's son."

Norah nodded. "She wouldn't have asked Arlene or Patrick. Jude and Arlene were never close. Jude and Patrick were great friends when they were children, but when Jude was older she wanted to distance herself from the family business and everything she thought it stood for. She considered Patrick spineless when he dropped out of graduate school to work with his father, and she let him know it."

"And she wouldn't have left Tommy with you because this would be the first place anyone would look for him."

"She had to be terribly concerned about the boy."

I pushed my cup and saucer away from me. "The police say her killer may think Tommy can identify him. So it's probably a good thing he'll be off to that school tomorrow."

"That school." Norah looked around the well-appointed room. "You know, I wasn't born into all this. I grew up in a big family in Ireland and I came to Canada to find work. I took a job at Seaton Ferguson and a year later I became Harold's father's secretary."

She covered her face with her hands. When she removed them, her eyes were filled with worry.

"Last summer Jude was seeing a man by the name of Clive Pettigrew. Did you meet him?" I asked.

"Clive Pettigrew? No. Do you think that's—"

"Clive says he and Jude stopped seeing each other in September. She may have been involved with someone else after that. Would you know…"

She shook her head. "She told me nothing about her love life. Oh, I assumed she had one, a pretty girl like her."

"Other than work, how did your daughter spend her time? Did she belong to any clubs? What were her hobbies?"

"She didn't belong to Arlene's tennis club. That sort of thing didn't interest her. She did volunteer work. She helped a nun who runs a refugee center."

"Sister Celia. But she told me Jude hadn't worked at Safe Harbor since Tommy was born."

Norah looked surprised. "She hadn't? Once when I called her at home, a foreign-sounding person answered. I assumed Jude had hired one of those refugees to do some work in her house."

I saw that her face was ashen. "How are you feeling?" I asked.

"I'm fine."

"You should lie down for a while. But make sure Tommy doesn't leave the house. Tell Mrs. Bonokowski to keep an eye on him."

Norah smiled wanly. "I've always wondered who Tommy's father was. He must have been a good man since you still care for him."

"Michael was a good man." My heart brimmed with sadness as I spoke the words. I touched Norah's hand. "Thank you for lunch. I'll say goodbye to Tommy."

In the car, I glanced at the back seat where Tommy had sat and blinked back tears.

Down the street, I looked at Norah's house through the rear-view mirror. I wondered how safe Tommy would be in there. Would he want to explore the neighborhood with Gigi while Norah rested? And would Patrick tell the school about his nephew's situation?

I thought of the black SUV the night before. Did the Seatons fully understand that whoever had killed Jude might wanted her son out of the way?

With a heavy heart, I rounded the street corner and headed for home.

Chapter Sixteen

Pat

I lowered the volume on the stereo in my study and reached for the phone. A pity to silence Schubert, I thought as I picked up the receiver. "Hello?"

"The cops have been bugging the hell out of me," a man said on the other end of the line. "Thanks to you."

"Who is this?"

"Clive Pettigrew."

Alarms clanged in my head. "How did you get my home number?" I'd given him my card with my office number.

He laughed. "I have ways."

What the hell did that mean?

"Ms. Tierney, I need to talk to you. Can we meet today? I understand you live in Moore Park. We could have lunch at Milo's."

"How do you know where I live?"

He laughed again. "I'll tell you when I see you. Milo's in an hour?"

Clive was the last person I wanted to spend any part of my Sunday with. But, if I didn't meet him, I knew I would spend the day wondering how he'd got my number.

"Okay. An hour." I slammed down the receiver.

His laugh hadn't a touch of mirth in it, I thought as I headed upstairs to change.

I got to Milo's first and claimed my favorite table by the window. I'd ordered coffee when the door opened and Clive walked in.

He gave me a curt nod, took off his leather coat and slid into the chair across from me. His idea of weekend casual was an open-neck white shirt under a tweed sports coat. A gold chain glinted around his neck.

The waitress brought my coffee and Clive ordered one for himself. No mention was made of lunch.

"Who gave you my phone number and told you where I live?" I demanded when the waitress had gone.

His smile fell short of his eyes. "The cops had me down to the station for a grilling. And they keep dropping by my office. You put them on to me."

"So what if I did? How did you get my number?"

"I called Norah Seaton last night. Told her I'd known her daughter and extended my sympathies."

"Did she ask about your relationship with her daughter?"

He threw me a look of dislike. "She did. And, again, I have you to thank. I told her Jude ended our relationship but we parted as friends. Then I asked how I could get in touch with you."

I groaned silently. Why had Norah told him anything? Didn't she realize he might be looking for Tommy?

Something else occurred to me as I stirred cream into my coffee. "You just said that Jude ended the relationship."

He waved a hand dismissively. "Don't even think about reading anything into that. She ended the relationship. One person usually does when there's a break-up. That doesn't mean I killed her."

He paused for a few seconds. "Besides I have an alibi. I was with someone the morning Jude was killed."

"Have you told the police? That should get them off your back."

He cleared his throat. "Bit of a problem there."

"Oh?"

"I was with a woman I've been seeing. She's married."

I took another sip of coffee. "And you're married as well."

"No. Why do you say that?"

"Because you didn't want Jude calling you, and you called her from pay phones."

He pursed his lips. "My background as a lawyer. You never know who'll try to pin something on you. I don't like to leave...tracks."

A Teflon man, I thought. Nothing sticks to him.

"Without this alibi of yours, the police will treat you as a suspect. Jude told me she was afraid of someone. And you were recently involved with her."

His eyes flashed with anger. "Jude knew all sorts of people, but you had to point me out to the police."

"The woman was murdered. The police need to talk to everyone who knew her. Tommy told them she'd been seeing someone by the name of Clive." I realized too late that I shouldn't have brought up Tommy. "So when I found your card in her home, I gave it to Detective Hardy."

"If they're looking for romantic interests, Jude may have been seeing someone after we parted."

"You're sure your friend won't talk to the police?"

He gave me one of his sour smiles. "I asked if she would tell the police we were together that morning. Because unless it comes out in court, and there's no reason why it should, it's unlikely that word of our involvement will get back to her husband."

"But she refused."

"She refused, but you may be able to help. Since it's because of you that I'm in all this trouble."

I saw red. "Let's get something straight, Clive. I'll do anything I can to help the police find Jude's killer."

"Would you...would you speak to her? Convince her to tell the police that she was with me that morning."

"How could I do that?"

"You were Jude's financial advisor. So she might listen to you."

"Who is this woman?"

"Arlene Dobson."

I smiled to myself in the car, thinking that Clive and Arlene made a charming couple.

I tightened my grip on the steering wheel when I realized that Clive and Arlene could be a deadly pairing. Arlene had been jealous of her sister and Jude had dumped Clive. If Clive had killed Jude, he would be afraid that Tommy would tell the police about his argument with his mother. And he would know from Arlene where Tommy was at any given time.

I sent a silent prayer to the Goddess: Keep Tommy safe at that school.

Chapter Seventeen

Pat

On Monday morning, I resolved to get my life back into gear. Devon was gone and Tommy's family had sent him to a boarding school. He was no longer my responsibility. My so-called holiday was over; I had my clients to look after.

I finished my coffee and looked at Laura across the breakfast table. She was dressed in jeans and a navy V-neck pullover over a crisp white shirt. Her long hair was pulled back from her face and gathered into a knot. Her eyes were riveted on her history book. She didn't even look up when Farah came into the kitchen.

"Hey, Farah," she said, her eyes still on the book. "Good holiday?"

Farah shrugged. "Yesterday, guy take me to movie."

"You have a boyfriend, Farah?" Laura was all attention now.

Farah gave her a half-smile. "Maybe."

Laura closed her book and pulled out the chair next to her. "Sit down and tell us everything."

Farah seated herself and I got up to clear the table.

"My brother, Raad, he help out at house for refugees. Saturday, he have me answer phone there. And I meet Oskar."

"Oskar Jacovic, Sister Celia's assistant at Safe Harbor?" I suddenly felt apprehensive.

"Oskar is not boss? He tell me he running that place."

"Sister Celia De Franco is Safe Harbor's director."

"This Oskar was trying to impress you, Farah," Laura said. "Always a good sign."

"He thinks he important guy. But Oskar, he is new in Canada just like me."

"You met him on Saturday and he took you to a movie yesterday. He's a fast worker," Laura said. "What movie did you see?"

I was sure Raad knew nothing about his sister's date. He would not have approved.

"First, he take me for lunch at a place call Sa-ra-yay-vo. Capital city of Bosnia country Oskar come from. He thinks this restaurant special, but it serve terrible food." She paused for a few moments. "Oskar have beer. Me, I have glass of wine."

Surprised, I turned to look at her.

"But you don't drink alcohol, Farah," Laura said. "You're a Muslim."

"Many things Muslims should be doing. Some doing them, some not. Canada free place."

"Things like going to movies with guys?" Laura had a twinkle in her eyes. "Is Oskar Muslim?"

"No, Oskar is Christian Serb. He call me free spirit."

That made Laura giggle. I sent her a warning look. Farah was trying to fit into a culture she didn't fully understand, and I didn't like Laura laughing at her.

Farah shrugged. "After lunch, we go to place call Bijou Cinema."

"Rep house on the Danforth," Laura said to me. "It had a Bogart festival this weekend."

"We see *Casablanca.*" Farah sighed. "Me, I like movie with big stars. Tom Cruise, Brad Pitt, Angelina Jolie. But Oskar, he like old movies and this guy, Humphrey Bogart."

"*Casablanca*'s a great movie," I said.

She frowned. "Ending, it is stupid. Why she not stay with that guy, Rick? Guy with nice dinner club."

Tracy had come into the kitchen, dressed for the law firm in her navy power suit. "*Casablanca* is about honor," she said. "Rick was an honorable man. He believed Ilsa's place was with her husband."

Farah gave her a long look before she got up from the table.

As she passed me, I heard her humming "As Time Goes By."

Luella Cruickshank fluttered into the branch, resplendent in a scarlet coat and a purple shawl. Her hair had morphed into magenta from midnight black since her last visit.

"Patricia, here's my son, Arnie."

A handsome, blond-haired man held out his hand and I found myself shaking it. Arnold Cruickshank III flashed me a confident smile that displayed cosmetically whitened teeth. His eyes sized up our premises.

"You're early," I told them. "Please take a seat."

Then I motioned to the man seated in the reception area into my office.

"But we have an appointment," Luella said.

"Your appointment's for ten and it's now twenty to. I'll be with you at ten sharp."

Scowling, Arnie loosened his scarf and lowered himself into a chair.

I closed my office door and smiled at Leo Cornacchia, a long-standing client who owned a chain of coffee shops.

"Everything okay?" I'd never seen Leo look so tired. He was fifty-six but looked much older. Dark circles stood out under his eyes and his face was almost the color of his gray pinstriped suit.

He took the client's chair and pulled an envelope from inside his jacket. "I had my will updated. Here's a copy."

I raised an eyebrow.

"No major changes." He placed the envelope on my desk. "A few more charitable bequests. And I've put the cottage in my kids' names rather than leaving it to them in the will."

"Barbara's only eighteen. And Mark's what, twelve or thirteen?"

"They love the place. They've been going there since they were babies."

"It's not a bad move, actually. It will be double its present value by the time they inherit it, and they'd take a big tax hit on the appreciation."

"Not necessarily." He heaved a sigh. "You see, Pat, I'm waiting for a kidney transplant, but I don't know how long I can hold on."

I was shocked. "Leo, I'm sorry. I had no idea."

He smiled wanly. "Even if I get a kidney, I could reject it. It's funny, I was always worried about money, whether the business would succeed, whether we'd have enough to put the kids through school. Now we're sitting pretty but I don't have my health. Life's a bitch, eh?"

I tried to give him a reassuring smile. "Let's hope everything goes smoothly. You get a kidney, the surgery's a success, you're back to normal."

"I hope that's what will happen." He got up from his chair. "I want to see my kids settled. And spend more time with Tonia."

I said goodbye to Leo and waved Luella and Arnie into the office. Arnie glanced at his watch and frowned.

Luella beamed at me when they were seated. "Arnie has an investment idea."

I braced myself for the worst.

Arnie crossed one leg over the other and cleared his throat. "I was in England just before Christmas. A house in London is worth millions of pounds these days. Makes Toronto real estate look like a steal. I'm convinced the market here hasn't even begun to take off."

I shrugged. "And some say it's peaked. The baby boomers may want to downsize in the near future. They'll be spending more time at their vacation homes. And the next generation?"

"Immigration," Arnie cut in. "Canada will raise its immigration quotas to replace the retiring boomers in the workforce. The newcomers will need places to live."

"But will they be able to afford current house prices? If they can't, prices will drop."

"In any event," Luella drew out the words, "I want to diversify my investments by adding some real estate. You're the one who always talks about diversification, Patricia."

I counted to ten. "What do you have in mind?"

"Arnie's found a small apartment building near High Park. Twenty units."

"I can arrange an appraisal."

"No need." Luella shook her head, her purple earrings bobbing around her face. "Arnie's already attended to that. He's had an engineering company go over it and they say it's sound."

"It's an older building?"

"Fifty years old," she said, "and we all know they don't make buildings today like they did back then. It needs a few things?a new furnace and new windows, although the windows can wait. But it will go up in value, just you wait and see. In the meantime, it will produce revenue. I'd say it's a steal at $5 million."

I wondered what Arnie stood to gain from this venture.

"And the best thing," she went on as if she'd read my mind, "is that Arnie will manage it. He'll live there, rent out the units and see that everything runs smoothly."

Arnie uncrossed his legs and flashed me a smile. "You don't seem to like this idea, Ms. Tierney."

"I'd like to take a look at the appraisal. Do you have it with you?"

"No, I don't. Look, Sanderson Brown gave it a thumbs-up. My mother's keen and it is her money."

"And it's my job to protect that money for her and make it grow."

At eleven, I grabbed my handbag and ran down the five flights of stairs. I was certain that Arnie was about to wreak havoc with his mother's investment portfolio. The only upside was that he hadn't mentioned working at Tierney Pratt.

On Eglinton Avenue, I grabbed a spinach salad at Greens and went into Starbucks for a latte. As I stood in line, I wondered if I should call Arlene. I cringed at the idea of talking to a woman I'd met only once about her lover. It was so distasteful that?

"Please, we must talk."

I whirled around and looked up at a tall man in a worn, black pea jacket. He had high cheekbones, full lips, and dark, almond-shaped eyes . A handsome face carved out of mahogany.

"It is about Jude Seaton." He glanced at the people who were seated at the tables.

"What?" Then I froze. "You were at the back of the church."

He appraised the clientele again. "We cannot talk here."

"My office?"

"I must go." A police patrol car had pulled up at the curb, and two officers were getting out of the vehicle.

I handed the man my business card.

He took it and hurried to the side entrance. He slipped out of the shop as the officers entered by the front door and got into line behind me.

"A little upscale here," one officer grumbled. "What's wrong with Tim's?"

"A change won't hurt," his partner replied. "Like I said, the Leafs..."

I tuned them out and paid for my coffee. Outside the shop, I looked up and down the street. The tall man had vanished.

But I had a hunch that I'd see him again. And when I did I'd ask him why he was on the run.

My last client of the day arrived at three o'clock. Then I settled down to paperwork. An hour later, Ray Leckie strode into the office suite.

"Glad to see you're free, Pat." He came into my office and closed the door.

I looked at the stack of folders on my desk, biting back a smart reply.

"I've decided to take on Cruickshank. And this branch is the place for him."

I stared at him in dismay. "Stéphane and I are fine as we are. Besides, there's a conflict of interest. We handle his mother's account."

"You'll continue to work with Mrs. Cruickshank."

"I don't think…"

"Give Arnie a three-month tryout. Pass some of your smaller clients on to him and you'll have more time for your A group. You know what they say about giving eighty per cent of your time to the top twenty per cent of your book."

I glared at him. "We built this business ourselves."

"And you don't want Cruickshank horning in. Fair enough. What would you say if I gave him some accounts?"

I should have replied that I didn't want Arnie Cruickshank at my branch. "We don't have space for a third advisor," I said.

Ray got out of his chair and opened the office door. "What's over there?" He pointed to a door behind Rose's desk.

"Our supply room."

He left my office and returned a few minutes later.

"I'll have a man clear it out and build shelves for your supplies in the kitchen. We'll bring in a desk, a cabinet and a computer." He smiled with satisfaction. "Cruickshank should be able to start work on Thursday."

I took a taxi home, seething with anger. How could I work with Arnie?

But what were my options? I could check out other firms, but I'd have to build up my business from scratch. Norris Cassidy claims that it "owns" its advisors' clients. When an advisor leaves the company, clients are reassigned to other people at the firm. I'd have to leave the flock I had spent years nurturing.

The house was in darkness when I opened the front door. Maxie barked a joyous welcome. A note on the kitchen table told me that Tracy would be working late and that Laura had gone to a movie with Kyle.

Maxie stood at the front door and barked.

"I get the idea. Laura forgot about you." I clipped on her leash.

I walked the dog around the block. I thought of the black SUV and that Hardy had warned me not to be outside at night on my own. But at six in the evening, the residents of our neighborhood were pulling into their driveways and taking their trash cans to the curb for the following day's collection. I was hardly alone.

Back at the house, I stowed Maxie in the back seat of the Volvo and turned the key in the ignition. While the car warmed up, I put on a CD. A Mozart piano concerto poured from the speakers.

On the Don Valley Parkway, I felt the tension in my neck dissolve. I was leaving Arnie and Ray behind in the city. With every passing mile, they grew smaller in my mind.

I decided I'd give it a try with Arnie. But, if I had to, I would start over somewhere else. I could do it.

I turned my thoughts to Tommy. The terrible stories I'd heard about boarding schools flooded through my mind. Was CCC one of those predatory places?

I knew the route to Central Canada College well. A few years before, when Tracy was in high school, she and her friends went to CCC dances. I drove the girls up to Norwood and another parent took them home later in the evening.

The school had been built in the countryside ninety years before, and Norwood had grown up around it. The school's three buildings now stood on five acres of land in the center of town. The property was enclosed by a high, chain-link fence. The gate was closed.

I got out of the car and pressed a button beside an intercom speaker. There was a rustle of static. "Who is it?" asked a male voice with a singsong accent.

"I'm here to visit one of the students. Tommy Seaton."

"No visitors for Tommy Seaton." He substituted a "w" for the "v" in visitors.

"I'd like to speak to the headmaster."

"Drive in."

The gate opened. I drove down a tree-lined drive and parked in a visitor's space in front of the main building. "I won't be long," I told Maxie.

I heard the doorbell chime inside the building, followed by more static on the speaker beside the door. "Who is it?" the same voice asked.

"Pat Tierney here to speak to the headmaster."

Seconds later, the door was opened by a man dressed in a uniform with a turban on his head. I stepped into the lobby and he closed the door behind me. "I'm not a relative but?"

The man reached for the telephone on his desk. "I will call Mr. Deschenes."

I thought of Tommy in one of these buildings, surrounded by strangers and missing his mother. A visit with Maxie would do him good.

Two minutes later, a door opened and a dark-haired young man in a gray hoodie came through the lobby bouncing on his feet as if they were made of rubber. "Gilles Deschenes, deputy headmaster. I'm very sorry, but Tommy can't have visitors."

I looked into a pair of intelligent gray eyes. "I'm Pat Tierney, a family friend. Would you call Tommy's grandmother? I'm sure she'll let me see him for a few minutes. I've brought my dog."

Deschenes looked sympathetic but shook his head. "No visitors. That's our policy for the first few weeks. Tommy can visit his family on weekends, but he has to settle into our routines during the week. If he sees you and your dog, he'll spend the evening thinking of home and his friends."

"Can I talk to him on the phone?"

He shook his head. "Sorry."

Outside, I looked up at the stone buildings and wondered where Tommy's room was. Was he missing his mother?

"I didn't pass muster," I told Maxie when I got into the Volvo.

I steered the car down the drive and out the gate. Tommy wasn't my responsibility, but my heart reached out to the little boy.

I slipped an Ella Fitzgerald CD into the stereo. "Someone to Watch Over Me" flowed from the speakers. My mood lifted as I realized that Tommy was safe at this school.

Back in Toronto, I drove down to the Gardiner Expressway and then headed west to High Park. I pulled up in front of Safe Harbor to find Sister Celia climbing the front stairs.

I got out of the Volvo. "Hi."

"Pat. What brings you here?"

"Can we talk for a minute?"

She motioned me to follow her inside. When she opened the door to her rooms at the back of the house, I saw that a lamp was lit on a small table.

"Oskar!" she cried. "What's going on here?"

Two figures sprang apart on the sofa. Oskar sat up and Farah jumped to her feet, her long hair in disarray.

151

Oskar really was a fast worker.

He smoothed his sweater. "Sister, this is Farah. My girlfriend."

"Farah and I have already met," Sister Celia said. "She and Raad brought dinner to the residents last week."

Farah stared down at her feet.

I looked hard at her. "And I know Farah too."

Sister Celia threw me a look of surprise. Farah put on her coat, her eyes still downcast.

Sister Celia's cat Benny jumped into Oskar's lap. "Scram!" He threw the cat to the floor and aimed a kick at it. The cat scampered out of his reach.

"Oskar!" Sister Celia cried. She touched Farah's arm. "Are you all right, dear?"

Farah nodded and glanced at Oskar on the sofa. He looked extremely uncomfortable.

"Raad knows about you and Oskar?" Sister Celia said.

"Please, my brother not understand."

Sister Celia studied her for a moment, then frowned at Oskar. "You'll have to meet somewhere else. These are my private rooms."

"I'll drive you home, Farah," I said.

"Farah, you come with me," Oskar said.

"I go with Pat." Farah looked at me for the first time. "Please."

"You wanted to talk about something," Sister Celia said to me at the front door.

"It can wait." I didn't want to talk about Tommy in front of Oskar and Farah. "I'd better get Farah home."

In the car, Farah sat straight-backed beside me. I waited for her to explain herself.

"Idiot," she said when we'd turned onto the Gardiner Expressway.

I glanced at her.

"Oskar big idiot. He take me to private room." She was silent for a few moments. "If Raad..."

"I don't think Sister Celia will say anything to him."

"Raad, he tell me to have nothing to do with Oskar. Serbians bad guys in war they have in Bosnia, Raad say. They kill many Muslims. Rape Muslim women."

I looked at her again and saw that her eyes were closed. She was way out of her depth with Oskar. As well as the religious and ethnic differences, he was a fair bit older than her. He was street-smart and Farah had lived a sheltered life. Different backgrounds, very different expectations.

"But Raad is wrong about Oskar. He not bad guy but...he just cannot wait. Get something in his head, he must do it now." She put a hand to her neck. "He give me beads tonight. Pretty." She was quiet for several moments. "And he take me for nice dinner."

A tingle went down my spine. "Did Oskar pick you up at our house?"

"He come when I finish my work."

I clutched the steering wheel, thankful that Tommy was in good hands at Central Canada College.

Chapter Eighteen

Yuri

Oskar snapped his cell phone shut. He held up two fingers to the waitress and pointed to the empty beer glasses on the table.

Yuri gathered that all was not well. "Boss not happy?"

"He ask when we take care of kid. Do it soon, he say. And find Ali. Boss want no more loose end."

Yuri grunted and rubbed a finger over the scar on his left cheek.

"Not fair," Oskar went on. "We do dirty work. He get rich." He pulled an old copy of the *Toronto Tattler* from his shoulder bag and pointed to the front page. "The Seaton woman, she was rich."

Yuri swept his long hair back from his face. Oskar had been effective in Bosnia when the enemy was in clear sight, but when it came to springing nighttime ambushes, he didn't have the patience to wait, quiet and still. He shook his head. If the boss knew that Oskar tried to run the blonde down the other night…

"The boy, he worth plenty," Oskar said.

"Boss want him disappear."

"Oh, he disappear. But, later, maybe one or two weeks, we get in touch with family. Boy alive, we tell them, and he come back…for a price."

Yuri's eyes brightened. Now Oskar was using his head. "What price?"

Oskar shook the newspaper. "It say here, boy is seven years old. One million dollars for each year of his life. Sound good?"

Yuri nodded.

"Then boss can find someone else to be supplier." Oskar grinned. "You and me, we retire."

"Where you keep this boy?"

Oskar smiled. "I have place."

"Who watch him?"

Oskar smiled again. "Don't worry, my friend. I have someone for that, too."

Chapter Nineteen

Pat

Arlene looked sulky. "I suppose you want to talk about Tommy."

I decided that inviting her to lunch on Tuesday had not been a good idea. I should have relayed Clive's request over the phone. Well, it was too late now, I thought, as the waiter brought Arlene's martini and my lime and soda to the table.

I waited until the waiter had gone. "It's not about Tommy. Clive Pettigrew asked me to talk to you."

Her eyes widened.

"He told me he was with you the morning Jude was murdered. He wants you to tell that to the police."

She banged the table with her fist. The silverware jumped and her martini sloshed over the side of its glass. "We've been over all that. Now he's got you involved."

The couple at the next table turned to stare at us. I took a deep breath and let it out slowly. "Husbands and lovers are always suspects when a woman is murdered. Jude was seeing Clive last summer and there doesn't seem to have been anyone else in her life since then. That anyone knows about, at least."

"Their affair ended months ago."

"That's what Clive told me."

"And he wants me to tell the police that we're an item? Ha! I'm not about to stick my neck out for Clive Pettigrew."

"Not even to clear his name? He's a murder suspect."

She glanced at the next table. The man and woman had gone back to their conversation. "Clive and I spent that morning in a Holiday Inn off the 401. We were pretty sure we wouldn't run into anyone we knew up there."

"What time did you get there?"

"Around nine."

My mind was racing as the waiter set shrimp and avocado salads in front of us. The police said Jude had been dead a few hours before Arlene found her. Had Clive killed her before he met Arlene at the hotel?

"I was half an hour late. There was an accident on the Don Valley Parkway."

"He was at the hotel at eight-thirty?"

"I assume so. That's when we'd arranged to meet. We both had things to do that afternoon. I was going over to Jude's to give her our Christmas presents."

She winced. I knew she was thinking about what she'd found at the house.

"Look, the reason I started this thing with Clive was because he'd been seeing my sister."

I couldn't help but smile at that.

"Jude did whatever she pleased. She didn't care how worried our parents were when she was in those godforsaken countries. Or when she had an illegitimate child. I always did the right thing. I even married a top gun at the family firm. When Clive came on to me, I decided to let go. For once."

By taking up with a man her sister had rejected.

She speared a piece of avocado. "Well, my little fling isn't worth wrecking my marriage."

"If you tell the police where Clive was that morning, they'll move on. But if he's charged with murder, he'll certainly talk to save himself."

"I'll deny it."

"The police will check out his story. They'll talk to the desk clerk at the hotel."

She looked down at her plate. "Nobody saw me. Clive gave me the room number when he called that morning. I went straight there."

"You can't be sure that no one saw you. One of the maids may have."

She seemed to consider what I'd said for a moment. Then she shrugged. "I'll take my chances. The police will find Jude's killer any day now."

I closed my eyes in the taxi I took back to the office. What would Clive do? If he told the police he was with Arlene that morning... I told myself to drop it. I had gone out of my way to help him. He could work it out on his own.

Yet my mind kept on clicking. Clive could have killed Jude early in the morning—at six, six-thirty, even seven—cleaned himself up and driven up to the Holiday Inn to meet his alibi. But the police said Jude had been dead a few hours before Arlene found her at one-thirty. If she'd been killed at six or six-thirty, she would have been dead for a good seven hours.

The taxi pulled up in front of my building and I glanced at my watch. Ten minutes to two. I had clients arriving at two o'clock.

Upstairs, I found four oversized boxes in the reception area. "Computer, desk, chair and filing cabinet for our new advisor," Rose said. "A carpenter will be here at five to put up shelving in the kitchen. I'll stay until he's done."

I glared at the boxes. Arnie wasn't making my life any easier.

"Have a taxi come for me at four forty-five," I told Rose. "I'll take some files home."

She motioned to the chairs on the other side of the boxes. "There's a young man here to see you. Doesn't have an appointment. Says it's something personal."

A figure rose up from behind the boxes—the man who'd approached me at Starbucks. His eyes bored into me. "Please, we can talk now?"

"How long till my next appointment?" I asked Rose.

"The Robertsons should be here in five minutes."

"Let me know when they arrive." I turned to the man. "Come into my office. You'll have to make it brief. I have clients who'll be here soon."

Seated in the client's chair, the man looked around nervously. I closed the door and settled myself behind my desk. "Who are you?"

"I am Ali Hassan." His English was formal and precise. "I saw you with young Tommy."

"At his mother's funeral."

He inclined his head. "Miss Seaton was a good woman. You are her sister?"

"No family relation."

"You have a kind face. I think I can trust you. I have to trust somebody." He clasped his hands together. "I stayed at Miss Seaton's house."

I opened my mouth in surprise, but waited for him to continue.

"I stayed there when I could no longer stay at Safe Harbor." He paused. "You know Safe Harbor?"

"Yes."

"The tribunal refused my("

Rose opened the door. "The Robertsons are here." Tim and Sherry Robertson had recently won a lottery jackpot worth a few million dollars, and another client had referred them to me. They would be a plum addition to my client roster. I couldn't put them off.

"I'm sorry, Mr. Hassan, but we'll have to continue this another time. Can you come back in an hour?"

He looked at his watch. "Somewhere I must be in one hour."

"How about tomorrow morning at eight-thirty?"

"Tomorrow morning?"

"Eight-thirty sharp. I have a client who'll be here at nine."

He threw up his arms. "You do not understand. This cannot wait."

I stood up. "It will have to wait until eight-thirty tomorrow. Good day, Mr. Hassan."

He stood and shook his head. Then he turned and left the office.

When I arrived home at five-fifteen, I found Farah talking to Ali in the front hall. For a moment, I thought they knew each other. But Ali's face brightened when he saw me and I realized he was there to finish our talk.

"I told you to come to the office in the morning."

"I heard lady in your office give taxi company your address. I need to talk to you. I cannot wait for tomorrow."

"Take a seat in here." I pointed to the front room. "I'll be back in a few minutes."

But instead of going into the room, he swung around to face Farah. He pointed to the amber necklace she was wearing over a white sweater. "Beads. Where did you get them?"

Her hand flew to her throat. "My boyfriend give me."

I headed upstairs wondering why Ali was asking Farah about her jewelry.

The doorbell rang as I came down a few minutes later with Maxie. From the staircase, I saw Farah open the door and Oskar step into the house. Maxie flew to the door.

"One day, I have house like this," Oskar said. He bent to pat Maxie's head. The dog snarled and Oskar backed away.

Then he noticed me and yanked off his tuque. "Mrs. Tierney, hello. I come for Farah."

Then he noticed Ali standing by the sofa. "You!" His face contorted with anger. "You give much trouble."

The tall man sprinted for the open door, knocking Oskar into Farah.

"Hey!" she cried.

Oskar bolted after the stranger. Maxie took off after them.

Farah and I ran out onto the porch. Oskar seemed to be catching up to Ali when Maxie sprang up on Oskar's back and threw him off balance. He slid on a patch of ice and fell to his knees. Ali disappeared around a corner.

Oskar pushed himself to his feet to find Maxie standing in his way, growling.

He reached into his jacket, pulled out a knife and slashed at the dog. Maxie backed away, barking. He lunged at Maxie, but she dodged him and ran back to the house.

Maxie dashed past Farah and me and bolted inside the house. I followed the dog in and found her on the kitchen floor. She was out of breath, but otherwise seemed to be okay.

Oskar returned a few minutes later, his face shiny with sweat. "I lose him. Damn!"

"What's going on?" I demanded. "Why were you chasing Ali?"

Oskar peeled off his jacket and collapsed against the hall wall. He pulled tissues from his jacket pocket and mopped his face. "Farah, how you know Ali?"

"I do not know him. He come here few minutes before you. To see Pat."

"What?" He looked at me.

"I asked you a question, Oskar. Why did you run after Ali?" I drew myself up to my full five feet, eight inches, and noted with satisfaction that Oskar was a couple of inches shorter than me.

"So sorry, Mrs. Tierney." He gave me a conciliatory smile. "Ali owe me money. When he see me, he run."

"Why did you threaten my dog with a knife?"

"I try to get Ali, but dog get in my way." He looked down at the floor. "Sorry."

I couldn't accept that. "I don't want to see you in this house again."

Farah fingered her necklace. "Ali ask about beads."

Oskar moved toward her. "Farah, you give me those. I get you other beads tomorrow."

She clasped a hand over her necklace. "No."

He gave her a hard look. "We talk about it later." He pulled on his jacket. "Come, Farah. We go now."

I poured a glass of chardonnay and wondered whether Ali would return. Glass in hand, I walked around the main floor of the house.

The girls would be gone soon. Laura would be at university and Tracy would want to set up her own home when she passed the bar admission exam. I would be alone with my memories of a marriage that was a sham.

I thought of the business trips Michael had taken over the years. What had he been up to while he was away?

Two glasses of chardonnay only made my thoughts more oppressive. In the kitchen, I fixed myself a plate of cheese, crackers and apple slices.

I thought about Ali as I ate my dinner at the kitchen table. He had wanted to tell me something. Something about Jude. I should have made the Robertsons wait while I heard him out.

He was clearly on the run. He'd left the coffee shop when he saw the police officers. He'd started to say something about the tribunal refusing...It had turned down his claim for refugee status. Ali was an illegal refugee.

I pictured him, slouched in a subway train, fighting off fatigue and wondering when it would be safe to get off. He was terrified of Oskar and now that he'd seen him at my home he probably assumed he was a friend of mine.

I put the empty plate in the sink and headed upstairs. In bed, I took several deep breaths and pushed away thoughts of Michael and Jude and Ali. I felt myself unwind, my thoughts slowed...Then the image of Arlene banging on the restaurant table flashed into my mind.

Arlene had said she was late for her *rendez-vous* with Clive because she was stuck on the Don Valley Parkway. There had been no accidents on the parkway when we drove to Haversham that morning. But we'd left the house at seven-thirty.

Drop it, I told myself. The police could sort it out.

With a jolt, I realized that I couldn't drop it. Not until Jude's killer was found and Tommy was out of danger. I knew I would never rest easy until he was safe and...

Happy?

I hoped that Tommy's family would come up with an arrangement that would give the boy a loving home. But, I thought in frustration, that was completely out of my hands.

Chapter Twenty

Pat

I waited for Ali in my office for a good thirty minutes the next morning, reading the *Toronto World* and the *Financial Times* to pass the time. At five past nine, I buzzed Rose on the intercom and told her to send in my first appointment.

"And, Rose, if that tall young man who dropped by yesterday comes in, have him wait. I'll see him between clients. His name is Ali Hassan."

After lunch, Arnie Cruickshank made an appearance. His desk, chair and filing cabinet had been unpacked, and a techie from head office was setting up his computer.

I was on the phone when he breezed in, sporting a Burberry trench coat. He gave me a jaunty wave from reception and said something to Rose, who immediately got up from her desk. When they disappeared from sight, I assumed he was checking out his new digs. Something told me that this wasn't going to be fun.

I had just put the receiver back in its cradle when Arnie plopped himself down in the client's chair. A scowl distorted his handsome face.

"What brings you in today?" I asked.

"Pat." He drew out my name as far as the single syllable would go. "I can't use that office."

"Oh?"

"There's no window."

"I'm sorry, but Stéphane and I have the only offices with windows. But there's plenty of ventilation in there.

We set that room up to function as an office, although we've always used it as a supply station."

"I can't work in there."

I gave a small shrug. It wasn't my fault.

"SAD. Seasonal affective disorder." He enunciated each word carefully as though speaking to a very slow child.

"SAD." I tried to suppress a smile. Arnie couldn't work with us. Ray would have to find another branch for his protégé.

"It's a type of depression caused by the short winter days. I need natural light." He smiled. "Do I need a note from my doctor?"

That wouldn't have been a bad idea. I didn't trust Arnie as far as I could throw him and I wouldn't put it past him to be faking this condition. But I ignored his question. "That is unfortunate, but I don't see what we can do…" I held up my hands in a gesture of helplessness.

He glowered at me. "Ray wants to give me a chance in the industry. But I can't work without natural light. Especially in January and February."

"Depression, you said?"

"That. Also lethargy and anxiety attacks."

I figured this guy would be a treat to have around.

"Don't you use some kind of lamp?"

"SAD lamps. For short periods of light therapy. Can't have them on all day, though."

"Pat?" Stéphane came into the office. "Sorry, I didn't('"

"Stéphane, this is Arnie Cruickshank. Arnie, my business partner, Stéphane Pratt."

"Pat told me all about you." Stéphane held out a hand.

Arnie shook Stéphane's hand and nodded glumly. Stéphane looked at me and raised an eyebrow.

I took a deep breath. "Arnie's office has no window and he suffers from seasonal affective disorder."

"*Mon Dieu!* That is unfortunate. Depression, lethargy, cravings for sweets, weight gain. A terrible affliction. A real cross to bear."

Cut it out, I wanted to shout. He was a terrible actor.

"We'd better get Ray on to this," I said. "He'll need to find another branch for Arnie. I'll call him right now."

I switched on the speaker phone, hit the key for head office and got Ray's assistant. After a short wait, Ray's voice boomed over the speaker. "All set for your new advisor, Tierney Pratt?"

"A problem, Ray. Arnie's office is set up but, as you know, the room has no window. Arnie suffers from seasonal affective disorder and he needs a room with natural light."

"Seasonal? One of those mood-swing things?"

"Mood disorder," Arnie corrected him.

"Terrible!" Stéphane chimed in.

"Ray, perhaps you can find a place for Arnie at another branch." On the other side of the city.

Ray grunted. "No can do. There's no room anywhere else." He cleared his throat. "Could one of you, ah, switch places with Arnie? Take the new office and let him have yours?"

Blood pounded in my temples. He was asking us to give up our offices. Arnie was grinning from ear to ear.

"Ray," I said as evenly as I could, "I don't think that would be wise("

"Pat," Ray barked, "we've got a man here who will be a valuable addition to your team. He needs a place to work. Tomorrow morning."

"He can have my office," Stéphane said. "The technician's here now, so he can switch the computers."

I glared at him.

"It's all set, then," Ray boomed. "Arnie starts work tomorrow."

Arnie stood up and bowed to me. "At your service bright and early tomorrow, ma'am. Eight-thirty or nine?"

"Nine." I said through clenched teeth. "Now, if you'll excuse us, we have work to do."

Arnie gave another bow and left.

"Why did you do that?" I ranted at Stéphane. "That's your office. He has no right("

"Better to volunteer and avoid an ugly scene. Ray would have forced one of us to give up our office, and you're the senior partner."

"Ugly scene? That was an ugly scene. Ray made us step aside for his boy wonder."

He patted my shoulder. "It's only an office, *ma chère*. Besides, something tells me Arnie won't be with us long."

But would he take us down with him? Feeling as though I'd been turned inside out, I swiveled my chair to face my computer monitor.

"Mis-sus Tier-nee? This Mis-sus Tier-nee?"

It was a woman's voice on the other end of the phone line, but not one that I recognized. "This is Pat Tierney."

"Sophie Konstantopoulos, neighbor of Jude. You say I call if I remember something."

My heart took a small leap. "Sophie, what is it?"

"Is possible you come to me?"

I realized that she was uncomfortable talking over the telephone. We rely on facial expressions and body language when we're speaking a language we don't know well.

Call display told me it was ten to five. The girls both planned to be home that night and I had said I'd make dinner. But I wanted to hear what Sophie had to tell me. I decided to take a taxi home, leave the girls money to order a pizza and drive over to Sophie's.

"I can come by around six, unless your family will be eating dinner then."

"No, I live alone. My Spiros, he die three years ago."

"I'll see you around six."

Sophie had set two places at her dining room table. She served me Greek salad with plenty of feta, and large pieces of spinach-and-cheese pie, the phyllo pastry tender and light.

She watched me eat. "*Spanakopita*. I make today. You like?"

"Delicious." I thought of the girls eating pizza at home. I wouldn't have them around much longer. I should be with them while I could.

Sophie handed me a glass of retsina wine. "You tired?"

"I was thinking about my daughters."

She looked concerned. "Young girls?"

"No. They're big girls now, but they're still at home."

"Nice to have family at home." She looked wistful. "My son, he is in Halifax. My daughter in Newmarket. She want me live with her, but I like this house."

"You've lived here a long time, Sophie?"

"Almost forty years. Good house, strong foundation. But walls very thin. Sometimes hear what people say in there." She inclined her head toward the house where Jude and Tommy had lived. "I try not to hear, but…"

"Sometimes you can't help it."

She smiled and topped up my glass. "I know you understand. That's why I call you, not police. They ask questions like...like I kill Jude."

"You heard something the day Jude died?"

"No, not that day."

My heart sank. "No?"

"Not that day. Jude..." She hesitated for a few seconds. "She sometimes have visitors."

"Friends? A gentleman friend?"

She shook her head. "She have no special gentleman after that Clive guy."

So Clive had been Jude's last beau.

"But every few weeks this guy bring someone to her house. Stay two, maybe three days. Then guy come and take them away. Always same guy, but he bring different people."

"Men, women, young, old?"

"Sometimes man, sometimes woman. And always young. Not children, but young people. They..."

"Yes?"

"They not Canadians."

"Not Canadians?"

"They poor, dressed bad. Look afraid."

"Immigrants." Norah had said someone with an accent had answered Jude's phone. "Maybe refugees."

She nodded. "Some have black skin, others yellow. You know, from China, places in Asia."

"How long had Jude been having these visitors?"

"Maybe one year. Once they go, I not see them again(except for last visitor."

She picked up the wine bottle.

I placed a hand over my glass. "No, thank you, I'm driving. What about the last visitor?"

"Guy bring him to Jude's house. Few days later, guy come back and they leave. Later that day, visitor come back in taxi. Alone."

"What did he look like?"

"Very tall. Man with black skin."

That could have been Ali.

"Sophie, do you remember when that tall, dark-skinned man was at Jude's house?"

"Day I go to my daughter's house. Six days before Jude die. Maybe he kill her?"

"I don't know." But I thought it unlikely that Ali would have approached me and told me he'd stayed with Jude if he had killed her.

"Sophie, you said Clive spoke of 'those people' when he argued with Jude. Do you think 'those people' were these visitors who came to Jude's house?"

"Maybe. Maybe Clive not want them stay with her."

"Why didn't you tell me this before?"

She lowered her eyes. "I not want you think I listen through walls."

I left Sophie just before seven. I figured Tracy and Laura would be home by then. In the Volvo, I put on Devon's Willie Nelson CD and hit a button at random. I smiled to hear Willie's version of "Don't Get Around Much Anymore." The girls, I decided, would be fine on their own.

I sat there until the song was over. Then I popped out the CD and punched Safe Harbor's number into my cell.

When Sister Celia told me I could come by, I slid the CD in again. This time I let it play from the beginning. Willie's mellow voice singing "Stardust" filled the car. The song was a favorite of Devon's.

I shook my head. Devon and Jude and Tommy, and now Arnie. All these people who had come into my life. With a flash of irritation, I turned off the music. I wished I had never heard of any of them. My life had been fine the way it was.

Sister Celia met me at the door and ushered me into her sitting room where a fire was burning in the fireplace.

"Cozy," I said. "Just the ticket for a winter evening."

She pursed her lips. "Very cozy. And, as you know, some of our people make themselves at home in here when I'm not around."

I smiled. It couldn't be easy living at your workplace. You would never get away from the job.

"Come, sit down." She dropped into a sofa and patted the seat beside her. "Something about Tommy?"

"About his mother. I just spoke to Jude's next-door neighbor, Sophie Konstantopoulos." I told Sister Celia what Sophie had said about Jude's visitors. And I told her about Ali's visit to my office the day before.

Sister Celia ran a hand through her short hair. "Ali Hassan."

"He said he lived here."

"For several months. He disappeared the day after Christmas, a week after his refugee claim was turned down." She got up and went over to the fireplace. "He can still appeal, and the appeal process usually takes months, sometimes even years. If you see him again, tell him to give me a call."

She stirred the fire with an iron poker. I glanced at the door, thinking I heard it open, but I figured it was just an old house's creaking joints. "Where is Ali from?"

She returned to the sofa. "Somalia. He was an IT student at Mogadishu University. He was visiting his family in Elasha, a town not far from Mogadishu, when he was picked up by a cell of al-Shabaab, the Islamic extremist militia. He was badly beaten, but he escaped. He knew it was just a matter of time before al-Shabaab found him again."

"He told me he stayed with Jude when he left here."

She looked at me sharply. "Jude? How would Ali know Jude?"

"He wouldn't have to know her. Someone brought him to her. The same man who brought all the other people to her. I should have quizzed Sophie more about this guy."

Sister Celia stared into the fire.

"Jude's last visitor arrived six days before she died. He was a dark-skinned man. Very tall, Sophie said. That sounds like Ali."

"The timing's right. He left here around then."

"Have other residents gone missing?"

A look of pain crossed her face. "Oh, yes."

"Then all the people Sophie saw at Jude's could have been from here."

"Jude hasn't worked here for years."

"She and Tommy came to your Christmas parties. Maybe she was in contact with someone here. The priest who celebrated her funeral Mass?"

"Father Jack hadn't seen her in some time. I had to brief him about her when he was writing his eulogy."

"What about Oskar?"

"Oskar?" She looked skeptical. "It's possible, I suppose."

Then I told her about Ali's visit to my house they day before. "He ran off when Oskar arrived to get Farah."

"I wondered how you knew Farah."

"She's my housekeeper."

She looked thoughtful. "Maybe Ali thought Oskar would turn him in."

"Oskar took off after him, but Ali got away. When Oskar came back to the house, he told me Ali owed him money."

"That doesn't sound like Ali. He's honest to a fault."

"Do people often disappear when their claims are turned down?"

She closed her eyes. "They don't understand that their claims can be appealed. They're terrified that they'll be sent back home so they light out and try to find work in the underground economy."

"Are appeals usually successful?"

She frowned. "Unfortunately, no." Her eyes bored into me. "Can I trust you?"

I met her eyes. "Yes."

"Our Sanctuary Coalition operates a couple of safe houses for refugees who've come to the end of the system. We can't let them go back where they came from. And we don't want them to go underground and drift into crime."

"Did Jude have anything to do with these houses?"

She shook her head emphatically. "She knew nothing about them."

"Sophie said people arrived at her place every few weeks."

"Residents have gone missing from here every month or so. When new people arrive, I tell them what will happen when they go before the tribunal. And I explain the appeal process in the event that their claims are turned down."

She shrugged. "A lot of good it seems to do."

"You tell the police whenever a resident goes missing?" I asked.

She was instantly defensive. "Of course, I do. If I didn't report people who were missing, I'd risk having Safe Harbor shut down."

Did the missing residents she reported include those who had been taken to the Sanctuary Coalition's safe houses? I knew she wasn't telling me the full story, but I let the matter drop.

"Jude may have been a maverick years ago," I said, "but her visitors seem to have been the only unconventional part of her life in recent years. She taught school and lived quietly with her son. And she harbored illegals."

"We're not sure they were—"

Suddenly, she sprang off the sofa and pulled the door open. "Oskar! What is the meaning of this?"

Oskar stepped into the room. His eyes darted around, then focused on me. He swung around to face Sister Celia. "You have grocery list, Sister? I go for groceries first thing in morning."

She glared at him. "I'll have the list for you then. And, Oskar, in this house we don't sneak around and listen to private conversations."

With that, she inclined her head toward the doorway and Oskar left the room. She shut the door behind him with a resounding bang.

"He heard what we were saying?" I asked.

"Not much. I saw the door open, and it's soundproof when it's closed."

I wasn't reassured. I thought of the creaking I'd heard earlier. But I had something else to ask her. I lowered my voice. "The people who came to Jude's house, where do you think they went when they left?"

"Ali should be able to tell us. Hopefully, he will contact you soon."

"I'll call Clive tomorrow and see what he knows about the people Jude took in."

I didn't see Oskar when I left Safe Harbor, but as I walked to my car, the hairs on the back of my neck started to prickle. I turned and looked at the house. The slats of a Venetian blind at the front window dropped into place.

He was watching me.

Chapter Twenty-One

Pat

Farah cleared the table after Laura and I had finished breakfast the next morning.

"How's Oskar?" Laura asked her.

Farah shrugged.

"Out with him last night?"

"Oskar very busy. Safe Harbor just one job he have. He also run business."

That got my attention.

Laura looked impressed. "Cool. What kind of business?"

"Secret business. He not telling me."

"So he's hot, this Oskar?"

"Laura," I said.

"I'm just asking Farah what she thinks of Oskar"

Farah put dishes into the sink, then faced us, fingering the amber beads Oskar had given her. "He make lots of money at his business."

Laura looked impressed.

"Yesterday, I go downtown on way home. I go to Tiffany's."

"Tiffany's?" Laura chuckled.

I shot her a warning look. Why shouldn't Farah have gone into Tiffany's or any other store she chose?

"I look at jewelry there. Amber beads, like Oskar give me, cost eight hundred dollars."

Laura whistled. "Your Oskar must be running one hell of a business."

Laura had made a good point.

177

Walking to work, I thought of Oskar listening at Sister Celia's door the night before.

And he was dating Farah. Coincidence? My gut feeling was no. On the other hand, an attractive young woman helped out at Safe Harbor and a man who worked there asked her out. Nothing unusual about that.

Arnie was seated at the desk in Stéphane's former office. "Good morning," he called out.

I gave him a half-hearted wave.

He followed me into my office. "Could I see the accounts I'll be taking over?"

"Let me get my coat off, please."

He sat down in the client's chair and drummed his fingers on my desk.

When I was in my chair, I took a deep breath and looked at him. "We'll have you sit in on client meetings for a while. Let clients get to know you. We don't want them to think they're being passed on."

"I'm sure they'd be happy to be passed onto a bright, young advisor full of energy and ideas."

Instead of working with two old dinosaurs.

"How old are you, Arnie?" It had to be ten years since Luella told me he'd graduated from university.

"Thirty."

"Well, Stéphane is only a few years older than you."

"Pat, I want my own clients. Ray said("

The door to the office suite opened, and Ray and Jan Vrancic walked in. "Pat, Arnie, my boy." Ray steered Jan into my office. "Pat, you and Jan have already met. Jan, this is Arnie Cruickshank, the young advisor I told you about. Arnie, my friend, Dr. Jan Vrancic."

Jan bowed to me and shook Arnie's hand. Jan looked like a character in an old movie in his out-of-date suit.

"Arnie," Ray said when they had pulled up chairs, "I look after Jan's personal investments, but he has a project you'll be interested in. He's set up a charitable foundation to help orphans in his homeland."

"Yugoslavia, right?" Arnie said.

"Bosnia-Herzegovina," Jan said. "Many people died in the war, leaving children without parents."

I couldn't help but think that that war had ended years ago. Bosnian war orphans would be adults now.

Jan frowned, as if he'd read my mind. "The war may be over, but many children there still need help."

"You and I will be two of the trustees," Ray said to Arnie, "and we'll manage the foundation's assets."

"Ray," I said, "Arnie has just started in the business. He needs time?"

"Arnie will be fine, just fine. What say the three of us go into Arnie's office and look at the files? Pat must want to get on with her day."

The little woman had work to do. I was more amused than offended by Ray's chauvinism.

Jan took a round gold watch from his vest pocket and glanced at it. The only person I knew who carried a pocket watch was my grandfather, and he would have been over a hundred if he were alive.

I shook my head and hoped Ray wouldn't be sorry he'd put Arnie on this team.

When I was alone, I called Clive Pettigrew's office. After a short wait, he came on the line. "Can I see you today?" I asked.

"I wondered when you'd get back to me. Have you talked to Arlene?"

"How about we do lunch?"

Clive was seated in the Bloor Street Diner when I arrived. I slid into the seat across from him.

"What did she say?"

I glanced at the menu. "Arlene refused to get involved."

He groaned and closed his eyes.

I let several seconds tick by. "If you're innocent, there should be nothing to link you to Jude's murder. You can't be charged just because you two were once an item. You said you hadn't seen her in months."

The waitress took our orders for veal parmesan sandwiches.

"I, ah, I did see Jude recently," Clive said when we were alone again. "Just before...she died."

I scrutinized his face. So he had lied. What other lies had he told me?

He pursed his mouth and examined his manicured fingernails. "I stopped by her house the day before New Year's Eve. I figured she might be at home seeing that it was the Christmas holidays. I had a gift for her. I wanted to see if we could, you know..."

"Start up again?"

"Something like that. But she was distracted. She looked frightened when she came to the door."

She was terrified. She and her son had been threatened.

"Was Tommy there?"

"I didn't see him. She was rushing off somewhere."

"You came by in the afternoon?"

"Yes."

"She was probably on her way to see me. She came to my office late that afternoon. But so what? You dropped in on her the day before she was killed. A dozen other people might have stopped by as well. But it's unfortunate that you withheld this from the police. When they find out…"

"Who will tell them(except you?" His eyes flashed with anger. A moment later, he looked deflated. "I don't want to be involved in the investigation."

"But if you have nothing to hide…" I paused. "Clive, that argument you had with Jude."

"What argument? I never said we had an argument."

"Jude's next-door neighbor heard you arguing about 'those people'."

"That snoop next door was listening through the walls?"

"Jude had refugees staying with her from time to time. Is that what you quarreled about?"

He groaned. "She was a bleeding-heart social-justice freak. Every few weeks, she'd take in a refugee until an opening came up at some place called a safe house. She'd have this foreigner hanging around her home, acting like a scared rabbit. Gave me the creeps."

I winced at his bigotry. The waitress set our food in front of us and I bit into my sandwich.

"In September, Jude told me another refugee would arrive the next day." He speared a pickle with his fork. "I said she was a doormat for those fakes and liars. If the refugee tribunal turned down their claims, it must have had good grounds for doing so. She told me to get out of her life."

He really didn't have much in common with Jude, I thought as I devoured my sandwich.

"She was a headstrong leftie. With all her family money, she lived in that east-end dump and babysat border jumpers."

"But you wanted to start up with her again."

He sighed. "I thought her sister would be like her, but Arlene is a pain in the butt. Turns out she was adopted. I guess I was attracted to Jude because she was so damn headstrong."

"Clive, were you around when that man brought the refugees to her?"

"No. I was never there when they arrived or left."

Then he did something that struck me as completely out of character.

"You said you're related to Tommy," he said.

I hesitated a few seconds. "Yes."

He took the watch off his wrist and handed it to me.

"He's a good kid. Give this to him. He thought it was pretty cool."

I finished my sandwich and slid to the end of the booth. "Got to get back to the office. I'll make sure Tommy gets the watch."

Snow was falling on my way back to the office. The taxi crawled through the downtown traffic giving me time to think about what I'd learned from Clive. Unless it had been a crime of passion, Clive had no motive to kill Jude and he didn't strike me as a passionate man. He also had a soft spot for Tommy, which counted for a lot in my books.

The cab braked suddenly at a pedestrian crossing, and I sat up straight in my seat. Jude hadn't told me who had threatened Tommy or why. She'd been evasive because she had been harboring illegals. That was why she hadn't wanted to get the police involved.

I punched Sophie's number into my cell. "Jude's friend Clive visited her the afternoon before she was killed. Did you see him?"

"No. That day I am with my daughter in Newmarket. Maria drive me home next morning."

"Sophie, the man who brought the refugees to Jude's house. What did he look like?"

"Ordinary guy."

"A young guy? White, black, Asian?"

"Not too old. White skin, brown hair. Ordinary guy."

Tommy would know who he was. If this was the man who had killed Jude, he would want to silence her son.

I punched in more numbers and reached Sister Celia. "Clive just confirmed that Jude took in refugees. He said they stayed with her until an opening came up at a safe house."

"Impossible. Jude wasn't involved with our safe houses. And people go straight to them from Safe Harbor. I take them myself or Father Jack does. No one else."

"Is there another group that helps refugees in the city?"

"I've heard that some ethnic communities take care of their people who have come to the end of the system."

"Sophie said the people who stayed with Jude had different backgrounds. Some were Asian, others were black."

"Then it wouldn't be the project of a single community."

"I hope Ali contacts me soon."

"What's my favorite financial advisor been up to?" Devon's voice was a warm caress over the phone line.

"I've been busy."

"Care to fill me in?"

"See what you make of this." I told him about Ali's visits to my office and home. And that Jude had taken in refugees.

"Tommy would be able to identify the fellow who brought refugees to his home. Which puts the boy…" He didn't finish.

"You got it."

"You told this to Hardy?"

"Not yet."

"Do it right now, Pat. Soon as you get off the phone."

"Maybe the police can get Tommy to talk about the people who came through his home."

"Speaking of coming through someone's home…" Devon paused. "I was, ah, calling to invite myself to Toronto for the weekend. I could catch a five forty-five flight tomorrow evening that gets in a little past seven."

"Oh." I needed time to myself that weekend, but I didn't know how to tell him that. "That would be…nice."

"I won't be intruding?"

"Of course not." I should have come up with an excuse. Told him I was busy.

"I'll take a taxi to your place. Then we can have dinner at Milo's."

"Sounds good."

I put the phone in its cradle, my anxiety level rising. I thought about the groceries I'd need to buy, the meals I'd have to make… No, Devon had invited himself. I'd had a hectic week and he would have to take me as I was.

I picked up the phone again and reached Hardy. I told him about the refugees who had been staying with Jude, and that Tommy would be able to identify the man who brought these people to his home. I told him he should speak to Sister Celia.

"You've done enough sleuthing," he told me. "Let us handle it from here. These are dangerous people."

Call display told me it was five-fifteen. I walked around the empty office suite. Stéphane's new office was tidy, but his plants looked forlorn in the windowless room. They needed a SAD lamp.

Arnie's office was a mess. File folders were stacked on the desk and chairs, and a pile of sports gear had been thrown into a corner.

I flicked on his computer and was surprised to see that head office hadn't yet issued him a password. Stéphane and I worked on the same network so that each of us could keep track of what the other was working on. But Arnie had been put on a different network.

His desktop displayed four documents, each labeled BYRF and numbered one through four. I did a "read only" on one and saw that BYRF stood for Bosnian Youth Relief Foundation. "Read onlys" on the others showed me that each document tracked a component of the foundation's investments. I was amazed to see that its assets totaled almost $6 million. I had no idea that Toronto's Bosnian community was so large.

I shook my head, puzzled that Ray had given a rookie an account of that size.

Chapter Twenty-Two

Pat

"Patricia, the apartment building closes on Monday." Luella's high-pitched voice assaulted my ear over the phone the next morning. "Is everything in order?"

I took a deep breath, and reached down to stroke Maxie by my feet. "I sold your Limex and Trendon shares. It's a seller's market these days, but…" As Arnie had reminded me, they were Luella's assets. "The check will be at the realtor's office at ten on Monday. You'll carry a sizable mortgage, but you should be able to handle it."

"It's a very smart move. The rents I collect will cover my mortgage payments. And my Arnie will be right there to look after everything. Nothing can go wrong."

She paused. "I've been thinking about changing my power of attorney. As you know, I've authorized my daughter to make decisions for me if I'm no longer able to. But Caroline lives way out in Calgary. Now that Arnie's in Toronto, I should transfer those powers to him."

What was Luella thinking of? "Do you think that's necessary?" I asked.

"Arnie is an investment specialist and Caroline doesn't know much about financial matters. But we can talk about that next week after the sale goes through."

I hung up and pasted a smile on my face. Time for the meeting I'd scheduled with Stéphane and our whiz kid.

Arnie's eyes were on Maxie when he and Stéphane came into my office. "I'm allergic to dogs."

I might have known. "That's too bad because Maxie will be coming to work with me on Fridays for the next little while. She's just made her home with us and my housekeeper has Fridays off."

Maxie got up and went over to Arnie.

"Maxie, come back here."

The dog licked Arnie's hand.

He jerked his hand away. "My allergies."

"I'll put Maxie in my office while we meet." Stéphane took the dog by the collar. "Come, *ma belle*. A change of scenery for you."

"Arnie," I said when Stéphane had returned, "Stéphane and I are each giving you two of our clients. You'll be the account manager, but we'll supervise you. With Dr. Vrancic's foundation, that should keep you pretty busy."

Stéphane and I went over the profiles of the four clients and the holdings in their accounts. Arnie's face grew progressively more sullen.

When we'd finished, he glowered at us. "Those accounts aren't worth the time I'll have to put into them."

"Think of their potential," I told him. "These four clients could become the cornerstone of your business. They're young professionals in high-income careers with years ahead of them to grow their money."

"Yeah, but they've got to educate their kids and pay off their mortgages before they can do any serious investing. Which means zilch in commissions for years."

"You're starting to build your business, Arnie," I said trying to hide my impatience. "These people have friends they can send to you. And they have families(parents, siblings, cousins(who may need a financial advisor. And three of them stand to receive substantial inheritances."

"When? Their parents are(what? In their fifties or sixties?"

"If you take good care of these people they'll be with you when that day arrives. Meanwhile, others will come your way."

"From where?" He brushed imaginary hairs off his suit. "Damn mutt."

"From referrals. Dr. Vrancic may be able to help you there. And you can call on your friends from school and on relatives. And you can contact service clubs and other organizations and offer to hold seminars for their members on different aspects of financial planning."

Arnie grinned. "And there's always my mother. But you've locked up her assets."

I'd figured he'd bring up his mother's account sooner or later. "Norris Cassidy won't allow its advisors to work with relatives. Company policy."

I watched him digest that and continued. "Down the road when you're more established, there are other things you can do to build your business. You can hold lunchtime seminars in restaurants that have private rooms. Invite your clients and ask them to bring a friend or a colleague along. That way, you'd meet several prospects at the same event."

"And who pays for this lunch? Norris Cassidy?"

"You'd pay," Stéphane said, "but it would be a tax deduction. A business expense."

Arnie snorted.

Stéphane and I exchanged glances.

"Look, Arnie, we all started out this way," Stéphane said. "When I joined Pat four years ago, I'd practiced in North Bay for a few years. I was fortunate to pick up three former clients who had moved to Toronto. And Pat passed some of her smaller accounts on to me. The rest was a scramble. You work at it and, sooner than you think, you've got a healthy book of business."

"Sure." Arnie gathered up his papers. "Anyone who wears the clothes you do must pull in some hefty commissions. Never mind treating clients to lunch, I'll barely be able to feed and clothe myself."

He'd be living in his mother's apartment building rent-free. And it would never occur to him to ask her for the occasional handout.

At the office door, he turned around. "Don't let that dog come anywhere near me."

At half-past twelve, I took Maxie for a short walk and tied her to a bench while I went into Greens. I kept my eyes peeled for Ali, but if he lived in the neighborhood, he hadn't joined the lunchtime crowd on Eglinton Avenue.

Back in my office, I closed the door, filled Maxie's bowl with kibble and settled down to lunch at my desk. In a few hours, Devon would be at the house. I should have told him I had other plans.

I was about to dig into my salad when the telephone rang.

"It's Leo Cornacchia, Pat. I have good news."

"You're getting a kidney."

"I am. It will be done at a private clinic. Tonia is packing as we speak."

"The surgery is today?"

"You move quickly when you get the call."

"At a private clinic? That means("

"You'll have to sell some stocks so I can settle the bill. Tonia will be in touch with you. And, if I don't come through this, do your best for her."

"Everything will go well, Leo. Give me a call when you feel up to it." I stared at my salad. A kidney transplant was a major procedure. What kind of clinic was Leo going to?

I dialed Tracy's office number. "What do you know about private health clinics?"

"They're out there, although they're only supposed to provide services that aren't covered under the provincial health plans."

"Like cosmetic surgery."

"Right. But I've heard that some clinics are getting into procedures that are covered. People who can afford them can bypass the waiting lists."

"What's all the talk we hear from politicians about safeguarding Canada from a two-tier health system?"

"It's bullshit. We already have a two-tier system. One for the rich and the well-connected. Another, with long waits, for the rest of us. And those who could afford it have had procedures done outside of Canada for years."

When I told her about Leo, Tracy yelped. "Mom, he's having a major organ transplant(not knee surgery."

"I take it that kidney transplants are normally done in hospitals."

"Well, of course."

Did Leo know what he was doing?

"Mom, it's not your problem. You're this guy's financial advisor, not his doctor. He made his decision and all you can do is hope that everything goes well for him."

I left the office at five and took a taxi home. I was touring the main floor of the house to see if everything was in order when I heard a tapping sound on the French doors in the sunroom. I peered out between two shutter slats. All I could see was the Toronto night.

The tapping sounded again and I turned on the deck lights. A man stood on the other side of a door. A very tall man. Ali!

I opened the door. "Come in."

He seemed to hesitate. I grabbed his hand and pulled him into the house. He looked around the room warily.

"It's okay. There's just the two of us here." I glanced over my shoulder. "Except for my dog. Don't worry, she's friendly."

"And brave." Ali stroked Maxie's head. "She saved me from…"

"You'll have to explain what happened here the other day."

He inclined his head toward the shutters. "You close, please?"

I closed them. "No one can see inside this room with the shutters closed. Do you want to take off your jacket?"

"I will keep it on."

I motioned for him to join me on the sofa, where Maxie lay down on the floor at his feet. I knew I had to proceed carefully. "My daughter will be home from school soon."

"Oskar will come here?"

I smiled. "Oskar from Safe Harbor? No."

"He was here on Tuesday."

"Oskar is a friend of my housekeeper and she is not in today. You ran out of here on Tuesday because of Oskar?"

"Yes."

"Let's start at the beginning. Ali, you left Safe Harbor when your refugee claim was turned down. What happened?"

He took a deep breath and let it out slowly. "Before I went to the tribunal, Oskar told me about a safe house where people go when they lose their claims. When the tribunal refused me, Oskar said I needed to go to the safe house right away."

"But Sister Celia told you that you can appeal."

"Yes, she told me that, but Oskar said the police sometimes arrive without warning and take refugees to the appeal hearing. If they are turned down, they take them straight to the airport."

"I don't think that's how it works. But you went with him."

He held out his hands palms up. "I cannot go back to Somalia."

"Where did he take you?"

"First, he took me to the house of Miss Seaton. He said I would stay there for a few days until a room opened at the safe house."

He kneaded his hands together and went on. "Miss Seaton, she was very kind lady. She showed me a metal box she hid under the roof of her back porch. In the box was money and a key to the house. She made me memorize her address. She told me if something went wrong to take a taxi back to her house. She told me to pay the driver with money from the box and wait for her inside the house."

So Jude was worried about what happened to the refugees who left her home.

"After three days, Oskar returned. He took me to a house in the east part of this city. Near Lake Ontario."

I nodded to let him know I was following his story.

"We went down into the basement of the house. He put me in a room that looked like a doctor's examination room. A table covered with a white sheet and a cabinet filled with medical equipment?syringes, gauze pads, that kind of thing. He gave me a blue shirt and said a doctor would come to examine me. He told me to take off my clothes and my watch and other things, and put on the shirt. Then he left me.

"I took off my watch and?" His hands went to his throat. "The beads my father gave me. I put them on the cabinet. Then I tried the door. It was locked. All I could think of was the day I was picked up by al-Shabaab. They put me in a room, locked the door." He paused for a few seconds, his eyes enormous in his face.

"I saw a bin in the corner of the room. I lifted the lid. Inside were many blue shirts like the one Oscar gave me. But I also saw a red shirt and jeans. I pulled them out. They reminded me of the clothes another refugee, Suleyman, wore. Oskar took him to a safe house. No one has seen or heard from him since."

He took a deep breath and went on. "And before Suleyman, Oskar took other people to safe houses. No one has heard from them either. Oskar said they have started new lives so they cannot make contact with their friends. But I looked at the shirt and jeans in my hands, and I knew there was no new life after this place. For unfortunates like us, it was the end."

"How did you get out of there?"

"There was a window that was covered outside with wire net. I opened the window and cut the wire with scissors I found in the cabinet. I climbed out the window and returned to the house of Miss Seaton."

Ali had been locked in a room stocked with medical equipment. What had been going on in there?

"I left my watch and my bag and my beads in that room." He paused. "On Tuesday, that woman I saw in your house was wearing my beads. I would know them anywhere. Silver and amber. My father wore them and he gave them to me when I left Somalia. The woman here said they were gift from her boyfriend."

Oskar had given Farah the beads that Ali left behind. "So you went back to Jude Seaton's house. When was that?"

"The twenty-sixth day of December."

Six days before Jude was killed.

"That evening, Oskar came to Miss Seaton's house. 'Where is Ali?' he shouted. I came down from my room when he looked in basement, but he saw me leave the house."

"And the next time he saw you was here on Tuesday?"

"Yes. He ran after me, but your dog jumped on him." He bent down to pat Maxie. "I ran through a yard and over to the next street."

My heart went out to this young man who was hiding from the immigration authorities and from Oskar. "Where are you staying now?"

"I am with friends from Somalia, but apartment is small. I cannot stay there long."

"Ali, you have to talk to Sister Celia."

"Later, maybe." He gave a shuddering sigh. "I cannot go to the police, but they must know about this terrible house. I saw you at the church. I watched you on the street near your office. I think I can trust you." He paused for a few seconds. "But how is it you know Oskar?"

"I already told you that Oskar is my housekeeper's friend. She met him when she was helping out at Safe Harbor. Her brother, Raad, volunteers there."

"Raad, yes. Raad is good man." Ali sat up ramrod straight on the sofa. "Mrs. Tierney, you must tell people about this house. It is very bad place. And refugees are disappearing. My friends know two Somalians who disappeared."

"Did they live at Safe Harbor?"

"No. They saw a doctor who does not ask for government health card. He takes cash. A few days later, they were gone."

"You know where this doctor works?"

He shook his head.

"Ali, did you get the address of the house Oskar took you to?"

"No, I got out very fast. But I remember how Oskar got there. He drove east on Danforth Avenue from the house of Miss Seaton. Then he drove on Kingston Road and turned onto smaller street."

The house was in the Scarborough Bluffs neighborhood. "Did you take Jude there?"

"She was going to drive me there, but Oskar came."

The front door opened. "Hi, Mom," Laura called out.

Ali was out of his seat, poised for flight.

"My daughter." I motioned for him to sit back down. I gave Laura a warning sign as she came through the kitchen.

"Ah...I'll be in my room." She headed for the stairs.

"Ali, why don't we drive over there now? See if you can locate the house."

He didn't answer.

"You're the only one who knows where it is. You were going to go there with Jude."

He bowed his head. "It is my fault Miss Seaton is dead."

"You told her what happened at the house Oskar took you to?"

"Yes. She was looking for another place for me. She said Oskar would find me at her house and she was right." He glanced at the back doors. "I must go."

"Will you give me a phone number where I can reach you?"

He shook his head.

"You need to show me where that house is before more people disappear." I scribbled down my numbers. "And, Ali, why don't you give Sister Celia a call before you go? Tell her you are staying with friends, but you will need to find another place soon."

I pointed to the telephone on the end table and went upstairs to speak to Laura.

When Ali had left the house, I ran a bath and I was about to step into it when the doorbell rang. It was too early to be Devon, and I was about to call out to Laura to go to the door. Then I thought of Oskar storming into Jude's home looking for Ali. I grabbed my housecoat.

Downstairs, I turned on the porch light and peeked through the front curtains. Ryan stood on the porch, holding a canvas carryall and a parcel that looked like flowers.

"Hi," he said when I opened the door. Then he stared down at his feet.

I held the door for him. "What are you doing here?"

He came into the house and thrust the parcel at me. "For you."

I saw that he had several stitches in his face above his left eyebrow.

196

"I, uh, I'm sorry about...the last time we met. Dad told me he'd be up here this weekend, so I thought I'd...come and apologize." He paused, stared at his feet again, then back up at me. "Especially to Laura." He looked around as if he expected to see her.

The boy had hopped on a plane and crossed the continent to apologize. Feeling slightly stunned, I led him into the sunroom.

He took off his jacket, and I saw that he was nicely turned out in jeans and a cable-knit navy turtleneck. The rings were gone from his nose and ear.

"I was in pretty bad shape at New Year's. I did a lot of dope last fall and got terrible marks, which will probably ruin my chances for grad school."

He paused. "Christmas was the season for parties, and that's all I wanted to do. Party and get stoned. I didn't want to see either of my parents. But Dad kept pushing the bonding-quality-time thing. He wouldn't let it go. So I thought I'd make sure it was the last time he asked me anywhere. I was determined to be a complete asshole."

"You succeeded."

"When I got back to L.A., I went into a bar to buy some dope. I was mugged in the washroom." He pointed to the stitches on his face. "I decided to clean up my act and start over." He extended his right hand. "Nice to meet you, Mrs. Tierney."

"And nice to meet you." I shook his hand. "I'm finally meeting the real Ryan Shaughnessy."

"Yeah, well..." He stared at his feet again.

"I'll tell Laura you're here. I have no idea if she'll want to see you."

"I could go to a hotel."

"No!" Laura cried when I told her Ryan was downstairs. "I never want to see that jerk again. Tell him to go away."

"He says he's sorry about New Year's. Go down and say hello. His dad will be here soon and we can all go out to eat."

"No way." She reached for her cell phone. "I'll go over to Jessie's if she's in."

"What the hell are you doing here?" was all she had to say to Ryan when she came downstairs. She left the house with Maxie and a bag of kibble.

I took Ryan up to the spare room. "She'll calm down and be back. You've surprised her. You should have let us know you were on your way."

"I was afraid you wouldn't have me."

Devon seemed as surprised as I'd been by Ryan's turnaround. After his son had made his apologies, he gave him a hug. "Pat and I are going out for dinner. Like to join us?"

"I'll stay here. Laura may come back."

To my relief, dinner was pleasant and low-key.

"Ryan," Devon said with a sigh when we'd given our orders. "Is he really turning a new leaf? Somehow I doubt it. He has a lot to learn about responsibility. Part of the problem is that his mother denies him nothing. She's given him a credit card and she pays the bill every month."

"She's doing him no favors. He has to learn to manage money."

"I've tried to talk to her about it. It's useless."

The waitress arrived with our wine. Devon clinked his glass against mine and took my hand. His hand felt good on mine. Maybe he wouldn't bulldoze his way into my life.

When our salad and bruschetta arrived, I told Devon about Ali's visit earlier that evening and how he'd escaped from the safe house. "The place he was taken to doesn't sound like one of Sister Celia's safe houses."

I pictured the room Ali had described. A doctor's examination table. Medical equipment in the cabinet. And Oskar had told him to put on one of those hospital Johnny shirts. Why?

"They're two different places," Devon said. "What Ali described is a prison."

"Oskar is desperate to get hold of Ali because he escaped from that house and he can tell people about it. And Oskar knew he would have told Jude."

"You'd better let Hardy know about this."

"Let me know what?"

We looked up to see the detective beside our table.

"Sorry to crash your dinner." He pulled out a chair and sat down. "I stopped by your house and Mr. Shaughnessy's son said you'd be here. What do you have to tell me?"

I told him about Ali's visit that afternoon and what he'd told me about the safe house.

Hardy looked grim. "We've got to get hold of this Jacovic."

I looked at the detective, suddenly afraid that something had happened to Laura after she left the house. Or to Tracy, who hadn't arrived home when we left.

"You came by the house. You wanted to see me."

"About Tommy Seaton."

"Tommy." My heart twisted. "What??"

"He's missing. This afternoon, his uncle took him to his grandmother's house for the weekend. She had a nap before dinner and, when she came back downstairs, the boy was gone. It looks like he put on his jacket and boots, and went out the back door. And vanished."

Chapter Twenty-Three

Pat

Devon and I arrived at Norah's house at nine-thirty the next morning. Mrs. Bonokowski took us into the living room. I nodded at Hardy and Mancini, who were seated across from Norah and Arlene.

Norah had aged a decade since I'd seen her the week before. The lines were etched deeper into her face and her eyes were rimmed with red. Her normally coiffed silver hair stood up in tufts. She looked as if the stuffing had been knocked out of her.

"The police ask me the same questions over and over again," the old woman said, stroking her poodle. "And I give them the same answers."

"We need to see if you can remember anything else that could help us," Hardy said. "Tommy's disappearance has top priority. We've put out an amber alert."

"You still haven't found Jude's killer," Arlene said. In contrast to her mother, she was smartly turned out with her hair swept up in a chignon.

The muscles around Hardy's mouth twitched. "There's a tap on your phone line. And you'll need to let us know immediately if someone contacts you about Tommy any other way."

I followed the detectives and Arlene into the front hall. "Have you talked to Oskar Jacovic?" I asked Hardy.

He frowned. "If you see him, let me know right away."

"Who is Oskar Jacovic?" Arlene asked when the detectives had gone.

201

"Someone Jude did volunteer work with."

"Have you...have you talked to Clive?"

"I told him you didn't want to talk to the police."

Her face fell. "I don't know what to do."

I gave her what I hoped was a sympathetic smile and we returned to the living room.

Norah looked up at us. "Tommy just...vanished."

"I'm worried about Mom's health," Arlene said. "Those policemen have been hounding her."

"I'm fine," Norah said. "I just want Tommy back safe and sound."

"What happened last night?" I asked.

Arlene looked put out. "Do we have to go over it again?"

"Tell her, dear," Norah said.

"All we know is that Tommy went out while Mom was resting upstairs. When she came down, he was gone. His jacket and boots were gone, and so was Gigi."

"Mrs. Bonokowski found Gigi in the backyard with her leash caught around a bush," Norah said. "Tommy must have taken her out, then..."

She began to cry.

"Can I take a look at the back of your house?" I asked Norah.

She pointed to the dining room and the doors that opened onto the yard. Outside, I saw a raised patio and an expanse of snow-covered ground that had been trampled by many pairs of feet. The yard was enclosed by a high wooden fence.

I drew a deep breath. Someone had been waiting out there for Tommy.

"Have the police looked at those footprints?" I asked.

"They certainly have," Arlene said behind me. "They were here until late last night with their lights set up, taking measurements and photographs. Most of those prints were made by the police."

I returned to Norah in the living room. "Does the fence have a gate?"

"There's a six-foot gate on each side of the yard," Norah said.

"They're both locked?"

"No. Our security people suggested that I have locks put on them, but we always set the alarm when no one's at home.

"I told Patrick on Thursday that I wanted Tommy here for the weekend," she went on. "The headmaster wasn't happy about it, but I put my foot down. Tommy needs to be with his family."

"Who knew that Tommy would be here for the weekend?" I asked.

"The police already asked Mom that several times," Arlene snapped.

I ignored her and addressed Norah. "Would anyone at the school know where he'd gone?"

"I never thought to ask them to keep it a secret. I figured Tommy and I would stay in the house all weekend, and Patrick would drive him back to school on Sunday afternoon. I'd forgotten how active young boys are."

Back at home, I found Ryan stacking the dishwasher. I felt my jaw drop. "You're handy around a kitchen."

"I guess. Dad's out with your dog." His face broke into a grin. "Laura's back. She's going to show me Toronto today."

I hoped the city's highlights didn't include a hotel room. But I gave him a smile and wondered at Laura's change of heart. And where Kyle was that weekend.

The front door opened and Tracy came in. When she took off her coat, I saw that she was wearing the same pantsuit she'd had on the morning before. I hadn't realized that she hadn't come home the night before.

"Where were you last night?" I asked.

She blushed. "We went out for drinks after work. It ran pretty late, so I stayed with a woman I work with. I should have called. Sorry."

"You should have. I was worried."

The phone rang and she rushed to get it. "Farah, it's your boyfriend."

Farah hurried into the kitchen and grabbed the receiver. I couldn't help but hear her end of the phone conversation.

"Look after kid?" she said.

Farah paused for a moment. "Mama and Raad, they not let me stay out all night." After another short pause, she added, "It is not possible, Oskar."

She paused again. "What movie?"

Another pause. "Okay, okay!" She slammed down the receiver.

I smiled. Farah was treating her new boyfriend the same way she treated everyone else.

Thirty minutes later, I was trying to chill out in the sunroom with Samuel Barber's "Adagio for Strings." Tommy's face drifted through my thoughts and my heart constricted.

Where was he? How was he being treated? Was he…alive?

A wave of compassion for Jude washed over me. I had been shocked by her murder. No one deserved to die before her time and so horribly, but it had been like hearing about a stranger's death on the evening news. I had only met the woman once, and the meeting had not been pleasant.

But now I saw her with new eyes. Caught in the middle of whatever trouble she'd been in, she was frantic with worry about her son. I knew what it was like to love a child, to be willing to give up your own life in a heartbeat to save that precious little life.

"Pat?"

I opened my eyes. Farah stood in front of me, wearing a sullen expression. I turned down the volume and braced myself for a complaint about the extra work our guests had given her.

"All right to leave early today?"

"Everything okay at home, Farah?"

She shrugged.

"Then I could really use your help today with Devon and Ryan here. How about some time off next week?"

"Must be today."

"I don't understand."

"I meet someone this afternoon."

I studied her face. "This someone is Oskar, isn't it?"

She bit her lip. "Please, I can leave at twelve-thirty?"

"I'd like an explanation. Who are you meeting?"

She looked at the ceiling, then back at me. "Cousin in Chicago, his boy come stay us. Raad, he work today, so I must meet young boy."

The word boy got my attention. "Oskar's cousin?"

She shook her head. "My cousin."

A child travelling alone? What parent would allow that?

She glanced at her watch. "One-thirty, we meet. Broadview Station."

"You're meeting a child at a subway station?"

Her eyes threw invisible daggers at me. "The boy, he travel with friend. I meet them at Broadview Station."

The "friend" was Oskar. Was the boy Tommy? "So you meet the boy and…?"

"Mama must get apartment ready, make dinner. Boy and me, we go to movie at Bijou Cinema."

The cinema where she saw *Casablanca* with Oskar. But I was asking too many questions. "Finish up the bathrooms and be on your way."

I watched her go upstairs, my mind racing. Farah knew very little about Oskar. She didn't know that he'd been taking refugees to a house in Scarborough. She didn't know that the police were looking for him. I wondered whether should warn her.

She stopped on the landing and turned to look at me. I smiled, and she continued up the stairs.

I debated whether I should go after her. But what would I say? Don't meet Oskar? He's up to something and it's not good? She would just toss her head and laugh. Besides, I had a feeling she would lead us to Tommy.

I went into my study and called Safe Harbor on my cell.

"Any news of Tommy?" Sister Celia asked.

"Not when I last spoke to Hardy a few hours ago."

"Hardy was here last night looking for Oskar. I gave him a photo that I kept in Oskar's file. Do you think?"

"I do. Ali told you about the safe house when he called you last night?"

"He did."

Ali's face, his eyes wide with fear, flashed through my mind.

"Farah told me that Oskar is running some kind of business. Do you know anything about it?"

"A business?" She sounded surprised. "No. Oskar's worked here for years, but I have no idea what he else does. I know he shares an apartment with a couple of fellows in The Junction neighborhood. And he has an uncle in the city."

"Does he know about your safe houses?"

"Absolutely not."

"We've got to find that house he took Ali to."

As soon as Devon had taken off his boots and jacket, I pulled him into the study. "I need to talk to you."

When I closed the door, he cleared his throat. "You don't want Laura seeing Ryan."

"It's not that. I hope they have a good time today."

"Then what?"

"I don't want to Farah to hear." I told him about her plans for the afternoon.

"We'd better call Hardy."

"No. He'll have officers all over the station. When Oskar sees them, who knows what he might do to Tommy. I can't take that chance."

"This is police business, Pat. What do you think you can do on your own?"

He had a point. What if something came up that we couldn't handle? "All right, I'll call him. You'll come to Broadview Station with me?"

He sighed. "You know I will."

I touched his face. "Thank you."

Then I punched Hardy's number into my cell.

Chapter Twenty-Four

Pat

At one-twenty, Devon and I huddled under a shop awning directly across the street from the Broadview subway entrance, debating our next move. He wanted to wait inside the station where Hardy had said he would meet us, but I didn't want Oskar to see me there when he arrived. Oskar had a car so I assumed that he would leave it in a parking lot and walk over to the station.

"We've got to go in there at some point," Devon said.

"Here comes Oskar. Across the street."

Oskar had just rounded the corner of Broadview and Danforth. He held the hand of a child who was dressed in a dark green snowsuit and a colorful balaclava that covered most of the face. The kid swayed like a sleepwalker.

Devon and I sprinted for the green traffic light. We had just made it across Broadview Avenue when Oskar picked up the child and went into the station.

We ran through the entrance several people behind them. Oskar got on the escalator with the child in his arms.

"We've got to keep them in sight," I said.

"Pat, we have to wait here for Hardy."

"Can't." I stuffed a five-dollar bill and a loonie in the collector's box and raced toward the stairs. Devon was right behind me.

We were halfway down the staircase when I spotted Farah on the busy platform. She went over to Oskar as he got off the escalator.

She looked at the child in his arms and surprise registered on her face. She gave Oskar a questioning look. I knew then that the child was Tommy.

She looked in my direction and her eyes widened. Oskar spun around and saw me on the bottom stairs. He scowled, grabbed Farah with his free hand and pulled her farther down the platform.

I elbowed my way through the crowd, leaving Devon caught behind a woman with a child's stroller.

"Hey, lady, what's your problem?" a man yelled at me.

"Pat, wait for me," Devon called.

"Oskar, put Tommy down," I cried.

Oskar shoved Tommy into Farah's arms and wheeled around to face me.

I sprang toward Farah, but Oskar pushed me aside. A blade flashed in his hand.

"Back off!" he shouted at Devon who had come up beside me. He snatched Tommy away from Farah. He held the boy against his chest with one arm and waved the knife in his other hand.

A woman screamed. Devon took a step back as Oskar slashed the blade through the air.

"Farah!" Oskar yelled and motioned for her to get behind him.

She stood rooted to the spot, her mouth open.

"Farah, come. Now!"

Two men in maroon Toronto Transit Commission jackets gestured to the crowd on the platform. "Emergency!" one of them shouted. "Move back against the wall."

The crowd began to back away from us.

"Oskar, give Tommy to me," I yelled.

Oskar took another step back. "Farah, get over here."

I lunged at him.

He whirled around and slashed at me. Stuffing spilled out of the shoulder of my parka. He brought up his right boot, but I stepped out of its reach. He lost his balance and staggered to the edge of the platform. While he tried to steady himself, Tommy slipped from his grasp and fell off the platform.

"No," I screamed.

"Get back, Pat." Devon scrambled onto the tracks. People around me gasped as he picked up the boy and hoisted him onto the platform. Devon grabbed two outstretched arms, and two commuters pulled him back onto the platform.

I knelt and pulled the balaclava off Tommy's head. "Are you okay, sweetie?" I ran my hands over his body.

"Mrs. T?" he mumbled.

He didn't seem to feel any pain, but why was he so groggy? I realized that Oskar had drugged him.

I stroked his brow. "It's okay, Tommy." I folded him to my breast and kissed his head. The drug he had been given made him completely relaxed. That and the bulky snowsuit had saved him when he fell off the platform.

I felt a hand on my shoulder. Looking up, I saw Mancini beside me. He picked up Tommy and I got to my feet.

Farther down the platform, I saw a wild-eyed Oskar take a few steps back, waving the knife. Then he turned and bolted down the platform. Devon ran after him, followed by Hardy and the TTC men. Devon lunged at Oskar, knocking the knife from his hand. They fell onto the platform just feet away from the edge. People around them screamed and pulled back. They rolled away from the edge and Oskar jumped to his feet.

Two TTC special constables in black uniforms strode toward him. Oskar leaped onto the tracks and headed for the tunnel. Suddenly he stopped, wheeled around and ran back toward us.

People on both platforms called out to him.

Lights from within the tunnel shone on the tiled walls. A collective gasp rose from the crowd. With a whoosh of air, the train roared down the tracks.

Oskar screamed.

The sound of metal on metal rang through the station as the train screeched to a stop.

Beside me, Farah moaned. She looked stricken and her face was wet with tears.

TTC workers herded commuters toward the escalator and up the stairs. Farah and I got on the escalator. Mancini, with Tommy in his arms, and the special constables were right behind us. Farah stared straight ahead. Tears ran down her face.

We found Devon and Hardy waiting for us outside the station. I took Tommy from Mancini, and inhaled the little-boy scents of citrus shampoo and chocolate. He was safe. Tommy was safe!

With a stab, I realized how much this child meant to me. It didn't matter that he was Michael's son. It didn't matter at all. It was just sad that Michael had never got to know him.

A police cruiser, driven by a uniformed officer, pulled up at the curb in front of us. Hardy opened the back door. "Inside, please."

Farah let out a wail. "I swear I not know. I not know Oskar have this boy."

I put a hand on her arm. "It will be all right, Farah. Just tell the police what happened."

"In the cruiser, please," Hardy said.

I locked eyes with him. "This woman is terrified. Where she comes from, being taken away by the police means torture or a firing squad."

"Please get in the cruiser."

Devon took Farah's arm and led her to the door. He followed her into the cruiser. I put Tommy on the seat beside him and fastened the seat belt around him. I got into the front of the vehicle, took my cell out of my handbag and punched in Norah's phone number.

Our driver pulled up outside police headquarters. An unmarked car drove up behind us, and Hardy and Mancini got out of it. Hardy opened our back door and poked his head inside.

"DC Mancini will take Ms. Alwan upstairs for questioning. Ms. Tierney, we'll have the boy checked out at St. Mike's Hospital."

"He's pretty groggy," I said. "Oskar must have given him something."

"Let's get to the hospital."

He led us down the street to his own vehicle, a black Mustang badly in need of a carwash. "Drove my son to hockey practice this morning," he said as he zapped the doors open.

"Hold on a minute." He swept an assortment of candy bar wrappers and paper cups from the seats and floor into a plastic bag.

When we were all inside, Devon in the passenger's seat, Tommy and myself in the back, Hardy exhaled loudly. "Why weren't you at the station entrance where I said I'd meet you?"

"Oskar came in with Tommy and they went straight down to the platform," I said. "You weren't there and I had to look out for Tommy. They could have got on the next train."

"So you confronted Jacovic." He shook his head. "That could have been you?or the boy?on those tracks."

I looked at Tommy in my arms. His eyes were closed. He seemed to be asleep.

Still shaking his head, Hardy turned the key in the ignition. I started to ask about Oskar, but he held up a hand. "Don't...say...another...word." He pushed the CD Play button. Strains of "Dust in the Wind" filled the car.

A pretty Asian-Canadian doctor who looked about fifteen years old took Tommy into an examination room. I followed them.

"I'm Dr. Wong," she said when Tommy was seated on the table. "How do you feel, young man?"

"Sleepy."

She pulled up one of his eyelids. "Do you know what day of the week this is?"

"Saturday."

"What city are we in?"

"Toronto."

"I'm going to take your boots off for a minute." She reached down and pulled off Tommy's snow boots. She ran a key along the bottom of his right foot. His big toe turned down.

She turned to me. "That's a good sign." She repeated the exercise on his left foot. "Well, young man, did you take any pills today?"

"Two white ones. And Oskar gave me one with apple juice before we got the movie tickets."

"We'll take a sample of your urine and do some tests." She met my eyes. "If anything changes, bring him right back here."

At police headquarters, Liliana Markowitz smiled at me and greeted Tommy like an old friend. "Just a few questions, son." She turned back to the video equipment. "It won't take long."

Devon and I went to sit at the back of the room.

After her introduction on the video, she smiled at Tommy. "On Friday night, did you leave your grandmother's house?"

He nodded.

"Tommy, remember you have to say it out loud for the tape."

"I took Gigi out the back door. I know I can't go out alone, but Gigi had to poo."

"Who is Gigi, Tommy?"

"Nana's dog. We went into the backyard and Gigi went poo. Then I saw Oskar."

"Oskar was in your grandmother's backyard?"

He nodded.

"Tommy, you?"

"Oskar was in Nana's backyard. He came out from behind the big tree. He scared me."

"Was he alone?"

"Yes."

"Did he say anything to you?"

"He said the people who hurt Mommy wanted to hurt me too. He said I had to go with him."

"You'd met Oskar before?"

"At my house."

"The house where you lived with your mother?"

"Yes."

"Why did Oskar come to your house?"

"He brought friends to see us."

"Friends?"

"Bedo, Semira, Cheeva."

"Who are these people, Tommy?"

"Friends. Then Oskar came and took them away."

"After they left with Oskar, did you see them again?"

Tommy paused. "Only Ali. Ali came back."

I squeezed Devon's arm.

"Tommy, on Friday night, you left your grandmother's backyard with Oskar. What happened?"

"We went to Oskar's car."

"Where was his car?"

"On the street."

"On your grandmother's street?"

He shook his head.

"His car wasn't on your grandmother's street, Tommy?"

"No. On the street behind Nana's street."

"What happened when you got to Oskar's car?"

"We got in it."

"And then what happened?"

"We drove to a house."

"Where was this house?"

"I don't know. We drove for a long time. I fell asleep."

"What did the house look like?"

Tommy shrugged. "A house. The bedrooms weren't upstairs."

"What happened when you got to this house?"

"Oskar gave me pizza and apple juice. I told him I wanted to call Nana to tell her that Gigi was outside. He said he'd already called her. I guess he called her on his cell, because I didn't see a phone in the house."

"Was there anyone else at the house?

"No, just me and Oskar."

"After you ate your pizza, what did you do?"

"I went to bed."

"And this morning. What did you do when you got up this morning, Tommy?"

"Cornflakes and apple juice. Watched cartoons on TV. Then I had a baloney sandwich and milk, and we left to watch movies with Farah. But we never went to a movie."

"Did Oskar hurt you in any way?"

"No, but I don't like his baloney sandwiches." He made a face. "He puts ketchup in them. Yuck."

"Thank you, Tommy," Markowitz said. "That's all for today."

Hardy had come into the room during the interview.

"What about Oskar?" I asked him while Devon was helping Tommy get into his snowsuit.

"Dead. Multiple traumatic injuries." Hardy grimaced. "It wasn't pretty…" He broke off as Tommy came over to us.

"Tommy's grandmother isn't well." I put an arm around the boy. "So Tommy will be with us until he goes back to the school tomorrow afternoon."

Tommy wrinkled his nose.

Hardy placed a hand on his shoulder. "I'll come by your place in a few hours," he said to me.

Tommy tugged on my sleeve. "Is Gigi okay?"

I gave him a fierce hug. "Gigi's just fine. They heard her barking so she wasn't outside long."

Chapter Twenty-Five

Pat

Tommy was asleep in the sunroom when Hardy arrived, so I led him into the front room.

"I assume that Oskar took Tommy because the boy could identify him," Devon said when we were seated.

"That's what we think." Hardy turned to me. "We need to talk to Ali about that house. Where can we find him?"

"He's staying with friends. He wouldn't give me a number where he can be reached."

Hardy's eyes probed my face. "You're sure about that?"

"Yes. And I asked him to take me to the house, but he seemed terrified of even being in the neighborhood."

"Keep away from that place. Let us handle it. And if the guy doesn't want to talk to us, have him write down directions."

"I will when I see him. But I'll have to wait for him to come to me."

He looked toward the back of the house where Tommy was sleeping. "I'll talk to the kid now."

"Tommy's asleep," I said. "Let him get the sedatives out of his system."

Hardy seemed about to protest. Then he wiped a hand across his brow. "Okay. In the morning."

An hour later, the doorbell rang again. This time, I found Sister Celia on the porch.

"Norah said Tommy is here."

I held the door open for her. "He's asleep."

She kicked off her work boots, then looked questioningly at me.

I pointed to the back of the house.

She made her way through the dining room and stood over the sleeping boy. She brushed a lock of hair from his face and placed a hand on his head. "Thank you, Lord."

Then she turned around. "Hey," she said to Devon who was watching her from the kitchen. "We met at the funeral."

"Glass of wine or a cup of tea?"

"I wouldn't say no to a nice glass of wine. Red, if you have it."

"How did you know where I lived?" I asked. "I'm not in the phone book."

"Norah told me."

Norah seemed to be giving my address and phone number to everyone who asked for it. I resolved to have a word with her.

Sister Celia took a sip from the glass Devon handed her and sat down at the kitchen table. "Umm, good. My dad used to make wine, but his was a lot rougher than this."

I sat beside her. Devon brought the chopping board, a bag of mushrooms and two red peppers to the table for the spaghetti sauce he had offered to make.

"Here's to Oskar." Sister Celia raised her glass. "That was no way for anyone to go."

"How did you hear about it?" I asked.

"The police came by an hour ago. I gather you were there when it happened."

I filled her in on Farah's phone call from Oskar.

"How long did Oskar work for you?" Devon asked.

"About eleven years. He had just arrived in Canada and he signed up for volunteer work with us. He was handy, so when he got his work papers, he became our full-time maintenance guy. That wouldn't happen today. The Sanctuary Coalition screens all volunteers and they undergo police checks. But things were a looser then and we were grateful for any help we could get."

"So he may have had a police record," I said.

"No, he didn't. I asked the detectives that last night." Her shoulders slumped. "Oskar was unreliable. He often came to work late or called in sick at the last moment. He brought friends to my rooms when I was out. The other night, Pat and I caught him and Farah doing a bit of courting."

Devon raised an eyebrow.

"I should have let him go a long time ago, but he was handy and cheap. He kept our furnace and fridge running, and repaired the roof."

She ran a hand across her brow. "It's an uphill battle to keep Safe Harbor afloat. I have to fight for every penny. The archdiocese refused to raise its grant this year and I'm afraid it will cut us off completely one day. We have an old building, an ancient furnace and a rickety van. Something always needs work."

She finished her wine and shook her head when Devon offered a refill.

"Ali needs to show us that house," I said.

We looked at one another, but nobody spoke for a few moments.

"I gave the police the name of the dentist who works with Safe Harbor residents," Sister Celia said. "He may be able to identify the dental work in some of the skulls they've found."

I put down my glass. The body parts that were turning up. The room that was stocked with medical equipment. "They're harvesting human organs."

Devon stopped chopping.

Sister Celia nodded. "Looks like it."

"If that's the case, there must be other people involved." Devon said. "Surgeons and lab technicians."

"Absolutely," she said. "And they'd need agents to scout out clients. Oskar didn't have the knowledge or the savvy. He was the supplier. He terrified those poor people by telling them that they were about to be deported, then he took them to stay with Jude until they were needed."

"They would have to match tissue with the recipients," Devon said.

"Of course. They were probably about to take samples from Ali. They must have access to lists of people waiting for organs. Or they may export them."

She held her hands over her face. After several moments, she took a deep breath and continued. "Trafficking in human organs is a major international racket. Marginalized people are targeted, and their organs are sent around the world. People who need transplants pay high prices for them."

"Did Jude ask if you knew a place where Ali could stay?" I asked.

"If only she had."

"She told Ali to go back to her house if he had any problems. She made him memorize her address."

"I'm sure she thought she was helping those people," Sister Celia sais. "She must have believed Oskar took them to a real safe house, although later she had her doubts."

"Have you met any of Oskar's friends?" I asked.

"Farah, as you know. Do you think she's involved?"

"No. She only met Oskar a week ago. Any other friends?"

"A few people have come by Safe Harbor over the years, but nobody really stands out."

I got up and took a few garlic cloves from an earthenware pot on the counter. I handed them to Devon. "The first time I visited Safe Harbor, I saw Oskar with a man with long blond hair."

"That would be Yuri. I'd forgotten about him. He comes from Russia. Can't think of his last name." She closed her eyes. "It's appalling what they were up to. And what's even more appalling is that it all comes back to Safe Harbor. Our house is meant to be a home for refugees."

"You've done wonderful things for people there," I said.

"I should have put two and two together when refugees started disappearing. What's happened is monstrous."

"It is." Monsters. That's exactly what Oskar and his gang were.

She pushed her chair back from the table. "And I'll never find another maintenance man for what I paid Oskar."

Sister Celia turned down my dinner invitation. She planned to visit her father that evening.

"Looks like we'll be dining alone," I said to Devon. "Laura and Ryan are taking in a movie. And Tracy has a date with someone called Jamie. He's a partner at the law firm, so he's probably my age and divorced three times."

"You worry too much."

"It's what I do best." I squeezed his shoulder and went to answer the phone.

Sophie Konstantopoulos was on the line. She'd just had a visit from the police.

"Same policemen that come here when Jude die," she said. "They show me photo and I know the guy. He the one bring people to Jude."

Oskar!

Chapter Twenty-Six

Yuri

"Yes….yes….I understand…It will be done." Yuri snapped his cell phone shut and stared out of Coffee Time's window. The boss was angry.

He took a sip from his cup. Oskar, what were you thinking? You wanted to cut corners and look what has happened. You learned no lessons from Bosnia.

The boss had asked Yuri how much Oskar's woman knew. Maybe nothing, maybe everything. Oskar liked to brag, so Yuri couldn't be sure.

Yuri had told the boss he had seen Oskar's woman at Safe Harbor, that she was the sister of a volunteer, an Iraqi called Raad. Her name was Farah and he knew where she worked.

A couple of days before he died, Oskar had picked Farah up at work and he had just missed getting his hands on Ali. Oskar had asked Yuri to keep an eye on the house where Farah worked in case the Somali returned.

"Find out what this woman knows and who she's told," the boss had just now told Yuri. "Let her know how…persuasive you can be."

Working for the boss had not been difficult and the money had been good. Yuri had kept his eyes and his ears open. He needed to learn the ropes so he could start up a similar business of his own one day.

But then the Somali had escaped and the operation had started to unravel.

He zipped up his black leather jacket. He needed to put matters right. Oskar had blown it, but he could get the job done. He would show the boss that he could take Oskar's place.

Chapter Twenty-Seven

Pat

The room was still dark when I turned on the bedside light the next morning. Six-thirty was much too early to get up on a Sunday. I snuggled down against Devon.

He turned and gathered me into his arms. "Like this?"

"Um…"

"I sensed some hesitation when I invited myself here."

He had been a wonderful help the day before. I couldn't have taken on Oskar by myself. And I didn't know what I would have done when Tommy fell onto the tracks. But I wasn't sure what I wanted from Devon in the grand scheme of things. In fact, I didn't want to think grand scheme at all.

"I was tired. Overwhelmed."

He stroked my face. "That's okay. We'll take it slowly, see what happens. You set the agenda."

Hey, this was different. I'd never set the agenda with Michael, I'd always followed his. But I had been in the driver's seat in recent years and I liked it.

I pushed away thoughts of Michael and ran a hand down Devon's back.

Two hours later, I glanced out the kitchen window. It had snowed overnight, but not enough to warrant shoveling the sidewalk and drive.

Tracy handed Tommy cutlery to set the table. "It's a full house this morning," she said.

I poured myself a mug of coffee.

225

Ryan came into the kitchen. "Morning. Laura up yet? We're going skating at City Hall."

I saw black stubble on his head. He had let his hair grow.

Tracy looked up from the bagels she was slicing. "You brought skates along?"

"No. I'll buy a pair." He pulled out a chair.

"Is that a good idea, son?" Devon said, joining Ryan at the table. "Maybe you can rent."

Ryan shrugged. "I'll put it on my card. Mom will pay."

"Ryan, there's a place that rents skates over on Mount Pleasant and it's probably open on Sundays." Tracy slid into a chair beside Devon. "Check it out after breakfast. Mom will let Laura take her car."

"Good idea," Devon said. "Your flight's this evening?"

"Tomorrow morning. No classes on Mondays this term."

"What movie did you see last night?" I asked.

"The first *Planet of the Apes* at a rep theater."

Laura appeared, stifling a yawn. "It was cool. And we stayed for the original *Star Wars*."

"I didn't see a movie yesterday," Tommy said.

I put a hand on his shoulder. "Maybe next weekend."

"I don't want to go back to that school."

"We'll see what your grandmother says." And the police. Oskar hadn't been working alone. There were others out there who might want to silence Tommy.

Laura appraised her sister. "Don't you look radiant this morning."

Tracy's cheeks flushed and she got up from the table. "Forgot the cantaloupe."

Tracy did have a certain glow. She seemed...very happy.

"So what's the name of this dude you're seeing?" Laura asked.

"Jamie. Jamie Collins."

"Mom says he's a partner at your firm," Laura persisted. "That means he's a geezer, right?"

"Laura," I said.

"It's a perfectly natural question."

"How old do you have to be to be a geezer?" Devon asked.

"Well..." Laura appraised him. "I guess about("

"My age." He chuckled.

The phone rang and Tracy hurried to answer it. "Mom. For you."

It was Hardy. "This a good time to come by?"

"It's fine. We'll have coffee on."

"Where is he?" Hardy took a sip from his mug.

"Walking our dog with Devon and Ryan. Have the results from his tests come in?"

"Urine tested positive for benzos. Benzodiazepine, a sedative available on the street. Is he still groggy?"

"He seems to be back to normal this morning."

"We matched Jacovic's boots with prints in Norah Seaton's backyard."

"And Sophie Konstantopoulos, Jude's neighbor, said Oskar was the one who brought refugees to Jude's home."

Hardy looked at me sharply. "She told you that?"

"She called after you left her place yesterday. Oskar took Tommy because the boy could identify him. So he must have killed Tommy's mother."

Hardy didn't reply.

"Oskar was part of a body-parts racket," I pressed on. "Human remains have been turning up around the city and beyond it. And Ali saw medical equipment in the house he was taken to. Seems like it's set up as a clinic."

Hardy's face remained impassive.

"Oskar appeared to be the only person who brought refugees to Jude so there may not be anyone else Tommy can identify."

"We can't take that chance," Hardy said.

"You don't think Oskar was working on his own."

"Jacovic was no doubt working with others." Hardy seemed to be choosing his words carefully. "And they may think Tommy knows something that could lead us to them. They may be looking for Farah Alwan too," he added. "We told her yesterday to keep out of sight for a while."

Of course. They would assume that Oskar had told Farah about his "business." I made a mental note to call her and tell her to stay at home for a few days.

"Norah Seaton wants the boy with her," Hardy said.

"Central Canada College runs a tight ship. They wouldn't let me even get a glimpse of him when I went up there last week."

"That's right. And, if we have to, we'll take the boy to the school ourselves. But it would be better to have the family's co-operation. I thought you could talk to Norah. She likes you."

A chorus of voices and barking at the front door announced that the dog walkers had returned. "Mrs. T, there's a dog that looks like Gigi down the street," Tommy called out. "Only she's black."

"Take off your boots, Tommy. Detective Hardy has something to ask you."

When Tommy was seated beside me, Hardy ran a hand over Maxie, who had positioned herself beside his chair. "Had a dog like this when I was your age,

Tommy." He reached into his brief case. "Do you know this man?" He handed the boy a photo of Oskar.

"That's Oskar. He said I'd see a movie yesterday, but Farah never took me."

"Tommy, you told us that Oskar brought people to stay at your house. Was one of them Suleyman Goven? He may have visited you before Christmas."

Tommy was silent for a few seconds. "Suley? Suley made neat things with my Leggo. Spaceships and castles and stuff."

Hardy reached into his brief case again and took out a fax. "Is this Suley?"

Tommy took the paper and studied a photograph of a man's face. "Yep, but his hair's short here. Did he get a haircut?"

"He must have. That's it then. Thank you, Tommy."

"No problem." Tommy ran off to the sunroom where Laura and Ryan were going through my movie DVDs.

Devon sat down beside me and I took his hand.

"Was Suleyman Goven at Safe Harbor?" I asked Hardy.

He didn't answer.

"Sister Celia gave you the name of a dentist that worked with the people at Safe Harbor. Was he able to match Suleyman's dental records with…human remains?"

Hardy took a deep breath. "No doubt you'll hear it from that nun. The dental work in one of the skulls has been identified as Goven's. He disappeared from Safe Harbor in November after his refugee claim was turned down."

"Suleyman left Safe Harbor and stayed with Jude," I said. "And then he was killed."

Hardy pulled another fax from his briefcase. "Immigration sent us this." He handed it to me. "Jacovic was sponsored into Canada by his uncle, a Dr. Jan Vrancic who recently retired from Mount Hope Hospital."

"Jan Vrancic."

"You know him?"

"I've met him. The doctor at Ray Leckie's party," I added to Devon. I turned back to Hardy. "Ray is a VP at my firm who is a friend of the doctor and manages his investments. A few days ago, he gave one of Vrancic's accounts to a new advisor at my branch."

"We went to Vrancic's home last night to inform him of his nephew's death," Hardy said. "He said he hadn't seen Jacovic since Christmas."

"I forget what Vrancic's specialty is," Devon said. "Ray mentioned it at the party."

"Nephrologist," Hardy said. "Kidney specialist."

Some of the haggardness had left Norah's face. Her hair was brushed, she had put on lipstick, and she was dressed in a mauve wool skirt and a matching cardigan. After she had fussed over Tommy and made him sit on the sofa beside her and Gigi, she turned to Devon and me.

"You can't imagine how relieved I am. But I don't understand what that man wanted with Tommy. He never asked us for money."

"Tommy says Oskar Jacovic visited his house." I didn't want to elaborate in front of the boy. "He knew Jude."

"So he(" Norah put a hand over her mouth.

"Maybe. But he may be one of several people who were up to something your daughter found out about.

The police think the boarding school is the best place for Tommy right now. The staff watches over those kids like hawks."

She put an arm around Tommy. "He needs to be with his family."

"Norah," I said gently, "after all this is over, Tommy may make his home with you. But not right now. He can't go back to his old school and he won't stay cooped up in this house. You know what happened on Friday night."

Devon and I drove Tommy to Norwood, and handed him over to Gilles Deschenes in the school's lobby.

"Can we go to the movies next weekend?" Tommy asked me.

"We'll see what your grandmother says."

My heart twisted when Deschenes took Tommy's backpack and held open the door to the school's inner sanctum. Devon put an arm around me as we left the building.

We drove the first few miles to the airport in silence. "I don't know," Devon said as we passed the turnoff to the Allen Expressway.

"What's on your mind?"

"I was thinking about what Sister Celia said yesterday. Her big concern seemed to be that she'd lost her maintenance man and how difficult it was to run Safe Harbor."

"Safe Harbor is her life."

"Exactly. What would she do to keep it going? Sacrifice a few for the good of many?"

My anger flared. "No way. How can you even think of something like that? Sister Celia wouldn't part with a single lamb in her flock."

"Okay, okay. Just playing devil's advocate. But here's something you might want to keep in mind. She didn't remember that Yuri guy until you described him, and she claimed she didn't remember his last name. She doesn't strike me as a woman who forgets anyone's name."

I stared at the road ahead, seething with anger. How dare he imply that Sister Celia had anything to do with the missing refugees.

In the airport parking arcade, Devon took his bag from the back seat. When I got out of the car, he moved to take me in his arms. But I shrugged him off.

"I have to get back."

"I could take a page from Tommy's book and ask what we're doing next weekend."

"I need some time to myself."

I hunched over the steering wheel as I drove back into the city. But my anger gradually dissipated. By the time I turned off the 401 at the Avenue Road exit, I leaned back in my seat and blew out a giant breath.

Poor Devon. I had vented all the anger and frustration that had built up over the past two weeks on him. He didn't deserve the cold shoulder I'd given him. Still, he shouldn't have implied that Sister Celia was involved in Oskar's operation.

I wondered again who Oskar had been working with.

Arnie was managing a $6-million foundation for Oskar's uncle. Arnie had neither the experience nor the knowledge to run an account of that size, even with Ray's help. I wasn't sure how well he would handle the four small accounts we had given him.

Oskar, Jan, Ray, Arnie. Was it a coincidence that Jan was Oskar's uncle? I remembered the axiom of equality from my high-school geometry: things equal to equal things were equal to each other. Jan was Oskar's uncle, and Jan and Ray were buddies from university. Was there a connection between Oskar and Ray?

I parked on a street that ran off Eglinton Avenue and let myself into the office building. With the blinds all closed, our suite was in twilight on that gray, winter afternoon. I turned off the alarm system and switched on the lights in the reception area. I dropped my parka and my handbag on Rose's chair, and headed for Arnie's office. While his computer warmed up, I looked around the room. Tidier than on Thursday, but no attempt had been made to personalize the space. There were no pictures or diplomas on the walls, no golf trophies or memorabilia on the desk.

Who was Arnie Cruickshank? He was Luella's thirty-year-old son who had already flubbed a couple of careers. A man with an overweening sense of his own importance. Other than that, I knew nothing about him. Did he have a special girl or guy in his life? Who were his friends? What were his hobbies? I'd seen sports gear in there a few days before. Did he work out at a fitness center, or play squash or soccer?

I turned back to Arnie's computer. He still didn't have a password, but I saw that he could now access the Tierney Pratt system. I found the client accounts Stéphane and I had given him.

The Bosnian Youth Relief Foundation files were on a separate system. I combed through the foundation's investments. Several of the stocks were real slowpokes.

I closed the investment file, then moved on to deposits and withdrawals, supporters, current projects and special events. Centered at the bottom of each page were the words, Greek Cypriot Wealth Management, and an address in Nicosia. Was Norris Cassidy holding an account for a brokerage firm in Cyprus?

I was about to print out the first document, when I heard the office door open. Quickly, I shut down all the files. The screen displayed only the desktop with its blue background when Arnie appeared in the doorway.

"What are you doing in my office?"

I felt a flicker of fear. I was alone with a man who was considerably bigger than me. A man who had found me logged into his computer. But I forced myself to smile at him.

"Hello, Arnie. I just finished up some work in my office. I thought I'd check your machine for virus screens. Just as I thought, there aren't any. I'll call IT first thing tomorrow."

I shut down the computer and stood up. "What brings you in here on a Sunday?"

He looked at me through narrowed eyes. "Work."

I smiled at him. "Well, don't wear yourself out. We're back in here tomorrow morning."

I ran down the five flights of stairs and cursed fate for bringing Arnie to the office just then. First thing in the morning, he would get himself a password and I would never get another look at those files.

Chapter Twenty-Eight

Pat

Maxie jumped on me when I opened the door.

"Down, girl." The dog raced around the ground floor, and did a frenzied dance in the hall while I hung up my parka.

"You can go out in the yard, but you'll have to wait for Laura to take you for a walk." I grabbed her collar, and led her through the house and out the French doors. Then I took a casserole from the freezer and the makings of salad from the fridge. Sunday dinner was a ritual. Seven o'clock sharp.

The clock on the stove told me that I had plenty of time. I let Maxie back into the house and sank down on a sofa. I took several deep breaths and tried to shake the black cloud that was pressing down on me. I turned on the lamp on the end table. The diamonds on my left hand sparkled under the light. They seemed to be mocking me.

With a surge of anger, I pulled off the eternity ring and the wedding band, and threw them across the room.

The cloud began to lift. It was about time that I took off those rings.

A rap sounded on the back doors. I turned on the outside light and lifted a shutter. Ali was standing on the deck.

He gave me an inquiring look when I opened the door.

"I'm alone." I held the door open for him.

"I watched your house. I saw you arrive." He held up a hand when I grabbed Maxie's collar. "It is all right."

But the dog wanted to play so I took her into my study.

I was the first to speak when we were seated in front of the fireplace. "Oskar is dead."

Ali's eyes widened. "How...how did he die?"

I gave him an abbreviated version of the events of the previous day. "He wasn't working alone. Did you meet any of his associates?"

"Only Sister Celia. And Jude Seaton and her son."

"What about Yuri? Tall guy with long blond hair."

"Yuri, yes. I saw him with Oskar at Safe Harbor."

"Does he know that Oskar was looking for you?"

He shook his head. "I do not know that."

"Be careful. You are probably still in danger. Did you see anyone at the house Oskar took you to?"

"All I saw was basement of that house. Oskar opened one of the doors and put me in that room." He let out a big sigh. "I cannot keep running. I thought about what you said. Mrs. Tierney, I will take you to the house."

I wanted to cheer. The house was the key to the gang's operations. And Tommy wouldn't be safe until all its members were put away.

"Can we go now, Ali? It would be better to see it in the daylight, but I'll be at work all week."

He was silent for a few moments. "Sister Celia must come with us. If people are held there now, she can talk to them. They will trust her. Later, you can tell the police."

"If people are being held there("

"Where I come from, men in uniform(army, police(do terrible things. It is same in the homelands of other

236

refugees. You will say it is different here in Canada, but these people may not know that."

"Okay, we'll get Sister Celia. We'll do what she thinks is best."

He stood. "She will know what to do."

I thought of the question Devon had raised: How far would Sister Celia go to keep Safe Harbor running?

No, I couldn't believe that of Sister Celia. Everything she worked for was completely at odds with what appeared to be going on in that house Ali had been taken to. My gut instinct told me that Celia De Franco was a person I could trust. I could trust her with my life(and anyone else's.

I inclined my head toward the French doors. "We'll go out this way." I knew that Ali liked to move in the shadows. "I've pulled my car up to the end of the drive. It's right beside the house."

Chapter Twenty-Nine

Yuri

Yuri sipped coffee from his thermal mug and studied the street through the SUV's tinted windshield. He wriggled in his seat, wishing that he could stretch his legs.

Patience, he told himself. The thrill of the kill would always make the wait worthwhile.

He peered at the house through his binoculars. A Volvo pulled out of the driveway with two figures inside it. He recognized the Tierney woman, but the head and face of her companion were hidden by a hood. He thought about following them, but decided it would be better to stay and watch the house.

Twenty minutes later he was regretting his decision, when a woman wearing a black head scarf rounded the street corner and walked up to the Tierney home. At the front door, she turned and looked up and down the street.

Yuri adjusted the binoculars. If it wasn't little Farah.

He watched her let herself into the house and waited. Ten minutes later, satisfied that she wasn't leaving, he started up the SUV and drove down the street. When he saw that there were no vehicles parked in the Tierney driveway, he pulled in to the end of the drive.

He reached into the glove compartment and took out a roll of duct tape and what looked like a cell phone. Smiling, he turned the device over in his big hand. His new stun gun. If the girl wouldn't come along quietly…Zap! She would be in no position to resist.

He looked up and down the street. Then he made his way around the house. The windows were all dark except for a light in the room at the back. He examined the lock on the double back doors and pulled a set of picks from his pocket. He jiggled a pick and swung one door open. He heard a dog barking somewhere in the house.

He glanced at the woman who was curled up asleep on a sofa. Then he darted around the main floor to find out where the barking was coming from. He didn't like dogs.

Satisfied that the dog was shut up in a room off the kitchen, he returned to Farah. He shook her shoulder and felt her stir beneath her coat. "Farah, wake up. We must go."

She mumbled something and pulled her coat up around her shoulders.

"Now." He pulled her into a sitting position.

"Ow." She rubbed her eyes and opened them. "Who are you?"

"Come." He held out a hand to help her stand.

She let him help her up and her coat slid to the floor.

"Must hurry. Oskar wait for you."

Oskar's name seemed to snap her out of her drowsiness.

"Oskar." Her eyes flashed. "He is dead. Train come?"

"Oskar hurt, yes, but not dead. He ask for you."

She eyed him, suspicion written on her face. "Oskar send you?"

"You not remember me?" Yuri tried to sound as though she had hurt his feelings. "I am Yuri, friend of Oskar. I see you at Safe Harbor."

He froze at the sound of a door opening and feet stamping at the front of the house.

"Hey, Mrs. Tierney," a male voice called out. "Laura gave me her key. She's over at Jessie's."

"Quiet," Yuri whispered to Farah. He placed a finger to his lips. Then he slipped out of the sunroom.

"Mrs. Tierney…Hey, who are you? What("

In the front hallway, Yuri held the stun gun on the side of the young man's shaven head. It sent him slumping to the floor. He hunched over him and wrapped tape around his ankles and wrists. Then he slapped a strip of tape across his mouth.

Behind him, he heard a gasp. Little Farah was too nosey for her own good.

She was cowering on the sofa when he returned to the back of the house.

"Intruder. You safe now." He held out the cell phone, and pressed a button on the device. "Speed dial. You talk to Oskar."

"I don't know…"

"Here." He thrust the cell phone at her.

She reached out for it.

Her body twitched and spasmed. She collapsed on the floor in front of the sofa.

Yuri bound her hands behind her and hoisted her up on his shoulder. She was a tiny little thing, hardly weighed more than a bag of potatoes. Cute too.

"Now Farah, you, me and young man, we go for ride."

Chapter Thirty

Pat

Sister Celia came to the door with a black smudge on her face. "It took you long enough to get here...Pat! I thought you were the guy from the Handyman Connection."

Then she saw Ali behind me. "Ali. Come in, come in." She took us to her suite.

"You're back here to stay, Ali?" she asked when she had closed the door.

"Yes," he said softly.

"You can have the room you shared with Enrique. We will appeal your case."

He bowed his head. "Thank you."

"So if you have bags with you?"

"Sister, we want you come with us."

"You're showing us that house?"

He nodded.

"We must shut it down," she said. "Where is it?"

"The east part of the city. I do not know the address, but I will be able to find it."

"When we get there, we can decide what we should do," I said. "If anyone is being held..."

"Understood." Sister Celia clapped her hands. "So what are we waiting for?"

Night had fallen when we turned into Jude's street. I pulled up in front of her house and turned the car around. In the passenger seat beside me, Ali moaned. I hoped he wasn't about to bail out on us. Sister Celia reached out from the back seat and placed a hand on his shoulder.

Then he told me to drive up the street and turn right on Danforth Avenue.

"A little farther," he said when we got to where the Danforth merges into Kingston Road. After a couple of traffic lights, he indicated that I should turn south on one of the streets that runs down to the Scarborough Bluffs, the cliffs along Toronto's eastern lakefront.

As I made the turn, he pointed to a variety store on the corner. "That was where I got taxi."

I noted the name on street sign, which was illuminated by the bright street light. "Far down this street?"

"End of street."

Two blocks down, I slowed the Volvo to a crawl. "Look familiar?"

He wrinkled his brow.

The houses all looked the same. Tidy, brick story-and-a-half cottages on snow-covered lawns.

At the end of the street was a wire fence. A sign posted on it read: "Danger. No trespassing. Toronto Hydro." Behind the fence, transmission towers loomed on an expanse of snow-covered ground that ran down to the bluffs.

"That is it." Ali pointed to the brick house at the end of the block. Its front door faced the street, and a tall cedar hedge screened it from its neighbors in the back and on the north side. A door on its south side was sheltered by a carport at the end of the driveway.

A low brick building surrounded by more wire fencing stood across the street from the house. "Danger. High Voltage," proclaimed another Toronto Hydro sign on its fence.

Ali stared at the fenced-off building.

"Hydro substation," I said.

He looked back at the house he'd been in. "Oskar found key above the side door. We entered that way."

The house seemed to be asleep. Its blinds were drawn and snow covered its front walk and driveway. Snow had fallen the previous night, and it looked as if no one had entered or left the house that day.

But that didn't mean the house was unoccupied, I thought.

I noted the street number on the wall beside the front door. "You're sure this is it?" I asked Ali.

"I ran out very fast." The whites of his eyes shone in the streetlight. "But I am certain this is the house."

The place looked so ordinary. A brick house with a Georgian door and flower boxes under the front windows. I shivered, chilled by the idea of what might be going on inside it.

I turned the car around and parked three houses up the street. "Let's go," I said.

Ali grabbed my arm. "No."

I shook off his hand. "We have to make sure it's the right house. You've been inside it."

"We'll all go," Sister Celia said. "There's safety in numbers."

I opened my door. "We have to be quiet. Don't bang the car doors."

The night was cold and our boots crunched on the snow underfoot.

"They will hear us," Ali said in a loud whisper.

"Shh," Sister Celia said.

I let the way to the back of the house in the shadows cast by the hedge. Sister Celia and Ali were close behind me and something darted across our path. I froze, my heart thudding in my ears. I exhaled in relief when I saw that it was a cat.

"Oh," Ali moaned. "Let us go back to the car."

From where we stood, I could see two back basement windows covered with bars. A light was on in one of the basement rooms. I led the way up to the window. One of the slats on its Venetian blind was ajar and I peered through the opening that it created. A doctor's examination table covered with a white sheet. Beside the table, a white cabinet. There was no one in the room.

"That is where Oskar put me," Ali whispered behind me. "There were no bars on the window then."

Beyond the room, I saw a darkened hall and the rest of the house seemed to be in darkness. Suddenly, the crooked slat fell into place, blocking my view. Fear sliced through me.

Ali jumped away from the window, ready to run. I grabbed his jacket. "Stand against the wall. If you run across the lawn, you'll be seen."

Sister Celia took his arm and we flattened ourselves against the wall.

I counted to sixty, then approached the window again.

Ali whimpered. "Let us go back to the car. Please."

The light was still on, and I couldn't see shadows or movements behind the blind. I figured that gravity had drawn down the slat. "Nobody's in there. And we're out of here," I said.

On our way back to the car, I realized that we were leaving footprints in the snow. I hoped that the police would arrive before Oskar's associates saw our tracks.

I turned to Sister Celia. "Think it's time to bring in the police?"

"You bet."

I looked at our tracks in the snow. The police would know that we had been to the house and looked through the basement window. But that couldn't be helped.

I clicked the car doors open with my remote. "I'll drive around the block and call Hardy."

I was about to turn the key in the ignition when my cell phone rang in my handbag.

It was Tracy and she sounded frantic. "Mom, I found Farah's coat and handbag in the sunroom, but she's not here."

"You're sure they're hers?"

"There's a wallet in the bag with a bus pass that she's signed."

Static cut off her voice.

"I can't hear you."

In a few moments the static died down. "You there, Mom?"

"Yes, the connection is better now. You found Farah's coat and bag. What else?"

"Maxie was going berserk. She'd been shut up in your study."

She paused. "And Raad called a few minutes ago. He said Farah went out this afternoon after telling her mother she was visiting a friend. But when he called the friend's place, Farah wasn't there. The friend said she hadn't heard from her in weeks.

"And there was a voice-mail message from Farah." The pitch of Tracy's voice rose. "She was babbling about what the cops had put her through yesterday. Said she was on her way over here to talk to you."

"What time did she leave the message?"

"Four-fifty."

"Hang on a sec." I turned to Ali. "While you watched my house, did you see anybody out there?"

His eyes grew wide. "Nobody, until you came in your car. I was behind the bushes at the end of the driveway. Why?"

"The woman you saw at my house the other day?Farah?seems to be missing." I turned my attention back to Tracy. "Where's Laura?"

"She just got in."

"Mom!" Laura shouted into the phone. "I had to wrap up some schoolwork at Jessie's place so I gave Ryan my key. But he's not here."

"When did he leave you?"

"Around five-thirty."

Farah missing, then Ryan. "He'll probably turn up soon. Put your sister back on."

"Stay inside, both of you," I told Tracy. "Lock the doors and don't open..." Static erupted again and the line went dead.

I snapped my cell shut and turned to Sister Celia. "Farah must have turned up at the house just after I left with Ali. She probably answered the door. They may take her?"

"Here," Ali cried. "To this house."

Sister Celia and I exchanged glances.

"And Ryan's missing," I said. "Devon's son. Laura gave him her house key, maybe an hour ago, while she finished some schoolwork with a friend. He must have got to the house when Farah was taken."

What if Laura had come back with Ryan? Or Tracy had arrived home just then? A chill ran down my spine.

"We must not stay here," Ali said. "It is too dangerous."

"Call the police. Now," Sister Celia said. "Murder, kidnapping...We're in over our heads."

"Okay." I took Hardy's card from the dashboard. I read the number with the help of the miniature flashlight on my key chain, and punched it in. I paused, then punched it in again.

"Bad news. Battery's dead."

Sister Celia groaned. "And I left my cell at Safe Harbor."

A vehicle's lights lit up the street. "Get down," I said.

We crouched down inside the Volvo. When the vehicle had passed us, I raised my head and watched a black SUV pull into the driveway of the house we'd been looking at. A tall figure with fair hair got out and surveyed the street. It was the man I had seen with Oskar at Safe Harbor.

"Yuri." I ducked back down.

When I lifted my head again, Yuri had his back to me. He lifted something heavy out of the hatchback. He slung it over his shoulder, as if he were carrying a rolled-up carpet. I spotted a shaven head at one end. Ryan. I ducked back down.

"What's going on?" Sister Celia whispered.

"Yuri's got Ryan tied up. He's taking him into the house."

I counted to one hundred. When I raised my head again, Yuri was helping Farah out of the hatchback. Her arms were bound behind her, but she wasn't trussed up like Ryan.

I ducked back down. "He's got Farah, too."

I had let Farah go off to meet Oskar the day before. And I hadn't warned her that she might be in danger.

"What will we do?" Ali asked.

"Celia, you and Ali take the car. Call the police from a pay phone."

"Hey," she said, "what about you?"

"I'm worried that Yuri will do something to Farah and Ryan before the police can get here."

"And what do you think you can do to stop him?"

I shrugged. "Nothing. But if he leaves the house, I'll try to get inside."

"Then you'll need my help. Ali, can you drive this car?"

"Yes," he said.

I was about to argue with her, but I didn't want to waste more time. "Okay. Celia and I will stay here. Ali, find a pay phone and call a police officer by the name of Neil Hardy. You don't have to identify yourself. Just ask him to send officers over here. Mention my name." I rummaged in my handbag and handed him some quarters.

"But?"

"No buts, Ali," Sister Celia said. "Go for help. Hurry."

"But?"

I handed him my car key. "Here."

He stared at the key, then wrapped his hand around it.

I took a business card out of my handbag and, by the light of the small flashlight, scribbled Hardy's name and phone number, and the address of the house on the back. "Hardy will need to know where we are."

He tucked the card into his jacket pocket. Sister Celia and I got out of the car and ran for cover behind a bushy spruce tree.

"Godspeed," Sister Celia whispered as Ali started the Volvo's engine.

We ran across snow-covered front lawns and came to a stop behind the cedar hedge that screened the north side of house.

"If Yuri drives off…" she said.

"We'll try to get Farah and Ryan out."

"But if he stays in the house?"

"The police will be here soon." I put a hand on her arm. "With all that's happened since Jude came to see me, the least I can do is stay here and wait for the police. Stand guard, try to protect Tommy, avenge Jude's death...all of that."

She put an arm around me. "I haven't been vigilant at Safe Harbor. I should have kept a closer eye on Oskar. I should have asked our residents some hard questions when people began disappearing. They fled one horror and walked into another, right under my watch. Some shepherdess I've been."

I gave her a hug and turned my attention back to the house. The lights were still out. "Looks like Yuri might have called it a night."

"You're not thinking what I think you're thinking? Getting Farah and Ryan out?"

I shook my head. "The police are on their way. Let's go around to the back. See if they're in the basement."

We followed our tracks to the back of the property. In the morning, I thought, there would be a well-worn path through the snow.

The light was still on in the basement window. I detected movement behind the blinds.

"He's got them in that room," I said.

A light went on in the house above us.

"Yuri's upstairs," Sister Celia said. "That's probably the kitchen up there."

"Ali said there's a key above the side door. We should get it for the police. Yuri won't let them in."

"The cops will kick in the door."

"A key would give them the element of surprise."

We continued on to the side of the house that faced the bluffs.

I slipped on a patch of ice on the driveway behind the SUV, but I caught myself before I fell. "Watch out for the ice."

At the side door, I ran my hand along the top of the doorframe. "He must have taken the key in with him."

The door opened. Yuri stood in the doorway. He held up a key in his left hand. "Looking for this, ladies?"

Sister Celia grabbed my arm and we both stepped back.

"I see Volvo on street, footprints in back of house, then no car." Yuri advanced toward us. "You think you smart, moving car to next street."

He didn't know there was a third person who had gone for help. C'mon, Ali!

"You like to call for help?" He held out a cell phone in his right hand.

"Here." He pressed it against Sister Celia's face. She gasped, writhed and fell to the ground.

He spun toward me and pressed the cell against my cheek. Pain shot through me. I blacked out before I hit the ground.

Chapter Thirty-One

Pat

"Get up!"

I felt something slam into my leg. I winced and opened my eyes. I was on my back on a cold floor. I had no idea how long I'd been out.

"On your feet." Yuri waved a gun at me. "You think I stand here all night?"

I pushed myself to my feet. My legs felt like noodles and my hands were trembling. A dull pain hammered at the back of my head.

I looked around and saw Sister Celia, her eyes half-closed, on a chair beside the white cabinet. She looked as dazed as I felt.

We were in the basement room we had seen from the back of the house. The room that was set up for medical examinations. Ryan and Farah were bound to chairs with duct tape, their arms behind them. Ryan's ankles were taped to the legs of his chair, but Farah's feet and legs were free. Strips of tape were plastered over their mouths.

Yuri thrust a roll of tape into my hands. "Tie her up." He pointed a handgun at Sister Celia.

I bound her wrists behind her chair as loosely as I dared.

"Tighter." He brandished his gun.

I wound the tape around her hands again.

"Now around her middle."

I bound her waist to the back of the chair.

If he'd given me rope instead of tape, we might have been able to loosen some knots.

"Now you." He pushed me onto a fourth chair. He taped my wrists behind me, and bound my torso to the back of the chair.

Then he surveyed us and grunted.

"You think you smarter than Yuri, eh?" He walked over to Farah and Ryan and ripped the strips of tape off their mouths.

"Ow," Farah cried.

Ryan sputtered and coughed.

Yuri grinned. "Go ahead, yell all you want. No one hear you here. This neighborhood, everyone mind own business. Like you should."

"I need toilet," Farah said.

Yuri laughed. "I think you have to hold it in."

She stamped her feet. "I need to go."

He laughed again and left the room.

"This psycho's going to kill us," Ryan said.

"Hang in, Ryan," I said.

Yuri returned with two handbags. "Your keys in here, Reverend Sister. Keys to Safe Harbor. Not so safe now, eh?" He gave an ugly laugh.

He waved the bag in front of her face. "Somali they call Ali. He back at Safe Harbor now Oskar is gone?"

Then he held up my bag. "And keys to your house, Blondie. You got two pretty daughters."

An icy hand gripped my heart. I sent up a silent prayer for Ali to get the police. Quickly!

"I see you ladies and gentleman tomorrow morning. Sweet dreams." He switched off the light and slammed the door, taking our handbags with him.

I heard him walk through the main floor of the house. Then the side door slammed and the SUV's engine revved. I jiggled my chair. I could move my hands and fingers, but not enough to rip off the tape. I groaned in frustration. I had to warn the girls.

Farah moaned. "I need toilet."

"Toilet's the least of your worries," Ryan said.

"It's so dark in here," Sister Celia said. "I can't see a thing."

I had my back to the wall in the armless metal chair. The door was directly across from me and I thought the light switch was beside it.

With the exception of Ryan, Yuri hadn't tied our feet. I jiggled the chair and dragged it forward on the linoleum, moving carefully. I didn't want to topple onto the floor. Taped to the chair as I was, I wouldn't be able to get up.

When I thought I was close enough to the opposite wall, I raised my left leg in what I hoped was the direction of the switch. Nothing. I dragged the chair forward again. Two more kicks and light flooded the room.

"Oh," Farah cried.

"Smart gal," Sister Celia said.

"You think we'll get out of here alive?" Ryan asked.

I saw the outline of the bars on the window. Ali had cut the wire mesh and climbed out of the window, but that exit had been blocked. I remembered the scissors Ali had found in the cabinet.

The cabinet was on my right and Sister Celia was on its other side. Farah was on a chair beside her. Ryan was across from Farah beside the examination table. It was a small room, and we were all fairly close together.

I dragged my chair back a bit, then veered to the right.

"What are you doing?" Sister Celia asked.

"Ali said there were scissors in this cabinet."

"I need toilet," Farah wailed.

Sister Celia started dragging her chair away from the wall. After what seemed like hours, she and I were both in front of the cabinet. Sister Celia was facing it and I had my back to it.

"A bit more to the right, Pat, and you can grab the door handle."

I jiggled my chair sideways and reached behind me. My fingers touched a metal handle. I hooked my fingers through it.

The stomping of feet sounded above us, followed by the loud bang of a door slamming shut.

"Fuck it," Ryan moaned. "He's back."

"The light," Sister Celia hissed. "How can we turn it off?"

The sound of whistling came through the door. Something dirge-like. I recognized the notes of Tchaikovsky's "Marche Slave" and grimaced. It was much too appropriate.

"Please don't come in here," Sister Celia said softly.

"Hey, you like pizza?" Yuri called down to us. "Come and get it." He gave a harsh laugh. "No? Then I save some for my breakfast." He laughed again and his heavy footsteps receded.

He'd gone out for food. Not for the girls.

The faint sound of music, laughter and clapping came from upstairs.

"He's got the TV on," I said.

"How will that help us?" Ryan asked.

"He won't check on us if he's distracted."

"I don't think he's locked us in," Sister Celia said. "That's a plus."

"How is it a plus?" Ryan asked. "We can't walk out of here. He didn't have to lock the door."

Farah groaned. "I need toilet."

"The cabinet, Pat," Sister Celia said. "Pull the handle on the cabinet."

I grasped the metal handle and pulled.

"Good. Now move your chair forward. I'll kick the door open wider."

I shuffled the chair forward. "What's in there?"

"Gauze, bandages. Scissors on the middle shelf. You should be able to reach them if you move your chair back again."

I jiggled my chair back and rotated my hand behind my back. I heard a small thud.

I saw the scissors on the floor near my feet.

I stared at them, helpless. "What now?" I was on the verge of tears. Time was passing. We had to get out.

With a surge of anger, I craned my neck and looked at Farah. She was doing nothing but complaining. "You've got to help us, Farah."

"I need toilet."

"Sooner or later, we will all need the toilet. Get your chair over here. Now."

She started to move her chair forward.

"That's it, Farah," Sister Celia said. "Good girl. Get over in front of Pat."

After what seemed like an eternity, Farah faced me. Sister Celia was parallel to me with her back to Farah.

"Kick off your boot, Farah," I said.

She scowled, but kicked the boot off her right foot.

"Get the other boot off, then take the sock off your right foot."

When Farah was in her stocking feet, she peeled the sock off her right foot with the toes on her left foot.

"Now pick up the scissors."

She put her big toe through one of the scissors' handles.

Sister Celia sucked in her breath. "Good."

"Now, very slowly so you don't drop them, put the scissors in Sister Celia's hand."

Farah slowly raised her leg.

I exhaled loudly. "They're about two inches from your hands, Celia. Push your chair back a bit and take them from Farah."

"Whoa." Sister Celia's fingers almost touched the scissors. "Take it slowly. Lift the index finger on your right hand. Careful, they look sharp."

I heaved a sigh when she had the scissors in her hand. "Great!"

Farah," I said, "you'll have to move your chair around now so Celia can cut the tape on your wrists."

When Farah and Sister Celia were back-to-back, I drew a deep breath. "This will be tricky. I don't want either of you to get cut."

"They're pretty sharp," Sister Celia said.

"With your other hand, Celia, can you touch Farah's wrist?"

She reached out with her left hand and her fingers brushed Farah's hand.

"Can you get a finger under the tape?"

She grunted an assent.

"Ow," Farah cried as Sister Celia pulled away a bit of tape.

"Okay, open the scissors. Let's do this in slow motion. Slowly, slowly, slowly. Farah, you'll feel the tip of a scissor blade against your skin. Don't jump. Celia, put one blade under the tape."

Farah scrunched up her face as if she were in agony.

"There, you've got it."

Sister Celia opened and closed the scissors.

"You may have to saw through it. That tape is pretty strong."

"Hurts," Farah said.

"Quiet. It's just a bit of tape burn. Farah, you're our only hope. Your hands will be free in a minute. Then you can cut the tape around your waist and get us loose."

"Now I use toilet." Farah rubbed her wrists.

The rest of us pulled tape off our clothing. I checked my watch; it was ten to nine.

"Hang on," I said. "We'll go out together. There may be a washroom down here."

Just as Sister Celia had thought, the door to the room we were in was unlocked. We found a small washroom across the hall.

"You're joking, right?" Ryan said. "A madman wants to kill us and we're stopping for a pee break?"

I glared at him. "You're free, thanks to Farah. So let her use the washroom."

"Shh," Sister Celia said. "Listen."

Loud snorts and grunts punctuated the drone of the TV program upstairs.

"His snoring is load enough to wake the dead," Sister Celia said.

"Perfect for us, though." I turned to Farah and waved her into the washroom. "Be quick. And don't flush."

"Come here, Pat." Sister Celia had another basement door open. She flicked on the light switch inside the room.

A steel table stood in the middle of the room under lights suspended from the ceiling. Cabinets with glass doors lined two of the walls. The shelves were filled with bottles and jars and white linens. What looked like a massive freezer was built into a third wall. A cabinet with drawers stretched across the fourth wall. I pulled a drawer open and saw steel instruments neatly laid out on a white towel.

I gasped. "Good God!"

"What's this?" Ryan whispered behind me.

"Tell you later."

Sister Celia opened the door to the next room. It held two hospital beds, neatly made up with white sheets and white covers, with a bedside table between them.

Then the toilet flushed. I groaned. I had told her not to flush.

Farah stepped out of the washroom, and I motioned for all of us to be quiet. I listened carefully.

The snoring had stopped. The TV had been silenced.

"Great," Ryan said. "Our chances of getting out of here just went down the can."

Chapter Thirty-Two

Yuri

Yuri sat up on the couch and rubbed his eyes. A half-eaten pizza and a half-empty bottle of vodka were on the coffee table in front of him. His gun and his zapper were next to the vodka.

He yawned, groaned and rubbed his temples.

He closed his eyes, then opened them again.

Flushing. He could have sworn he had heard a toilet flush. But that was impossible. The women and the boy were tied up.

He picked up the remote and clicked off the TV. Had the flushing been part of a commercial?

He walked over to the front window and looked out at the street. The Tierney woman's Volvo was now parked down the street. There was a figure inside it.

He hurried back to the coffee table, grabbed his gun and ran into the kitchen. The door to the basement was closed. He shook his head. There was need to check the basement. The prisoners were tied up tight.

Gun in hand, he returned to the window to watch the street.

Chapter Thirty-Three

Pat

"Why isn't he coming down here?" Sister Celia whispered.

"I don't know, but that's good for us," I said. "Something must have his attention upstairs. The police may be outside."

"But he's awake," Ryan said. "He'll hear us if we try to get out."

I held up a hand. "Keep quiet. I'll see what's going on. Then we can figure out our next move."

"Some plan," Ryan said.

I slipped off my boots and eased myself up the basement steps. I stopped in front of the door to the main floor. I took a deep breath and pulled the door open a crack.

The side door to the house was directly in front of me. Opening the basement door wider, I poked my head out and saw another short flight of stairs that led to the kitchen. Beyond the kitchen, light spilled from what I assumed was the living room.

I took a deep breath and scrambled up the stairs. From the kitchen, I could see Yuri at the living-room window, his back to me. He had the gun in one hand. A pizza box, a bottle and the stun gun were on a coffee table.

I retreated down the stairs to the basement.

"He's by the front window with his gun," I said. "He's watching something outside."

"Ali? The police?" Sister Celia asked.

"Can't say. But he's holding his gun, so it's not his buddies." I paused. "And that zapper thing that knocked us out("

"Cell-phone stun gun," Ryan said. "They sell them back home."

"(it's on the coffee table."

"Maybe we should make a run for the side door," Sister Celia said.

I shook my head. "He's got a gun so one of us could get hurt."

"We all get hurt if we stay here," Farah said.

"We've got to get his gun. Ryan, your dad said you played high-school football."

"Yeah. How's that gonna help us?"

"How are your tackling skills?"

From the kitchen door at the top of the stairs, I saw Yuri standing at the front window. I motioned for Farah to come up the basement stairs and into the kitchen.

"Okay I use washroom?" she called out when she got to the middle of the room.

Yuri wheeled around. "How you get out?" He raised his gun and moved toward her.

Then Ryan sprang into the kitchen. Keeping himself low, he slammed Yuri in the stomach. Yuri crashed into the fridge. His hand flew up and the gun went off.

Yuri smashed Ryan's head with the butt of the gun. Ryan grunted and slumped to the floor. Then Sister Celia ran at Yuri and sent him crashing to the ground. The gun flew out of his hand. Sister Celia kicked it to the back of the kitchen.

I sprinted into the living room and snatched the stun gun off the coffee table.

"Quick!" Sister Celia cried. "Farah and I can't hold him."

I pressed the stun gun against the back of Yuri's head. He writhed and went limp.

There was pounding on the door. "Sister Celia! Mrs. Tierney!"

Chapter Thirty-Four

Yuri

"Police are coming…how did…Ryan, you're bleeding."

The jumble of voices seemed far away. Yuri blinked his eyes open, then quickly closed them. Playing dead had once saved his life.

It was coming back to him. He was at the house, his prisoners had somehow freed themselves and the Tierney woman had knocked him out with the stun gun. The murmur of voices continued, but he sensed no one near him. He slowly raised his head. Their backs were to him. They were talking to the Somali.

He rolled over and sprang to his feet. Farah was closest to him. With his left arm, he grabbed her in a chokehold and pulled her to him. With his right hand, he fished his switchblade from his jacket pocket and snapped it open.

"No one move. All raise hands."

The others turned to face him, their hands in the air.

"You can't get away, Yuri," the nun said. "Oskar's dead. It's all over."

"Let her go," the Somali said. "Take me."

Yuri shook his head. "Women make better hostage."

The Somali took a step toward him. Yuri pointed the tip of the knife at Farah's temple. The Somali glowered, but stepped back and put his hands in the air.

"You won't get far," the nun said. "The police are on their way."

Yuri backed toward the side door, dragging Farah with him, keeping the knife blade near her head. The door was slightly ajar. He pushed it open with his boot.

Outside, he dragged Farah down the driveway to the driver's door of the SUV. The car keys were in his pants pocket. He would have to shift the knife to his left hand and release his hold on the girl.

"No tricks." He eased his left hand away from her throat. He started to lower his right hand when she grabbed his wrist with both hands, yanked it toward her and bit down on it.

"Bitch!" He dropped the knife. Farah kicked it under the vehicle, gave him a shove and ran to the back of the house.

He shook his hand to relieve the pain. Then he pulled the keys from his pocket. He glanced down the street and saw a car with flashing lights approaching. He decided that he would settle scores later.

He scrambled into the SUV, turned the key in the ignition and gunned the engine as he put the vehicle into drive. He had outraced enemies before. He would do it again with the Toronto police.

The SUV hit a patch of ice. In seconds it had spun out of control. He clutched the steering wheel and cursed. The vehicle's momentum carried it onto the street and over the curb. It crashed into a utility pole in front of the substation. An air bag popped up pinning him to the seat. He heard a thud on the roof. He saw a wire with sparks shooting from its end jump onto the hood of the vehicle.

He had to get out! He clawed away the air bag, pushed open the door and stepped onto the ground.

The dancing sparks were the last thing he saw.

Chapter Thirty-Five

Pat

We gave our separate statements at police headquarters, then assembled in a boardroom on the tenth floor. Ali wasn't with us. He had slipped away from the house when the police arrived. I hoped he had been able to make his way back to Safe Harbor.

"Ms. Tierney." Hardy's eyes bored into me across the oak table. "I asked you let us get on with our work. As soon as you knew the location of the house in Scarborough, why weren't you on the phone to me?"

I had gone over this in the statement I'd just given, but I figured I had better answer his question. "Ali didn't want to talk to the police. He was afraid he'd be sent back to Somalia. I thought if he showed me the house, I could tell you where it is."

"And did you tell us, Ms. Tierney? No. You and your friend here," he looked at Sister Celia, "got out of your car and nearly got yourselves killed. I'm going to charge both of you with interfering with a police investigation."

"We tried to call you," Sister Celia said, "but Pat's cell had died."

"And that was the only phone in the city of Toronto?" He wasn't joking.

"We were outside the house then," I said, "and Yuri drove up with Farah and Ryan. We sent Ali to call("

"Ali, he was afraid to call police," Raad cut in. "Instead, he call Safe Harbor. I am there looking for my sister and I answer phone."

Hardy turned to Sister Celia. "Ali Hassan disappeared from Safe Harbor a few weeks ago."

"Yes." She looked him in the eye. "Oskar Jacovic took him away and he hasn't returned."

"Do you know where he's staying?"

"No."

I was sure that God in Her infinite mercy would forgive Sister Celia for her lie. "Ali came to my home early this evening," I said, "and said he would take me to the house."

I went over how Ali had escaped from the house in Scarborough and returned to Jude's home. Hardy had already been told this and I had also given this information in my statement, but he seemed to want to rehash everything as a group. No doubt to see if all versions of events aligned.

"What did Ali say to you on the telephone, Mr. Alwan?"

"He tell me what happen, that Yuri has taken Farah. He give me address of house. He say he wait for me outside house in Mrs. Tierney's car."

"And you called us," Hardy said.

"Yes. Right away I call police. Then I look up directions on Safe Harbor computer and I drive to house. When I get there, police have barrier across street. I tell them my sister is in that house, but they make me wait more than one hour before I see Farah."

Hardy looked at Sister Celia and me. "Why didn't you two go with Ali?"

We looked at each other but said nothing.

"You wanted to play detective, eh? You could have ended up dead."

"What happened to Yuri?" Sister Celia asked.

I looked at her, surprised. We'd had a ringside view of Yuri's final moments from the living room window.

Hardy glanced at his folder. She gave me a wink and I realized that she was trying to get him off our case.

"Plowed into the hydro pole. He would still be alive if he had stayed in his vehicle until a hydro crew arrived."

"With that live wire on the hood?" I asked.

"The SUV was grounded. When he stepped out, he was touching both the vehicle and the ground, and became a conductor of electricity. The charge shot through him to the ground."

"Who was Yuri?" Ryan ran his hand over the spot on his head where Yuri had slammed him with the gun.

"We're checking with the Russian authorities. Yuri Vlasenko?that's what his driver's license has him down as?may have been a Russian mercenary or a member of the Russian Mob."

"Did Mob connections get him that zapper?" I winced, remembering the pain that had shot through me when Yuri had held it against my face.

"Possibly, but not necessarily," Hardy said. "They're sold as self-defense weapons in some American states, so he may have bought it there. They're restricted here in Canada."

"Sister Celia and I weren't out long, and neither was Yuri when I used it on him."

"It takes seconds to bring someone down," Hardy said. "How quickly a person recovers depends on weight, and how much of a charge the device has."

"And the house?" I wondered when he was going to clam up.

"We'll get a search warrant. We have officers outside it now."

"Who owns it?" I knew I was pushing my luck.

He ignored the question and took two handbags out of a large brown envelope. "I believe these are yours."

I took my bag and gave the other bag to Sister Celia.

He held up my car key. "We found this in your Volvo. We'll keep it and bring your car to your home tomorrow." He stood up. "There are other members of the gang out there. You'll need to be careful. I'll station an officer at Safe Harbor and another at your home, Ms. Tierney."

"My sister," Raad said. "She is in danger?"

Hardy looked at Farah, who had been silent in the boardroom. "We'll check security at your apartment building. Stay in your unit for the next few days, Ms. Alwan." He opened the boardroom door. "An officer will drive you home."

"I leave my car on that street," Raad said. "I need it for work tomorrow."

"The officer can drive you over there," Hardy said.

Farah tugged at Raad's arm. "My coat, my purse. They are at Pat's house."

"We all go with officer," Raad said. "After I get my car, I drive Mrs. Tierney home and get my sister's things."

"That's fine."

Hardy hadn't charged us, I thought when the elevator door closed on him. But I knew that was the least of our worries.

It was one-thirty in the morning when Raad pulled up outside our house. Tracy and Laura ran out, followed by Maxie.

"Mom." Laura opened the passenger's door and threw her arms around me.

Tracy opened the back door for Ryan and Farah. "I can't believe what you went through. Farah and Raad, come into the house for a few minutes."

Raad turned off the engine. "Farah will get her things. And there is something I must understand."

On the sidewalk, I swept my girls into a bear hug. Then Tracy and Laura hugged Ryan and Farah.

"Come inside," Tracy said. We followed her in. She took our coats and Laura headed for the kitchen. Soon we were all sipping tea in the sunroom while I told them how Sister Celia and I had got into the house.

"That creep Yuri could have killed you, Mom," Tracy said.

"Me too," Ryan put in. "I come to Toronto for the weekend and I nearly get snuffed." Laura moved beside him on the sofa and put an arm around him.

"Mom, tell us how you got out of there," Tracy urged.

I gave a short account of our escape.

"Incredible," Tracy said. "Yuri, the stun gun, the handgun...It's amazing that you got out."

"You wanted to talk to me," I said to Farah. "That's why you came over here this afternoon."

She shrugged. "Not matter now."

I figured it was about Oskar. Farah wanted to know what Oskar had been up to, but she wouldn't talk about him in front of her brother.

"Don't come back to work until this is all cleared up," I told her. "Stay in your apartment. And don't open the door to anyone you don't know."

"You must all be completely whacked," Tracy said.

It would be time to get up in a few hours. "I'll take the morning off," I said.

Raad drew a deep breath. "I not understand why Yuri take my sister from this house." He turned to Farah. "You know this guy?"

"No." She lowered her eyes. "But I think he work in Oskar's business."

"He did," I said.

"What business Oskar have?" Raad cried. "Farah, what you…"

"I don't know nothing about Oskar's business." Then the words rattled out of her. "But he say it pay him lots of money."

"When Oskar tell you this?"

Farah kept her eyes on the coffee table. "I go to movie with him last week."

"Farah!" Raad added something in Arabic.

"You make me answer telephone at Safe Harbor."

"One afternoon, you work there one afternoon. You do not(" He broke off, glaring at her.

Tears rolled down Farah's cheeks. "I did not know Oskar was up to bad business."

Raad turned to me. "My sister, she have big, empty head. She do what she want, not think what will happen. Not think of her family."

"In Canada, single men and women go out to movies and restaurants and get to know each other before they marry," I said. "Unfortunately, Oskar…"

Farah stared at me. She seemed to be surprised at what I was saying.

"That is not our way," Raad said. "Muslim families arrange marriage for their girls with sons of good Muslim families." He turned to Farah. "Come, we go home now."

To me, he added, "Here you have saying when you punish foolish young people. You make them stay at home. How you say? You are...?"

"Grounded," Laura said. "You are so grounded."

"Grounded. So it will be for Farah."

The doorbell rang soon after they had left. Tracy jumped up to answer it.

"Ryan, go with her. And look outside before you open the door." I wondered if we would ever feel safe in our home again.

Tracy and Ryan returned with a uniformed woman officer, her honey-colored hair pulled into a knot at the back of her head.

"I'm Constable Lewis." She surveyed the ground floor of the house. "I'll sit in the front room. Leave the lights on down here when you go to bed."

Laura lingered in the sunroom after Tracy and Ryan had gone upstairs. "Mom, about Ryan."

I braced myself for another bombshell. I couldn't take much more of this.

"That night. It wasn't what you think."

"The night in the motel?"

"Yeah. Ryan conked out. The dope he was doing, I guess."

"He was driving stoned?"

"I drove. Mom, I'm sorry we lit out like that. It wasn't very("

"Responsible."

"Yeah, it was irresponsible, taking off like that. I knew you'd be worried. And I thought I should tell you that we didn't, ah, do anything."

I smiled at my daughter.

"I guess I'm not ready."

"Nothing wrong with waiting till you're ready." I wasn't sure whether I bought this story of hers, but she had admitted that she hadn't behaved responsibly.

"That's what Ryan said today."

"You like Ryan?"

"He's okay when he's not doing dope. We had fun this weekend. But, hey, he's in California, I'm in Toronto." She shrugged. "Besides, there's Kyle. Good thing he was out of town this weekend." She jumped up and held me close. "We could have lost you tonight, Mom. That man could have killed you."

I patted her back. "Go to bed, honey."

"I shouldn't have said all that shit about you and Devon. I guess you're old enough to know what you're doing."

I gave her a hug. "We'll all take taxis for the next few days. Let Maxie out into the yard in the morning. I don't want you walking around the neighborhood alone."

Laura headed upstairs and turned around on the landing. "Love you, Mom."

Too revved up for sleep, I went to the liquor cabinet and poured myself a double St. Rémy Napoléon. I put on an Ella Fitzgerald CD and turned the volume down low.

"Mrs. Tierney."

Startled, I turned to see Constable Lewis in the doorway.

"I didn't mean to frighten you." She handed me a piece of paper. "Constable Avari will relieve me in a few hours and I'll be back here at four in the afternoon. These are our numbers."

I took the paper.

With Maxie stretched out on the floor, I curled up on the sofa as Ella crooned, "Someone to Watch Over Me." I took a swallow and felt the brandy course through my body. I closed my eyes and tried to clear away my thoughts, but my mind wouldn't turn off. The song made me think of Devon, looking hurt at the airport.

Poor guy. He had planned a New Year's holiday and we'd ended up going to a funeral. Yeah, we finally made it into bed. We had some good times, we went to Ray's party...

I sat up straight, spilling brandy over my shirt. Maxie sat up too, her tail thumping on the carpet. Ray's party had made me think of Jan Vrancic, who ran the Bosnian Youth Relief Foundation. And who also happened to be Oskar's uncle.

I pictured myself in front of Arnie's computer screen. Mentally, I booted up the machine and opened the foundation's files.

Where were the names of its trustees? Where was its charitable registration number? And where was the breakdown of its granting activity, the names of its recipients, its fundraising expenses? Of course, Ray may have stored this information somewhere else.

The foundation had over three hundred thousand dollars invested in Reginald Enterprises, the diamond miner with properties in Africa that had been linked to the trade in "blood diamonds" to finance terrorist groups' activities. Surely, a foundation with a mandate to help children wouldn't invest in Reginald. It also had sizable holdings in Macron, the technology firm whose stock had been dropping steadily in recent weeks. Its auditing practices were under investigation.

I have always been a buy-and-hold investor, but why keep a stock that was on a clear losing trend? Why hadn't Ray sold it and claimed the loss to reduce the taxable gains on the other holdings?

I went into my study and turned on the computer. The Bosnian Youth Relief Foundation wasn't listed under the Canada Revenue Agency's Charities Directorate. Or under Philanthropic Foundations Canada.

But Google brought up Greek Cypriot Wealth Management, which claimed to be a full-service brokerage house based in Nicosia. If Norris Cassidy was holding an account for an offshore firm, that might explain the slowpoke stocks. They may have been there to muddy the money trail.

It was ten past three when I went upstairs to bed. On the landing, I thought of the fifty-thousand-dollar deposits that had been made into the foundation on the first day of every month for the past eighteen months. Fundraising doesn't consistently bring in rounded sums like that.

But money launderers tended to move dirty money around in even amounts.

Chapter Thirty-Six

Pat

"You know the answer, kid."

Michael was seated at the foot of my bed wearing the Pal Zileri suit I'd bought him a few months before he died.

Died? He was right there on my bed, his brown eyes smiling at me.

He patted the blanket over my foot. "You've always had a good head on your shoulders. Use it."

I opened my eyes, my heart hammering. My bedroom door was ajar, although I remembered closing it before I went to bed. I heard the shower running in the bathroom down the hall.

I lay under the covers and listened to the girls get ready for the day. What did Michael mean(that I knew the answer? I threw back the covers, suddenly wide awake.

I turned on the bedside light and called Sister Celia. "They're going to make another move. Maybe today. You have a police officer at Safe Harbor?"

She assured me that an officer was there.

"And Ali came back last night?"

"He was here when I got in."

"I'm worried about what could happen to both of you when you leave the house."

"I'll be out of town today and tomorrow. Another sister will pick me up any minute now. We're off to our annual conference at our motherhouse in Ottawa. But I'll tell Ali to stay inside." She gave me her cell number.

Then I called Farah. "Don't leave your apartment." I told her. "The big guys are still out there."

"Big guys?"

"The bosses. Oskar and Yuri were just helpers."

She let out a howl. "In Iraq, we think Canada safe place."

Downstairs, I found Tracy at the front door. Another woman police officer, this one with dark hair, was seated in the front room.

"Mom, this is Constable Avari. She'll be here until later this afternoon."

I nodded at the officer and turned to Tracy. "Take a taxi home tonight. Have the driver wait till you're inside the house."

"I'm meeting Jamie for dinner. I'll get a lift home."

A car honked its horn outside.

"My taxi's here." She gave me a hug. "It should be over soon, Mom. That was a huge breakthrough last night. The title to that house should be registered in the name of someone from the outfit."

"Let's hope so." I kissed her cheek.

After a slapdash breakfast, I called two more taxis. Ryan left for the airport in the first one that arrived. I got into the second with Laura and Maxie.

"Stay in school at noon and call me on my cell before you leave this afternoon," I told Laura when the cab pulled up in front of the high school.

"I'll be seeing the guidance counselor after my last class to look at university applications. I don't know how long that will take."

"Call me when you're through."

I took the taxi downtown to the Land Registry Office. At the information desk, a young man with glasses and a crew cut smiled at Maxie, then turned to me. "How can I help you?"

I handed him a piece of paper with the address of the Scarborough house and told him I wanted the title searched. He pointed to the self-serve computer terminals across the room.

I put my Visa card in the slot, typed in the address and the machine spat out a page. The house was owned by 698763 Ontario Inc.

A numbered company. I groaned in frustration.

"Can I find out more about this company?" I asked the young man.

"You can request a corporation report from the Ministry of Government Services' companies branch on University Avenue. Or you can ask for a report online." He wrote an address and a website on a Post-it note. "You'll get the names of the company's officers and directors." He peered at me through his glasses. "But they won't necessarily be the people who put up the money for the property."

Arnie was coming out of the kitchenette with a mug of coffee when I arrived at the branch. He gave Maxie a baleful look.

"Good morning, Arnie."

He didn't answer.

In my office, I called up the Government Services' website. I went to the Gateway for Business section and asked for a corporation report on 698763 Ontario Inc.

Moments later, the report appeared on my screen. Oskar Jacovic was listed as the general manager. Yuri Vlasenko was its president.

I thought about what the clerk had said. Oskar and Yuri hadn't put up the money to buy the property. But I was pretty sure I knew who had.

I closed my office door and opened my cell phone. Hardy picked up on the second ring.

"I told you yesterday that one of our VPs recently turned over a large account of Jan Vrancic's to a new advisor at our branch."

"You did."

I filled him in on some of the holdings in the account. And about the deposits that had been made into it.

"All this appears irregular?"

"Yes." And I told him why.

"Your VP, what's his name?"

"Ray Leckie. And the new guy is Arnie Cruickshank."

"I'll see if we've got anything on them."

"Have you searched the house in Scarborough?"

"Let us do our work, Ms. Tierney. You do some financial advising." And he hung up.

With a sigh, I turned back to my computer. Would the police find anything in the house that would lead them to the organizers? Maybe, maybe not. Meanwhile, my daughters, Farah, Ali and myself might be their next targets.

I looked up Macron Networks on Morningstar.ca, the investment research firm's website. On Friday, Macron had closed almost a dollar down from the day before.

I placed an electronic order to buy five hundred shares. I knew that would get Ray's attention. All Norris Cassidy advisors' trades go through the company's compliance department.

I punched in Stéphane's extension on my telephone. "D'you have time to step out for a coffee?"

"What's up, *ma chère?*"

"Over coffee."

We ordered lattes in Starbucks. Stéphane added two chocolate croissants to our tray and carried it over to a window table where we could watch Maxie outside.

"Well?" He took a big bite of his croissant.

I locked eyes with him. "I need your help."

When my last client left at four forty-five, I closed my office door and called Hardy on my cell.

"You put in an order to purchase some stock," he said, "and you think that will flush these guys out?"

"I know who's behind this operation. You want proof and I should be able to give it to you."

"Okay. We'll set up at your office tomorrow morning?"

"They're on their way as we speak. They'll show up at our branch when the others have gone home."

"You've put yourself out as bait?" His voice thundered over the line. "Leave the building, Ms. Tierney. Immediately."

"They'll come for me at home and my daughters will be there." And I couldn't let that happen.

"I'll send a car to your building?"

"No."

"Ms. Tierney, our motto is To Serve and Protect, and I take the *protect* part to heart. I can't let?"

I glanced down at Maxie, chewing on a rawhide bone under my desk. "Detective, I need you and another officer over here right now. Without sirens."

"What?"

"My partner Stéphane Pratt will wait for you downstairs. If the front door is locked, he'll let you into the building. He'll have the key to the office suite. Then you can lie low and listen to our conversation."

"Just like that?" I could picture him shaking his head. "Your suspects waltz in and you sit them down for tea."

"Not quite but?"

"Give me the names and let us do our job. Go home."

I swallowed hard. "I'll see you soon, Detective." I hung up before he could protest further. And before I changed my mind.

I took a couple of deep breaths. Then I called Laura's cell and reminded her to take a taxi home. "Call Constable Lewis and make sure she comes to the door before you leave the cab." I gave her Lewis's cell number.

Then I opened my office door and returned to my desk.

Rose left at five. A few minutes later, Stéphane and Arnie got ready to head out. Maxie abandoned her rawhide bone and stood sentry by the main door.

"Coming, Arnie?" Stéphane bent down to stroke Maxie's head.

Arnie pulled on his Burberry and grabbed his canvas gym bag. Maxie pranced around him as he approached the door.

Arnie held up his bag as a shield. "Get that dog away from me."

"Maxie," I called. "Come here."

The dog remained in front of Arnie.

Obedience school for you, I thought as I held up the rawhide bone. "Maxie."

She saw the bone and trotted over to me.

Arnie scurried out. Stéphane gave me a wave and followed him.

I locked the door and toured the suite with Maxie at my heels. The only lights on were in the reception area and in my office. Anyone who was watching from the street would know I was alone.

I sat down at Rose's desk and opened her desktop recorder. The telephone rang, and my heart skidded around in my chest.

"Tierney Pratt Financial."

"Pat, it's Devon."

I closed my eyes. "I'm really busy right now."

"Give me thirty seconds. You're angry at me. It's understandable, I shouldn't have said what I did about Sister Celia. It was unfair and I'm sorry. But you overreacted. I just want to ask you to give me another chance."

I had to get him off the line. "You're right, I overreacted. Look, I don't mean to be rude, but I have to go."

"Ryan filled me in on last night. I can only say thank God you're all okay. Now get back to work."

I swiveled the chair to face the door. Maxie settled herself at my feet. Where was Hardy?

A good five minutes later I heard a key turn in the lock. I turned on Rose's recorder. "Stay here," I whispered to Maxie under the desk.

I stood up as Ray Leckie and Jan Vrancic, carrying a briefcase, walked into the suite.

"Looks like you're alone, Pat." Ray wore a genial smile on his face. He locked the door behind him.

Maxie danced around Ray and Jan. Jan eyed the dog nervously, but Ray reached down to stroke her coat. "Good dog."

Maxie gave a soft woof and went to fetch her rawhide bone. Some guard dog.

"You remember Dr. Vrancic, Pat."

"Madam." Jan bowed from the waist.

"It's the third time we've met." I moved from behind Rose's desk. "What can I do for you?"

Ray took a chair in the reception area across from me. Jan perched on the edge of another. Maxie went over to them and dropped her bone at Ray's feet.

"Damn dog." He smiled as he picked up the bone and pocketed it. Then he pointed to the floor beside me. "Sit."

Maxie whimpered.

"Sit." Ray pointed to the floor again.

Maxie went over to me and lay down at my feet.

"You'll have to give me the name of your obedience school," I said.

"This dog, I don't like him," Jan said.

"I'll handle the dog." Ray smiled at me. "Now, where were we? Ah, yes. We have a small problem, Pat."

I raised an eyebrow. "Oh?"

"You put in an order for five hundred shares of Macron today."

"Yes?"

"For whom? You didn't give a client's name."

"I must have forgotten. Why do you ask, Ray? I've never had to account for my stock picks before."

"They're usually on the conservative side, sometimes too much so. But Macron's price has been falling. We don't know where it will end up after the investigation."

I held his gaze. "The Bosnian foundation has a big stake in Macron, so I assumed..."

"What do you know about the Bosnian Youth Relief Foundation?" Jan asked.

"Only what I've seen on Arnie's computer. You've done a great job of fundraising. Almost $6 million."

Ray got up from his chair. "What were you doing on Arnie's computer?"

"I'm the manager of this branch. I was checking to see whether his computer had a virus screen."

I glanced at my watch. Five twenty-five. Where was Hardy?

"You were at a house in Scarborough last night," Ray said.

I remained silent. If I could get them to talk...

Jan stood up. "Madam, we understand that something unfortunate happened to you there. A certain hot-headed young man..."

"Yuri Vlasenko worked for you. So did Oskar Jacovic."

Jan's face grew dark. "My nephew messed things up by taking people to that woman's house."

"Jan." Ray shot him a warning look.

"You didn't know that Oskar took them to Jude?" I asked.

"The first we heard of her, she was dead and the police were nosing around. None of this would have happened...you would not have been involved, madam, if Oskar had not enlisted her."

"Jan, will you("

Jan put his briefcase on Rose's desk. "It doesn't matter what she knows."

I backed toward the door.

Jan opened the briefcase and took out a small leather case. He removed a syringe. "Adrenalin."

Ray stared at him, surprise written on his face. Then he shrugged.

"When they find you," Jan continued, "you will have suffered a fatal heart attack. A middle-aged woman with too much stress in her life. Did you know that women now account for nearly half of all coronary deaths? Many of them had no previous symptoms."

Ray seemed mesmerized by the syringe Jan was holding.

I inched closer to the door. I had to keep them talking. "How long has it been going on?"

"Couple of years. Jan got the idea from some pals of his back in Bosnia. We set up at the house, started with kidneys, Jan's specialty. Then we found a heart surgeon from the Philippines who couldn't get licensed here. We didn't take on too many patients, just those who could pay well. Sent some product out West and to the States. We made good money."

I clenched my teeth. For Ray and Jan, human organs were marketable commodities.

"We had a dumping ground on a farm we bought up near Sudbury," Ray said, "but Oskar got lazy and started dumping around Toronto. Why we ever took that idiot on."

Jan looked at Ray reproachfully over the top of his glasses. "Oskar had his faults, but he was my nephew."

I heard a key turn in the door lock. Ray picked up a metal stapler from Rose's desk and positioned himself behind the door.

"Watch it." I yelled. "Ray's behind the door."

Stéphane hurried into the suite. "Pat?"

Ray slugged him on the head with the stapler. Stéphane crumpled to the floor. Ray grabbed his feet and dragged him into the suite.

I sprinted for the open door.

"Not so fast." Ray came up behind me and pinned my arms.

Where was Hardy?

Maxie was up on her feet.

"Maxie, over here," I called.

"Stay," Ray ordered.

Maxie hesitated, then sat, keeping an eye on me and Ray. Ray kicked the door shut.

Jan locked the door and approached me with the syringe in one hand. Maxie growled and stood up.

I lifted my left leg and drove my heel down on Ray's foot as hard as I could. He winced but didn't release his grip on my arms.

"Maxie," I called as a last resort.

To my amazement, a golden streak flew across the room. The dog sank her teeth into Ray's leg.

"Aggh!" He dropped my arms.

I dashed to a chair in the reception area. I held it in front of me, its metal legs pointed outwards.

"Madam, you are outnumbered," Jan said. "You might as well give up. This won't hurt much. A clap of pain in the chest, then…"

I tightened my hold on the chair.

Ray reached down for Maxie's collar. She danced away, then turned and snarled at him. Ray swiped at her with his foot.

Jan lunged at me with the syringe. I kept him at bay with the chair.

Maxie jumped up on Jan and leaned her front paws against his back. Surprised, Jan dropped the syringe. Maxie pounced on it. It rolled across the floor and under a filing cabinet.

Ray scrambled over to the cabinet and got down on his knees in front of it. Maxie jumped on him, barking loudly.

Banging sounded on the door. I ran over to it and flipped up the lock.

"You okay?" Hardy asked.

"Glad to see you."

Behind him stood Mancini and two uniformed officers, their guns drawn.

"You. On your feet," Hardy said to Ray.

Ray stood up, and the uniformed officers took his arms.

Two more officers appeared in the doorway. Hardy gave them a signal and they went over to Jan.

Stéphane sat up and rubbed his head.

Maxie loped over to me and I stroked her back.

"A syringe rolled under that filing cabinet," I said. "Vrancic said there was adrenalin in it."

Mancini took a ruler from Rose's desk and poked it under the cabinet. The syringe rolled out. He prodded it with the ruler and got it into a plastic bag.

Hardy turned to me. "I told you to let us get on with our work."

I pointed to Rose's recorder. "It's all there. What they were up to at the house. What Vrancic planned to do with that syringe."

I collapsed into Rose's chair and reached down to hug Maxie. "My special assistant."

Chapter Thirty-Seven

Pat

"You handled that well, kid. I'm proud of you."

I raised my head from the pillow. "Michael?"

He bent over the bed and kissed the tip of my nose.

I started to reach out to him, but he drew back and shook his head.

"It's time you let go. Remember the good times, but get on with your life." He hummed a few bars of "They Can't Take That Away from Me." "Continue as you've been doing. The girls have turned out great. And the boy...well, do what you think is best."

He was talking about Tommy.

I propped myself up on one elbow, but he was gone. I closed my eyes and slid down under the covers. A wave of happiness washed over me. I hummed the Gershwin tune. Michael and I had a good marriage. Nothing(and no one(could take that away from me.

I arrived at the office a little after ten.

"*Ma chère.*" Stéphane winced as he got up from his desk.

"You're supposed to be resting today."

He shrugged and patted the bandage on his head. "And miss all the excitement around here?"

I glanced at Arnie's closed office door. "He in?"

Stéphane shook his head. "When I got here at nine, he was in there throwing things into a cardboard box. Wouldn't answer when I asked what he was doing. Then he stormed out with the box. I don't think he'll be back."

I poked my head into Arnie's office. Drawers were pulled out from the desk and the filing cabinet. Papers covered the floor.

The door to the suite opened and Keith Kulas walked in.

"A word, Pat." He inclined his head toward my office.

When we were alone, he cleared his throat. "You won't be surprised to hear that Ray Leckie is no longer with the firm."

"No."

"We're grateful for your astuteness. How did you figure it out?"

"The foundation's holdings. It had a sizable stake in Macron that's lost a lot of ground lately. And the regular deposits(fifty thousand dollars on the first of each month. Too tidy. They were holding a big bag of cash so they plunked it into a brokerage account in Cyprus. And Jan Vrancic's nephew, Oskar Jacovic, worked at a home for refugees. Some of them have disappeared."

"I was down at police headquarters last night. The cops had your rookie, Arnie Cruickshank, in for questioning. He was managing some $6 million, but he'd been at the firm for what, four days?"

"Three. He started last Thursday. Ray was keen to hire him and he gave him that account right away. Did they already know each other?"

"I'm not sure. The police will see what Cruickshank was up to in Vancouver. Anything's possible with people who ran that kind of a scheme."

"Has Ray been up to anything else here at Norris Cassidy?"

"Other than laundering the proceeds from his racket? We're looking into it. He was chief compliance officer so it wouldn't have been difficult for him to cover things up."

He ran a hand over his brow. "I let Cruickshank go. I'm sorry, Pat. I don't like to go over our branch managers' heads, but he had to have known something was wrong with that account. We'll get you someone else."

"We're fine just as we are." I gave him a big smile. "It was Ray's idea to bring in a third advisor."

"Hooray!" Stéphane cried, when I told him he could move into his old office. "Back to normal. Just the two of us and Rose."

"It doesn't sound like Arnie has been charged with anything."

"Not yet."

"Arnie was an opportunist, but I don't think he was part of the racket. Ray knew he would be willing to turn a blind eye to what was going on in that account."

"You don't think Ray and Jan planned to use Luella's apartment building for their...activities?"

I shrugged. "But guess what?"

He raised an eyebrow.

I smiled. "The sale didn't go through. I was so preoccupied yesterday that I forgot to get the check to the realtor. Someone else got the building."

"And Luella's on the warpath."

"She left a phone message. She didn't sound happy."

But Luella had other concerns when I reached her. "Arnie's left your company. He wants to go back to Vancouver."

"He won't be going anywhere for a while. The police are talking to him...for an investigation."

She sighed. "He says he'll go to Vancouver as soon as he can. And I thought he'd look out for me here in Toronto."

"Did you give him power of attorney?"

"No. Arnie's a good boy, but he sometimes gets carried away with his ideas. It may be for the best that we didn't get that apartment building."

I kept my thoughts on that to myself.

"Well, I've decided that Caroline can be responsible for my health care and my living arrangements. And I'll give you authority over my finances. Should I ever be unable to make decisions on my own, that is."

"As your investment manager, that would be a conflict of interest for me. But you can make Norris Cassidy a corporate trustee. The company will look after your money."

I groaned as I hung up the phone. Luella would have plenty of investment ideas to run by me until Norris Cassidy's power of attorney kicked in.

Stéphane had mugs set out in the kitchen and was about to pour coffee when Rose hurried in. "There's money missing from the safe," she said.

"Arnie, no doubt," Stéphane said.

"How much money?" I asked.

"Ten thousand dollars," Rose said.

Stéphane put down the coffee pot and loosened his tie. "I was holding it in trust for Peter Eisen. I told Arnie what I was doing and why. And I showed him the combination to the safe."

"It's worth ten thousand dollars to be rid of Arnie," I said.

"We need to tell the police," Rose said.

"Head office can do that." I picked up the pot and poured the coffee. "And it can come up with Peter Eisen's money. One of this firm's top guns put Arnie in here."

Keith Kulas told me he would have a check for Peter Eisen at the branch later that day. And he said he'd report the missing money to the police. As soon as I was off the phone, Rose buzzed me on the intercom. "I'm transferring Norah Seaton to you."

I stared at the ceiling thinking that I should have called Norah the night before. I apologized to her.

"Not to worry, Pat," she said. "Mr. Hardy told me the people who wanted to harm Tommy are in jail. What a relief that is."

"You can take him out of that boarding school."

"I'd like to talk to you about my plans for Tommy. Can you come by tomorrow afternoon?"

Later in the morning, I called Devon and filled him in on the events of the previous day.

"It's all over?" He didn't sound happy.

"Pretty much. Ray's associates have all been rounded up. Sol Alvarez, who was a heart surgeon in the Philippines. Lab technicians. A few guys who drummed up business, one of them in Vancouver. Ray and Jan had ties in Bosnia, too. God only knows what's happening there."

"What you did was foolhardy, Pat."

I smiled. Michael would never have let me get involved in any of this. He would have taken charge as he always did. It was ironic that Michael(or rather Michael's son(was the reason that I got involved. I wanted to help Tommy.

"You knew what Leckie and Vrancic were up to," Devon went on, "yet you invited them to your office."

Devon wasn't the least like Michael. He didn't have Michael's panache and easy confidence; on the other hand, he was far less controlling. And that suited me just fine. Devon might have complained that I acted foolishly, but he never tried to stop me.

I pictured his dark eyes boring into mine. I wanted to see him again.

"If the police hadn't arrived when they did…"

"Stéphane waited across the street. When Hardy hadn't shown up at five twenty-five, he propped open the front door with a wooden crate and came upstairs. Ray slugged him when he entered the suite."

Devon groaned. "Where was Hardy?"

"A transport truck jackknifed on Mount Pleasant. They had to take side streets."

"You could have been?"

"I had to do something, Devon. The police wouldn't tell me anything. The house was owned by a numbered company. Forensics would probably have found fibers that linked Ray or Jan to it. But in the meantime, the girls and I had to watch our every move."

Devon was silent for a moment or two. "Who gets the money in the foundation?"

"It wasn't a real foundation…"

"The account then?"

"I'm not sure what happens to the proceeds of this kind of crime. But I'll lobby for it to go to the families of Suleyman Goven and any other victims that can be identified. Wherever those families may be."

"And Tommy? What happens to him?"

"Norah wants to talk to me tomorrow. No doubt she has something in mind."

"Have you told the girls about Tommy's dad?"

"Soon. I'll get around to that soon."

He cleared his throat. "I've got something to say."

"If it's about Sister Celia("

"No, I blew that big time. I'm sorry."

"What then?"

"I don't like the risks you take. I worry that you'll get hurt."

I smiled.

"But I know you'll always follow your own mind when you believe strongly in something. So if we keep seeing each other, I guess I'll have to put up with being worried." He paused. "That is if we…"

"Keep seeing each other? I'd like nothing better."

For the present, at least.

I treated the girls to dinner at Milo's and waited until we'd ordered dessert before I gave them an account of the previous day.

When I'd finished, they stared at me for a few moments. Laura was the first to speak.

"Mom, you've got to be more sensible. You have to act("

"More responsible?"

"That's right. Join a book club or take up yoga. Marry Devon. But stop putting yourself out on a limb. We only have one parent. You don't want me and Trace to be orphans, do you?"

Tracy reached across the table and took my hand. "It looks like the police have nabbed most of the gang."

I smiled. "We can breathe easy now."

"By the way, how's your client who had the kidney transplant?"

I felt a stab of guilt. In the past few hectic days, I'd forgotten about Leo. "Thanks for reminding me. I'll call Leo's wife tomorrow."

The waiter set glasses of zabaglione and a plate of sponge fingers on the table. I took a spoonful of the thick, frothy custard and savored the Marsala flavor. Then I offered up a silent prayer for the right words to tell my daughters about Tommy.

I took a deep breath and told them about Jude's visit to my office. "She asked me to take Tommy for a few days. She said she was worried that someone would hurt him, and that she didn't think I'd turn him away."

I paused, took a sip of water and looked at the two pairs of eyes fixed on my face. Was I doing the right thing?

"When I asked why she would think that, she told me that Tommy was your father's son."

Tracy and Laura were quiet for several moments. What had I done? They adored their father. I shouldn't…

"Jude wasn't a client after all," Tracy said.

"No. I told you that the next day because I was still trying to come to grips with what she'd told me."

"How could he?" Tears filled Laura's eyes. "Dad cheated on you. He betrayed us."

Laura was angry with him, but I was afraid that later she and her sister would blame me. They would think their dad had turned to another woman because he wasn't happy with me.

I took Laura's hand and put on what I hoped was a brave face. "I was furious with your father at first, and what made it even worse was that there was no one I could yell and scream at. But I've come to realize that we all make mistakes. In the end, your father chose to be with us. Jude told me they never saw each other after we came back from England that summer. I believe what she said."

Tracy shook her head. "It's pretty hard to come to terms with. I always thought Dad was perfect. Now..."

"Nobody's perfect. What is sad is that he never knew he had a son. You've got to admit Tommy is a special little guy."

Tracy reached into her handbag and placed something on the table. My eternity ring.

"Saw it on the sunroom floor, twinkling in the lamplight. I guess you were trying to get rid of...Dad."

I scooped up the ring and dropped it into my purse. "Keep your eyes peeled for my wedding band. It's somewhere in that room."

The girls looked at each other.

I smiled at them. "We've learned a fair bit about Jude in the past little while. From all accounts, she was a good woman. She had strong convictions and stood by them. Impulsive, but good-hearted."

"She was sleeping with a married man," Tracy cried.

It was on the tip of my tongue to ask about her mystery man's marital status, but I checked myself in time. We seem to demand higher standards of our parents than we have for ourselves.

"She was desperate to protect Tommy, or I don't believe she would have approached me. Her family didn't know who Tommy's father was."

Laura looked thoughtful. "It makes sense, I suppose. Tommy looks so much like Tracy. I noticed that when we first met him. I just didn't make the connection."

"And Tommy?" Tracy asked. "What will happen to him?"

"I think his grandmother wants him with her."

"Puleeze." Laura made a face. "She's an old lady. Too old to raise a kid. Can we take him, Mom?"

"Yes, Mom." Tracy's eyes shone. "Tommy's our brother. He should be with us."

"It's not as simple as that. His mother's family has first claim on him."

"But we're his sisters," Laura said. "He'd be way happier with us."

I held up a hand. "Listen, you two. You'll both soon be gone. Tracy, you'll want to get a place of your own when you pass the bar admissions exam. And, Laura, you're off to university in the fall and you're talking about going out of town. It would be just Tommy and me in the house, and I don't know if I want to be a hands-on parent again."

The girls looked so dejected that I said, "Let me think about it. I'll be seeing Norah tomorrow afternoon."

Laura's face brightened. "You'll tell her that we'll take Tommy?"

"I'll listen to what her plans are for him."

"And then you'll tell her how much happier he'd be with us." Laura took my hand. "Please, Mom. I'll go to university here in Toronto if it means Tommy can live with us."

I made no answer to that. But, as I signed the credit-card slip, my thoughts turned to the small boy with Michael's eyes. I wanted to hold him in my arms.

And we did have a spare bedroom.

Chapter Thirty-Eight

Pat

Sister Celia was seated in the waiting room when I got to the branch the next morning. She jumped to her feet when she saw me. "Do you have a minute?"

"I do." I opened my office door. "You're my first client of the day."

"When I got back from Ottawa last night, Ali was in a terrible state." She settled herself in the client's chair. "He'd received a letter from his father. His younger brother was killed by al-Shabaab."

"His poor family."

"And he's not with them."

We were silent for a few moments. Then she leaned forward placing the fingers of both her hands together to form a steeple. "It gives us a good case for his appeal. If we can document his brother's murder, it would explain why Ali can't return to Somalia."

"It would." I shook my head. "But this news, after all he's been through."

Her brow furrowed. "I'm worried about him. That's why I'm here. It would be good for him to live in a real home with other young people. I wondered...?"

I held up a hand. "Can't."

Her face fell. "No? You wouldn't have to..."

"The girls want Tommy to live with us."

She clapped her hands. "That's what I've been praying for." She smiled. "You received a gift of a boy child this Christmas."

I felt like saying I'd had a boy child thrust upon me. But I didn't.

"I'll see what else I can come up with for Ali before I go."

"Go? Where are you going?"

It was a few moments before she replied. "The archdiocese(our major source of funding(is extremely, ah, displeased by the articles that have appeared in the newspapers. Articles about a human-organs racket linked to Safe Harbor."

"Linked to Oskar."

She held up her hands. "Somebody had to take the fall. I'm the director so("

"That's not fair."

"I'm being transferred."

"After the great work you've done…"

She smiled. "It's all right. Poverty, chastity, obedience. Those are the vows I took. Obedience means we can be taken off a project at any time. I'm just thankful that Safe Harbor won't be closed down. Someone else will carry on there."

"Where will you go?"

"I don't know yet. Somewhere outside the archdiocese. My superior thinks I'll be restricted in what I'll be allowed to do here."

"I'll miss you."

"We'll keep in touch."

As soon as Sister Celia had gone, I phoned the Cornacchia home. A woman answered.

"Mrs. Cornacchia? It's Pat Tierney at Tierney Pratt Financial."

"I'm Barbara, her daughter. Mom's in New York with Dad."

"How is your father?"

"Dad's doing well. His surgery was on Friday night. He was disoriented on the weekend, but the doctors say he's making good progress. Thank God for that wonderful woman."

"Woman?"

"The woman who donated her kidney. A complete stranger in Winnipeg. Dad had signed up with Living Donors Canada. This woman volunteered to donate a kidney and they got matched up. A miracle! No one in our family could donate. Mom has high blood pressure. I'm diabetic and my brother Mark's only thirteen."

Leo had a living donor.

"You said your father's in New York."

"In a private hospital. The donor wanted the procedure done right away. With no lead time, Dad couldn't have it done here in Toronto. So he had to shell out megabucks to go out of the country. I wish I could be down there with them, but I've got to keep an eye on Mark."

With a sigh of relief, I hung up the phone. Leo hadn't fallen into the hands of a Jan Vrancic.

I looked up from my computer early that afternoon to see Tracy and a striking-looking woman with burgundy hair in the doorway.

"Mom, can we come in?"

"Of course." I got out of my chair as they came into the office.

Tracy took the woman's hand. "Mom, I want you to meet Jamie. Jamie Collins."

I took a step back. Call me old-fashioned, but I'd assumed Jamie was a man.

Jamie smiled and held out her other hand. "Tracy figured it was time we met."

I took her hand and looked at Tracy. Her face was beaming as she looked from Jamie to me, and back to Jamie again.

Was this a dream?

"Yes, well, I…" I tied to find the right words.

Rose came into the office. "Keith Kulas on the line, Pat."

I dropped Jamie's hand and reached for the phone. Keith's call would give me time to adjust to this bombshell. "I have to take this."

The smile left Tracy's face. "We'll leave you to it." She took Jamie's arm and they moved toward the door.

My heart sank as I watched them leave. I had let my daughter down.

I stared out the taxi window. Men and women scurried down sidewalks and across streets, determined to reach their destinations. The sky was leaden and night was falling even though it was just past three. The weather forecasters had been calling for a snowstorm.

I closed my eyes and rested my head on the back of the seat. Tracy's lover was a woman. Why hadn't I been aware of my daughter's orientation?

Tracy only had one boyfriend that I known about: Brian Borovoy, back when she was an undergraduate. Then Michael had died. Months later, when the fog had lifted, I realized that Brian was no longer in the picture. Tracy had thrown herself into her studies to get into law school. Then she was away at Queen's for three years.

I stifled a sob and held my face in my hands.

I'd always considered myself a champion of diversity. Racial, religious and sexual. Stéphane, my business partner and friend, was openly gay, and I had gay and lesbian clients. It was easy to be open-minded...until your own kid came out.

Then something inside me shifted.

Why hadn't I known about Tracy's preference? Why hadn't she told me? I thought there were no secrets between the girls and myself. I didn't want them to keep things from me.

I pictured the look on Tracy's face as she'd left the office. I had let her down.

This woman was important to her and Tracy was important to me. I promised myself that I would get to know Jamie. If she was the one for Tracy, I would stand by her choice.

The taxi slowed and came to a stop in front of Norah's house. The driver turned to me. "You okay, lady?"

"Can you drive around the block?"

I had dried my eyes when the cab pulled up in front of the house again.

Arlene opened the front door, wearing a dark mink coat. "Mom has tea waiting for you. I'm going home."

But she stayed in the hall as I took off my coat and boots. "Have you...have you heard from Clive?"

"No, I haven't. But the police won't be bothering him anymore. The man who killed Jude is dead and his associates have been rounded up."

"That's what I hoped. I didn't see Clive's name in any of the newspaper articles."

I touched her hand. "Clive is off the hook."

"Is that Pat?" Norah called from the room to the right of the hall. "Come in here."

She was smartly turned out in a navy dress and a pearl necklace. Her silver hair was coiffed; her fingernails manicured and painted a pearly pink. In front of her, a silver tea wagon was laden with pots of tea and coffee, sandwiches and small pastries.

I sat down and watched as she poured tea into a china cup.

She passed the cup to me. "You're a good mother, Pat."

I winced and took a sip of tea.

"You've been a second mom to my Tommy." She held out a plate of dainty sandwiches.

I put the cup and saucer on the coffee table and took a pinwheel sandwich. "Will he stay at the boarding school?"

"Mr. Bonokowski has gone to get him. It's only Wednesday, but there's no reason to keep him there when he'll be back at his old school on Monday."

I waited to hear more.

"Arlene seems to think she has her hands full with her two children. And Patrick's wife is a career woman." She sniffed.

Wives and mothers have careers these days, I wanted to remind her. Like me. With a start, I wondered if I'd spent too much time at work after Michael's death and not enough at home.

"What it comes down to is neither his aunt nor his uncle want to be bothered with the boy. Sad, isn't it? His own family."

She picked up a sandwich. "Well, I want Tommy here. But I realize I can't keep up with a young lad. So I'd like to have a companion for him. A young woman, a university student who could attend classes during the day when Tommy is at school, and be here for him after school and on weekends. She would have a bedroom and a study, and a small salary. And I'd pay her university tuition."

"That's not a bad idea."

She smiled. "I have your daughter Laura in mind."

"Laura?"

"I've never met your girls, but I know they must be fine young women. Laura could come to us now while she finishes high school. She could bring her dog too. Maxie, is it?"

"Laura has a home of her own."

"She's Tommy's half-sister."

I gave her a stern look. "And she's my daughter. Unless she decides to study in another city next year, I want Laura with me."

She studied her hands. "Well, I could inquire at the University of Toronto. I'm sure there's an office that arranges accommodation for out-of-town students. But I wouldn't know what kind of person I'd get."

"I told my daughters about their father and Jude last night."

"Oh?" Her blue eyes were filled with concern. "How did they react?"

"They were upset at first. They felt betrayed, probably by both of us. But they thought it was terrific that they have a brother."

Her face brightened.

"They'd like Tommy to live with us."

She shook her head. "His place is with his family."

"Think about it. Laura said she would stay in Toronto for university if Tommy was with us. There would be young people in the house. And Moore Park is just across Mount Pleasant Avenue from Rosedale. Tommy can visit you whenever you like."

The old woman's shoulders sagged.

"Tommy should finish the year at the school he's at now," I continued. "But in September, he could go to the public school that's just two blocks away from our house. My girls went there."

The front door opened. "Take off your boots, Tommy," a man's voice said.

Norah gave a small sigh and sat up on the sofa. "There's someone here who wants to say hello to you, Tommy."

Tommy ran into the room, his brown bear in his arms. "Mrs. T!"

My heart soared.

"Come and give me a kiss, Tommy," Norah said. A tear slid down her face. She wiped it away with the back of her hand.

The boy went over to his grandmother and kissed her cheek. Then he ran over to me. "How's Maxie?"

"Maxie's just fine." I gave him a hug and he wiggled with delight.

"When can I see her?"

"Tomorrow afternoon, if you like."

My girls would soon be gone. Tracy would go first, maybe with Jamie. Laura wouldn't be long behind her. This little boy needed a home.

"Tommy," I said, "there's something we want to ask you."

Acknowledgements

Many people helped with the creation of *Safe Harbor*. My heartfelt gratitude goes to my husband, Ed Piwowarczyk, for his belief in me, his patience and his superb organizational skills.

Thank you to author Louise Penny and Crime Writers of Canada for founding the Arthur Ellis Award for Best Unpublished Crime Novel (a.k.a. the Unhanged Arthur). I was one of five finalists for the inaugural award in 2007. That honor, and the kind words of two of the judges, author Maureen Jennings and Marian Misters, co-owner of The Sleuth of Baker Street bookstore, spurred me on to more writing.

Three years later, support came from another group of writers, this one in Britain. *Safe Harbor* was shortlisted for the Crime Writers' Association's Debut Dagger award in 2010, and the encouragement and generosity of CWA members, especially authors Margaret Murphy and Liz Evans, was invaluable.

Back in Canada, Gail Bowen, author of the *Joanne Kilbourn mystery series*, provided sage advice on the *Safe Harbor* manuscript. Author Rosemary Aubert shared her love of writing and the written word at her 2011 summer workshop at Loyalist College in Belleville, Ont.

A big "merci" to fellow writers in my writers' circle: Catherine Dunphy, Madeleine Harris-Callway, Lynne Murphy, Joan O'Callaghan and Sylvia Warsh. They provided deadlines and terrific suggestions.

Thanks, also, to fellow Sisters in Crime in the Toronto chapter, and to fellow Crime Writers of Canada members. These two organizations have nurtured many crime-writing careers over the years.

My hat is off to Donna and Alex Carrick of Carrick Publishing for their work and dedication in publishing the Mesdames of Mayhem's crime fiction anthologies and the second editions of the *Pat Tierney mysteries*.

I would like to convey my high regard for members of Canada's financial services industry who I met and wrote about in my career as a journalist. They shared their enthusiasm for the important work they do.

If you enjoyed this book, please consider writing a short review and posting it on Amazon. Reviews are helpful to other readers and greatly appreciated by authors. When you post a review, drop me an email and I may feature part of your review on my blog. Thank you!

—*Rosemary*

http://www.rosemarymccracken.com/Contact.html

Born and raised in Montreal, Rosemary McCracken has worked on newspapers across Canada as a reporter, arts writer and arts reviewer, editorial writer and editor. She is now a freelance journalist who specializes in personal finance. She advocates greater investor protection and improved financial services industry regulation and enforcement.

Rosemary's short fiction has been published by Room of One's Own Press, Kaleidoscope Books, Sisters in Crime Canada, the Mesdames of Mayhem, Darkhouse Books, Down & Out Books and *Mystery Weekly Magazine*. *Safe Harbor* is Rosemary's first published novel. It was a finalist for Britain's Crime Writers' Association's Debut Dagger award in 2010, and it was first released by Imajin Books in 2012. *Black Water*, the second book in the Pat Tierney mystery series, was first released by Imajin Books in 2013, followed by *Raven Lake* in 2016.

Rosemary lives in Toronto with her husband and teaches novel writing at George Brown College. She is a member of Crime Writers of Canada and Sisters in Crime.

Visit Rosemary at her website and blog, and on Twitter and Facebook.

www.ingramcontent.com/pod-product-compliance
Lightning Source LLC
Chambersburg PA
CBHW030933260626
47169CB00002B/455